Already
Freakn'
Mated

(Freakn' Shifters, Book Three)

Eve Langlais

Copyright © September 2012, Eve Langlais
Cover Art by Amanda Kelsey © August 2012
Edited by Brandi Buckwine
Copy Edited Amanda Pederick
Produced in Canada

Published by Eve Langlais
1606 Main Street, PO Box 151
Stittsville, Ontario, Canada, K2S1A3
www.EveLanglais.com

ISBN-13: 978 1988 328 21 8

Prologue

Somehow, when Jiao pictured her death, it didn't involve drowning, bone crushing impact, or a heart attack caused by fear.

Eyeing the sheer drop, laced in darkness due to the late hour, she could too easily picture the several hundred feet of empty space, a scary chasm, bordered by ragged cliffs that funneled into the raging river below.

Jiao bit her lip. "You can't seriously expect me to jump? I'm a cat not a bird. What if I hit a rock? Or get eaten by a fish?" *Or die of fright on the way down?* A distinct possibility given the way her heart pounded, her palms sweated and her stomach roiled.

"To the first, you'll bounce. As for the second, you're too scrawny for most predators. Are you done making up excuses? We don't have much time. The guards will be making their sweep in less than four minutes."

Ah yes, the guards. Getting caught outside their cell, no matter the excuse they used — *we were taking a midnight stroll, looking for fishing worms, going for a pee* — would mean at least a week's worth of punishment. But still… Suicide versus scrubbing the communal bathroom on her knees? Tough choice.

"I haven't swum in years. What if I don't remember how?"

Clasping her hands, Sheng faced her, his dark gaze intense. "I promised to never let anything happen to you. That includes drowning, no matter how crazy you make me. I know you're scared, but you need to push your fear aside, just like we do in the ring and the woods. We'll survive the jump. You'll remember how to swim. And we will escape. We don't have a choice. Or would you prefer the alternative?"

Just the reminder of what awaited her if they didn't escape was enough to give Jiao a shiver and bolster her resolve. *There are worse punishments even than death.* Taking a deep breath, Jiao stepped onto the thick stone parapet. The wind tugged at her, whipping strands of her hair free from her ponytail.

"Will you hold my hand?" she asked, with just the slightest quaver. At sixteen, she didn't quite have the courage to do it alone.

"I will so long as you promise not to drown me," Sheng quipped, as he laced his fingers through hers.

Despite the situation, Jiao's lips curved in to a smile. "Of course I won't. I might need to use your meatier frame to save me from a hungry fish." Hand clutching his, she turned to face the edge and the very scary drop. *Will we survive the fall?* Did it matter? Sheng was right. Now or never. The opportunity might never present itself again. Freedom awaited if she could locate her courage – hiding really deep inside, underneath the panic and fear.

Easy. All she had to do was leap. A giant, freakn' leap of faith.

How bad could the plunge be?

Before she could take a deep breath and prime herself to jump, the scuff of footsteps broke the stillness of the night. Oh no! The guards arrived, earlier than scheduled.

Forget counting down, or having second thoughts. Sheng lunged forward, legs pedaling, one arm outstretched as if he meant to grasp freedom. Tethered by the hand, Sheng yanked Jiao after him.

Biting her lip, hard enough to draw blood, she halted the shriek threatening to spill from her lips – *I mustn't let the guards know we escape* – but she couldn't stop her heart from pounding a mile a minute as they plummeted in the darkness.

Down. Down. Down. The cool air whistled by her ears, but did nothing to slow her fall. Nor did she miraculously sprout wings. Or reverse the law of gravity despite her fervent wish. As for Superman? He was probably busy saving Lois Lane again.

The impact when she hit the river stalled her rapidly beating heart and she lost her grip on Sheng. Closing her mouth and eyes against the water trying to rush in and fill her orifices, she kicked until her head broke the surface and she drew in a gasping lungful of air.

What do you know? I survived the fall. Uninjured too, or so she assumed, considering she felt no pain. Felt nothing in fact but cold; a bone chilling, teeth-chattering misery as the river took her and swept her toward liberty – or death.

Chapter One

Years later ...

Drumming his fingers on the steering wheel to the hard bass of an AC/DC song, Chris cruised up the street towards his next job. A doozy of one, too. The guy who called, Asian judging by the accent on the phone, wanted an estimate on turning his basement into a veritable jungle gym with climbing ropes, wall pegs, balance beams, gymnast rings and more. Why he'd build one at home when he could just get a monthly membership to a gym for less wasn't something Chris concerned himself with. As a handyman-slash-contractor, he took whatever jobs came his way, anything to help him sock away for the time he'd leave home, which he didn't intend on doing anytime soon.

While his sister couldn't wait to leave the family nest, Chris found it quite comfortable. Sure, he needed to do his part keeping his own room tidy, helping out with the house and lawn work, but the home cooked meals and laundry – folded and ironed – totally made up for it. Oh, and you couldn't beat the cheap rent. Despite his father's wishes – grumbled loudly and often – his mother insisted Chris and his brothers only chip in enough to cover groceries. They were supposed to put the money they saved on rent aside for a down payment on their own home.

And Chris did that, most of the time. But, who could blame him for going on that trip to Cuba when he got such a smoking deal. Or the UFC tickets he'd bought, front row seats, for him and his buddies.

Yeah, so his nest egg suffered a few minor depletions, he was now determined to get his act together and start putting some dough away. The big screen, 3D television he'd seen in a flyer had nothing to do with it.

Arriving at his destination, a sprawling ranch style home – which meant a ridiculously large basement, ka-ching – Chris parked at the curb and swung out of his truck. He ambled his way to the back of his work vehicle and pulled the squealing tailgate down so he could heft out his toolbox. Clients liked it when he looked prepared, even if all he needed sometimes was a screwdriver.

Slamming the gate shut with another metallic scream begging for the lubricating miracle of WD-40, Chris grimaced at the noise. Of all the things he spent money on, the one he kept neglecting was his vehicle. Somehow, he didn't think his dad would very well handle him arriving home with a big monster truck. But then again, Chris could justify it as a work expense. Unfortunately, he could too easily imagine what his dad would say – ahem, yell.

Trudging up the front walk, comprised of builder grade, two-by-two concrete squares and unattractive stairs, he inhaled the crisp, clean air. The afternoon sun waned, the chill of autumn hard at work on turning the leaves. Some people loved summer for the sunshine and heat. Others loved winter for the crisp snow and skiing. Chris, however, would take the fall anytime. The brisk breezes which rifled through the colorful foliage. The crunch of leaves when he dove into the pile his brothers made when it was their turn to rake. Screwing outside without fear of bug bites on the ass. Football season. Oh, and his favorite holiday – Thanksgiving, with juicy turkey, savory stuffing, mom's fluffy mashed potatoes, delicious pan gravy, and whipped cream topped pumpkin pie.

Only two weeks away and already his stomach rumbled in anticipation.

Of course, fall also meant shorter days, cooler weather, and the grasshoppers of summer, a.k.a. his clientele, suddenly deciding they needed work done, NOW. Look at his current case. Called out on a service call by an intense gent who didn't want to wait, and expected a quote yesterday. Chris tried not to sigh as he thought of the lacrosse game he'd probably miss out on tonight because of this last minute job. *What's the point of having brothers-in-law who give me free tickets if I can't use them?*

Dammit, there weren't that many games left, the lacrosse season now in the final round of playoffs. But then again, he couldn't complain too much. He'd gotten to see more than his fair share of sporting events lately because of his sister's mates. He wondered if they had some pull when it came to getting cheap – or even better, free – hockey tickets.

And why the pessimism? Maybe he'd get done taking measurements quicker than expected. After all, the neighborhood was brand spanking new. How much work could there be? Chances were the basement wasn't yet finished leaving him with a clean slate. Piece of pumpkin pie. He'd get a list of what the guy wanted, take some measurements, and promise to fire him off a quote within a day. Then, race out of here and see if he could still make it in time for the game.

Knocking on the door, Chris bounced on the balls of his feet, surveying the neighborhood still under construction. He remembered it from Francine's house warming party a few weeks back. God, the fun he had bugging the hell out of his brother Mitchell when, on the tour of the house, he caught sight of the king-size bed in the master bedroom. The broken nose was well worth the ruddy-cheeked embarrassment on his big brother's face, though, when Chris asked him who slept in the middle.

What bad luck Mitchell had to share his woman with another guy. Not that Chris disliked Alejandro, Francine's other mate. On the contrary, he found Javier's brother, Alejandro, highly entertaining, especially since he excelled at driving Mitchell nuts. But still, while the threesome thing sounded kind of kinky, Chris wasn't the type to want to share, especially not his mate and for life. No way, not him.

Hopefully, with two polyamorous pairings in the family, chances were good they'd hit their quota and if he was really lucky, fate would hold off a few years before introducing him to his lucky lady wolf. He still had quite a few oats he wanted to sow and one was a blonde who'd given him her number yesterday. Maybe he'd give her a shout if he couldn't make the game, and see if he could salvage his evening partaking in a different kind of sport.

No one answered his knock, so Chris pounded harder, wondering if the guy who'd seemed so anxious to get him over here changed his mind.

The clicking of tumblers as locks disengaged told him someone finally answered the door. He didn't immediately turn, not wanting to appear too eager beaver or in their face. Like his dad told him, a hundred times or so, before it sank in, 'If you look too desperate for a job, people will either think you're incompetent, or try to pay you less.' Sound advice, much as he'd never admit it out loud to the old wolf.

The door swung open and the smell hit him first. Flowers of some sort with a hint of animal, cat he'd wager, but blended into something exotic he'd never scented before. It tantalized, but not as much as the underlying musk of the woman to whom it belonged. Toe-curling, cock-hardening woman.

Damn, that's one freakn' delicious aroma. Not just his man side reacted to the smell, his wolf did too, stirring in his mind with a rumble of excitement. *Lick her. Bite her.* His wolf had a list of things it wanted to do to the as yet unseen woman, most of them naked.

Uh-oh. That could only mean one thing.

Whirling, Chris gaped at the petite female in the doorway. His mate. Or so his yipping wolf seemed to think. Not even reaching his chin, she appeared of Asian descent, with dark, slanted eyes, high cheekbones, black hair twined atop her head in a bun, and rosebud lips, rounded into an 'O' of surprise.

Welcome to the club. Of all the things Chris expected to encounter today – hard to please client, a naked blonde, a late night burger at Al's – he didn't count on meeting the woman he'd spend the rest of his life with.

Inhaling her scent, Chris fought an urge to gather her in his arms and taste her mouth. Would she think him presumptuous if he pinned her against a wall and devoured her luscious lips? Or even better, dropped to his knees and worshipped her with his tongue. Or … Damn, the list of things he wanted to do went on and on. Best to find out her name now so he knew what to yell later when he got her into bed. Girls really hated it when you called them by the wrong name.

"Who are you?" Chris asked, pairing his query with his often used, panty dropping smile. Some guys opted for come-on lines. Chris preferred a naughty grin. And it worked every time.

"Taken," growled a male sporting the same Asian complexion as he came up behind the woman and placed a hand on her shoulder possessively. Chris noted the glint of gold on the man's finger and inwardly groaned.

Ah, freakn' hell. She's married. That would make things complicated.

*

Jiao blinked at the imposing figure in front of her. Reeled actually, as his scent, a masculine thing comprised of wild animal and a sharp soap, tickled her nose. Roused her senses. Made her feline stir with ear pricked interest.

Who is he? What's happening?

Through the cacophony in her ears – caused by her inner cat, which yowled in excitement and clawed to get out – she thought she heard the stranger ask who she was. The smile he bestowed in her direction brought a tingle to parts south of her waist and she fought an urge to purr under his admiring gaze. Her cat, not restrained by human habit, didn't hesitate, flopping down in her mind to contentedly rumble and roll in pleasure at the attention.

Who am I? he asked. *Yours,* came to mind as a reply, but thankfully didn't pass her lips. Luckier, she managed to stifle the meow of her cat before it left her lips. Before she could recover from the overwhelming presence of the stranger, or think of something intelligent to say other than 'Um', Sheng's heavy hand came down on her shoulder and he rumbled, 'Taken,' as a reply. She tucked her hands behind her back lest she give in to her wild side's impulse to swipe at Sheng for his rude answer.

Disappointment clouded the stranger's face, a quick lapse that he instantly recovered from, his expression smoothing into a jovial smile. He took the news well. Too well, and it miffed her feline half. Even odder, Jiao found herself somewhat disappointed too. Surely she didn't crave this unknown's attention?

Gently, but firmly, Sheng tugged until Jiao stood behind him. Yet, because of the stranger's great height, she could still clearly observe him at the door. Towering over her, which really didn't take much with her short five foot three stature, he possessed sun-streaked brown hair, hazel eyes framed by dark lashes, impossibly wide shoulders, a friendly smile, and a scent she found much too interesting.

Of course, while she admired all this, Sheng gave the guy, the contractor he'd called for the basement, a hard time.

"You're the handyman?"

"Yup. I'm Chris of Howling Good Reno's at your service. You called me about getting the basement converted into a home gym."

Ah yes, Sheng's brilliant plan to placate her. Since he wouldn't let Jiao shift and exercise her cat outside, he'd decided to give her a private option to morph inside. Given the amount of work involved, and Sheng's ineptness when it came to power tools, he decided to hire outside help. The most highly recommended guy for the job stood at their door. He was also the most handsome man she'd ever met and the first to ever intrigue her cat.

Jiao's teeth tugged at her inner cheek. If Chris got the contract, he'd end up at the house every day, working on the basement for as long as it took to complete the job. Weeks probably. Plenty of time to explore the strange reaction he evoked. If it were up to her, Jiao would hire him on the spot, but she said not a word, knowing Sheng would do the opposite if he knew of her interest.

A frown marred Sheng's face, a look she caught when he briefly glanced back at her. "I expected someone older."

Someone married, Jiao thought with a sigh. Sheng seemed determined to keep her away from men, all men. Single, married, young or old, fat and even human, he did his best to keep her secluded. Protecting her, he claimed. Keeping them both from discovery. He didn't seem to understand they couldn't live in hiding forever. Lies could only carry them so far.

Eventually – sooner rather than later if Jiao got a say – things would have to change. For six years they'd run and hidden from those who would take them back to their cloistered life. Frantic years spent looking over their shoulders, not trusting anyone. Relying only on each other without a friend, other than Patricia, an RCMP officer and shifter they'd befriended during their escape. Jiao tired of the subterfuge. Tired of living under the radar, in the shadows, never experiencing life.

But Sheng knew best. He'd gotten them this far after all.

Chris didn't seem daunted by Sheng's skepticism in his skills. "I've got years of experience. And references too, if you want them."

"You did come highly recommended," Sheng admitted, but grudgingly.

"What do you say you show me the space? Tell me what you need. I'll do up a quote and then we can go from there."

Sheng appeared torn, something about Chris setting off his radar, but then again, everybody set off his paranoia meter. Placing a hand on Sheng's arm, Jiao said, "He's one of us and Patricia approved him." Sheng trusted Patricia. After all, she was the one who gave them a new life, new identity, and more.

Lips tight, Sheng shook his head. "Sorry. But I don't think you'll do at all."

Then, her husband slammed the door in the contractor's face.

Chapter Two

What the hell?

Chris stared at the closed door, his jaw dropping as disbelief froze him. What was buddy's problem? Did he somehow sense Chris's interest in his wife? An interest Chris now felt sure was mistaken. He'd specifically requested, in his mind at least, to have a mate all to himself. Surely Fate heard him? Given his adamant stance on the whole subject of ménages – *not for me!* – it stood to reason, the female – hot and delectable as she smelled – didn't belong to him. Nope. She was taken. Off the menu. Not his concern.

If he knew that, then why did his feet refuse to move? Because he had unfinished business, that was why. And no, it wasn't his wolf's demand to sniff her again that had him raising his fist to knock. Then pound as no one answered the door.

I deserve an explanation. Or a valid reason, at any rate, for the dude's rejection of his services. Services, he might add, buddy asked for. But it seemed Chris wouldn't get an answer because the door remained shut.

Stepping back, Chris flipped a bird in the direction of a twitching curtain. *What an asshat.* He pitied the guy's wife. It must suck to live with such a jerk. He also thanked his lucky stars he'd gotten the shaft because given his attitude, working for the dude would have probably sucked large.

On a happier note, he'd make the lacrosse game after all. Jumping into his truck, toolbox tossed onto the passenger seat, Chris started the engine, the heavy rumble caused less by the dying diesel motor than the exhaust with its fist sized hole. As he shifted into gear, Chris turned his head to look one last time at the house where he'd gotten the rude treatment. A more hotheaded guy would have kicked down the door and beat the crap out of the little prick inside. Chris, though, preferred to think he could handle things in a more mature fashion. Holding the brake pedal down, he hit the gas, revving his engine and spinning his tires. The noise and smoke show, not to mention the probable tire marks, would hopefully annoy the Asian dude.

Keeping his eyes on the living room window, he hoped buddy would peek out so Chris could give him a single finger salute, but instead, the pretty Asian girl appeared, her head canted to the side. A smile curved her lips and she shook her head, as if chastising him.

Dammit. He was acting like a child, a petulant one who didn't get his way. With a growl, he let go of the brake pedal and took off.

What he couldn't escape? The dark eyes of the exotic female and her lingering, oh-so-yummy scent. Despite her taken status, his wolf rumbled at him to go back. *Ours.* Not likely. The woman was married which meant off limits. Out of bounds. No way, no how.

Despite that, he couldn't muster any interest to call the blonde who'd so eagerly given him her number. He blamed it on his annoyance at losing the job. Tried to convince himself he didn't bother offering to pick the woman up because it would make him late for the lacrosse match.

Liar. Liar. Wolf's on fire.

In truth, he couldn't call the big breasted blonde because a pair of dark eyes kept appearing in his mind, full of reproach. Wait a second. He didn't owe anything to the Asian girl. Yeah, she was hot. Yeah, he would have liked to tap her. But, that wasn't happening. Time to move on.

He scrolled through his contacts and found Brandy's number. His finger, however, refused to push the button to dial. Even more messed up, his wolf growled at him. Him!

"I'm in charge here, buddy," he reminded his canine half. "And I will call whomever I damned well like." He mashed his finger on the call button. It rang once. His stomach tightened. Rang a second time. His entire mouth went sour. A third time, and at the click signaling she answered, he quickly pressed the red hang up button.

What just happened? Why did the act of calling someone else make him feel sick? It made no sense.

I need a beer. Make that a dozen. And a chili dog, too, so he could forget the Asian couple – more specifically the petite hottie with the perfect mouth – and get back to normal. Well, as normal as possible for him considering his shifter status.

What he wouldn't give for a full moon tonight and a run through the woods. Nothing like howling up a storm and chasing down a rabbit to make him feel better. *But I bet I'd have more fun chasing a certain cat.*

*

Watching out the window, long after the handyman left, Jiao visibly jumped when Sheng laid a hand on her shoulder.

"You scared me," she admonished, a twinge of guilt assailing her at having gotten caught staring.

"The immature idiot is gone, so why are you still watching?"

"A better question is why you acted like such a jerk?"

The hand slid off her shoulder with the accusation and she turned to regard Sheng as he paced the living room. Sparse, because of their recent move here, it contained a red pleather couch – because no shifter with an ounce of morality would own the real thing – a plush armchair in black crushed velvet – which attracted hair like crazy – and an oval glass table in need of cleaning. Again. She hated the damned thing. Stupid dust collector.

"I saw no point in wasting his time. I didn't like him."

His response didn't surprise her. Sheng didn't like anyone. Jiao rolled her eyes. "Gee, I hadn't noticed. Still, it didn't mean you had to slam the door in his face. He showed up at your request."

"He wasn't right for the job."

"Why? Because he was young and good-looking?"

Sheng shot her a dark look. "Exactly."

So shoot her for noticing. *Hello, I'm married not dead.* "So we can only use an ugly contractor, even if he's not the best option for the job?"

Lips tight, Sheng glared, but didn't reply.

"Wow. Can you say control freak? This is going overboard, even for you." Throwing up her hands, Jiao stalked out of the room, but not without a parting shot. "Just so we're clear, if we're not allowed to have cute guys working in the house, then the same goes for cute girls."

Although, on second thought, maybe if confronted by an attractive woman, Sheng, her husband these past few years would lighten up. Just because someone was attractive didn't mean Jiao was going to rip his clothes off and betray Sheng. He should know her better than that.

Or at least that proved true up until now. Seriously, her instant attraction to the handyman defied all rational explanation. And even now that he'd left, despite his temper tantrum out front, she couldn't quite shake him from her mind, or quell the reaction of her body. The things she wanted to do... Guilt suffused her.

I'm supposed to be a married woman. Dissatisfied with her married life or not, though, didn't give her the right to lust after another.

It was probably for the best Sheng turned the Chris fellow away. Having him underfoot, his sizzling presence a constant reminder of her attraction ... Talk about a sure recipe for disaster.

Still, she felt bad at how Sheng handled the situation, and felt an even deeper chagrin that she wouldn't see the handyman again, a fact her cat complained about, loudly.

But what could she do to change the situation? Or an even better question, how much longer could she keep up the façade?

Another new town. Another new life. But things still hadn't changed.

Where's the freedom Sheng promised me?

She understood his caution, but at what point did they stop constantly looking over their shoulders and start living? When would they finally call somewhere home?

Chapter Three

The whack against the back of his head snapped Chris's attention back to the arena and the game at hand. Craning his head, Chris scowled as he saw the culprit, his sister Naomi. Wearing a baby in a chest sling, she smirked at him.

"Hey, little brother."

"What was that for?" He rubbed his noggin. Not that her little tap hurt. But still ... For a girl who screamed loud and often about her delicate sensibilities, his sister possessed a rough streak.

"Pay attention to the game. My mates are playing."

"So?"

A moment later the reason became clear as a missile sailed across the partition glass, the white, Indian rubber ball whistling past his head.

"That's why." Naomi grinned as she waved at Javier, number sixty-nine on Loup Garou, Ottawa's shifter lacrosse team. Chris could see her mate's answering smile even through his helmet, which the league insisted they wear because it minimized the blood on the floor.

"He did that on purpose," Chris growled.

"Of course he did. I told Javier to snap a ball at you during the last intermission when I saw you staring off into space. And he always listens," she bragged, sitting herself in the empty seat beside him. She shifted the sling she wore, not that the baby

21

nestled within stirred. Somehow the little bugger snored, a blissful slumber with a thumb tucked in a little mouth, and this despite the screams of the crowd.

"Where's the other one?" Chris asked.

"The other one has a name," Naomi remarked in an annoyed tone. "Melanie is staying with Francine. She gets too riled up when I bring her to the games."

"Too noisy?"

Naomi snorted. "Nah. Little Mellie gets mad when she sees people hitting her daddies and screams bloody murder, which in turn, upsets Ethan, and he ends up crushing the other team's defense. Literally. I was asked nicely by the league to keep her away so that the opposing teams wouldn't run out of able bodied players."

"And you agreed?"

"Only once they hired me to manage the league finances." Her bright grin at her maneuvering made him smile. His sister might lack the muscle to make people do things, but she possessed the smarts and right leverage to get them to give in.

"You know you're evil, right?"

"It's a gift. So hey, you never said what had you looking like a slack jawed idiot. Usually, at a game, you're pressed against the glass screaming advice to the opposition."

Yeah, he usually did. He liked doing it because it annoyed his brother-in-law Javier to no end. "Just thinking about a job I lost."

"What? Someone didn't hire you? Why not? Don't they know you're the best? Did you quote them too high? Wait, was it another one of those housewife's wanting work done on their *personal* plumbing?" She arched a brow suggestively.

Chris choked. "You did not just accuse me of being a handyman pimp."

"If the condom fits …"

"You have a foul mouth. And to think you kiss your children with it."

"According to my mates, my mouth is perfect. And there's nothing dirty about telling the truth."

Damn her, but she had a point. Yes, he did great work, but yes, he often got ridiculous calls from lonely women who needed a light bulb changed, then gave him a tip, usually on their knees. However, he drew the line at married women – most of the time.

"Well, it wasn't a wife wanting to hire me, but her husband. And he took one look at me, told me I was too young and slammed the door in my face."

"He didn't." She almost whispered the words, her eyes wide with shock.

"He did."

"Did you kill him?"

"I'm too classy for that," he replied. He almost managed to say it with a straight face too, but Naomi immediately snorted, and he erupted into laughter. "Okay. I'll admit, I might have clocked him if he'd opened the door back up. I had to content myself with leaving rubber marks in front of his house."

"Want to go back after the game and egg his house?"

A chuckle left him as her suggestion brought to mind some of the pranks they'd pulled in their youth. "No. But thanks for the offer."

"Anytime. But seriously, I wouldn't worry about it. Sounds like the client would have been a freakn' douchebag to work for. Probably a good thing you didn't get it."

"Tell me about it." He knew that, agreed wholeheartedly, yet he couldn't stop the dejection. "I don't need that kind of hassle."

"So why are you mooning about it?"

It occurred to him to deny her observation, but really, he was kind of gloomy. Without the job, how would he see the woman again? Find out why she drew him and his wolf. Should he tell his sister about his odd reaction to buddy's wife? Get her opinion?

Before he could decide, the game ended with a final buzz and a roar from the crowd. The home team won again thanks to Naomi's mates, or as she affectionately referred to them, 'my dumb jocks'.

The baby chose that moment to wake with a stretch of chubby fists. Only a few months old and he looked around with a serenity his sister lacked. His nephew, Mark, inherited his daddies' genes. Guess who took after their mother most? Chris's mom liked to cackle that Naomi got just what she deserved in Melanie, a mini version of herself.

I hope when I finally settle down and have kids, they end up nothing like me. He didn't think his paycheck could cover the damage.

But thinking of kids somehow brought his mind back to the Asian girl and his wolf sent him a thought. *Pups.* His wolf seemed to think she'd make the perfect mother, and damn him if he couldn't easily picture a girl, a miniature version of her mother that would wind him around her little finger. And a boy, with a gap toothed smile and shaggy brown hair, throwing him a football and –

Smack!

The ball hit Chris in the forehead and snapped his head back. Game over or not, his damned brothers-in-law thought he should pay attention. Never mind they saved him from his own thoughts. Chris needed to vent.

With a growl, he leapt over the row of seats and tackled the player's door into the arena. The impromptu chase and wrestling match with Javier didn't really solve anything – the damned jaguar was light on his feet – but at least it changed his focus for a while. A fat lip, black eye and bruises all over worked as a great distraction – until he pictured his Asian lady kissing his booboos better. Naked.

*

Days later …

The full moon emerged, bathing the backyard and the ravine bordering it in a soft glow. Sitting in the window seat, which spanned the length of the bay window in the family room, Jiao stared mournfully outside, but not as sadly as her cat.

"Why can't we go out?" she asked for the hundredth time, unable to mask the plaintive tone. The yard and the shadowy woods edging them looked so tempting. So perfect. The temperature crisp. The smells inviting. The chirrups of night birds taunting. Oh how she twitched to get out and stretch. Run a little. Chase something up a tree. Find some soft grass to roll in.

"I've told you a hundred times. We can't let anyone see our felines. If word gets back to Kaleb …"

"Yeah. Yeah. Everyone is a spy. Blah. Blah. Blah. We'll get kidnapped. Or stuck in a zoo. Or become the main act in a three ring circus. Hey, wait, that's happened to us before and we survived," she said sarcastically.

"You're not being funny or fair, Jiao. I'm doing this to keep us safe."

She knew that. Just like she knew six years ago she would have never joked about their time in captivity, objects brought out to entertain those rich and perverse enough to pay for it. She would never go back to that life. Ever. But freedom, or at least their version of, wasn't as much fun or liberating as she'd hoped. In many ways, she was more bound now than when she lived in Kaleb's prison.

Dejected – and her cat twitching – Jiao sighed and leaned her chin on the sill. "I know you're protecting us. But I miss running outside. I don't even remember what it feels like to climb a tree or do my nails, or hunt something."

"I miss it too," Sheng admitted in a low tone, putting his arm around her shoulder. "But, we can't risk exposure."

She gestured out the window where the distant howl of a wolf echoed. "They're not afraid." And by they, she meant the shifters who'd claimed the wild strip of forest backing the houses in this neighborhood as their own.

"They're also not rare species. Wolves, foxes and bears are common to the area. No one would think twice about seeing them. Clouded leopards, though, are not indigenous to this area, which you already know, not to mention they are rare even in captivity."

"Wouldn't people mistake us for a mountain cat? Or a lynx?"

"With our coloring?" Sheng arched a brow at her ridiculous hope. "No. We need to stay inside. Just have a little more patience. I know it won't be quite the same, but I'll get the basement done as soon as I can. Then you can at least let your cat out to exercise."

Ah, yes the basement project. Good for him for diverting her attention. Her arms crossed over her chest. "And how is that coming? Fired any more good looking guys before they even have a chance?" Oh how she loved sweet sarcasm, a girl's best friend in any fight.

Sheng's lip drew into a tight line. "No. And I didn't technically fire that Chris guy. I just didn't want to hire him. I have had another shifter in." An old guy with a belly to outshine most pregnant women. "And I'm expecting his quote any time. I've also got a line on a few humans."

Her lip curled. "Humans? Really? And how are you going to explain you want a scratching post?"

"I'll figure something out," he mumbled.

"Did you talk to Patricia about other shifters who could handle the work?" Patricia, the only one who knew their secret.

"Yes. She again recommended the guy from Howling Good Renos." Something Sheng didn't sound happy about at all.

"You should give him a chance."

"But –"

However, she'd had enough. Not only could she not change into her cat and hunt like she was meant to, she couldn't stop thinking about Chris. Oh how she wanted to see him again. Smell him. Rub against him until he wore her scent. To call her irritable was putting it too mildly.

"No more buts," she snarled, eyes narrowed and her claws extending as her cat rose to the surface. "I need something, Sheng. I can't live like this. Can't go on caging my other half. I want to tear my skin off. Gouge the walls. Kill something to stop this horrible ache inside. My cat is going mental. I need that gym. So stop imagining problems that don't exist and call the guy everyone keeps recommending. Or I swear, dangerous or not, I'm going to strip naked in the yard, shift and run until the sun comes up. Maybe even chase that stupid neighbor's tea poodle." Yappy little critter. Worse, a shifter owned the dumb thing. What carnivore named its snack?

"He won't come back." Sheng stated it with a little too much pleasure.

Men and their pride. Her lip curled. "Oh yes, he will, because you're going to apologize."

"Am not."

Jiao planted her hands on her hips. "Are too."

"Forget it. Not happening."

And that quickly, she snapped. Her body twisted and reshaped as she leapt at Sheng, her nightgown fluttering to the floor. Taken by surprise, she hit Sheng hard and took him down. He recovered quickly, his own cat springing forth until they tussled on the floor in a snarling, spitting, furry tangle.

Hair flew – probably in a direct beeline to that stupid velvet covered chair. Claws raked – and turned the maple hardwood floors into a distressed version. Teeth tugged, not hard enough to cause true damage, but she got her point across. Despite Sheng's larger size, Jiao used her annoyance and his inability to harm her against him. While she didn't manage to pin him, she did get her sharp teeth around his tail. Or as she well knew, his personal Achilles tendon.

He yowled.

She growled and shook her prize.

He tugged lightly hoping to get free.

Her teeth sank in deeper.

Beaten, he lay down on the floor and sighed, his spotted fur rippling.

Releasing his tail, she pranced around the room in victory. *I won!* Sheng would call. And she'd get to see the handyman again. In person. Not in her dreams or fantasies – and probably wearing more clothes than she'd imagined him in. A shame. But hey, at least if Sheng finally hired him, she'd get her gym. But that came second on the pleasure scale as far as her cat was concerned.

Excitement made her race around the room. She couldn't wait to see if Chris still affected her. If what she'd sensed with him before would happen again, or if was an anomaly. If he did make her cat, mind, and body, go haywire again, then what? She'd deal with that hurdle when she encountered it, whether Sheng approved or not.

I didn't escape one cage to live in another. It was time to stop hiding from the world. Time to let herself live – and maybe even love.

Chapter Four

On four feet he chased the scent. Sweet. Exotic. It promised so many things. Fun things. Naked and sweaty things.

Chris never quite got a glimpse of the one he followed, but she also did nothing to hide her trail. The minx! She wanted him to catch her. Taunted his canine side to hunt her feline one.

Eager to end the teasing pursuit, he quickened his pace, leaping through the foliage, taking care to move as soundlessly as possible through the fallen leaves. He didn't quite succeed, the crinkle of his passage loud in the still night.

She moved much more quietly, slinking and springing with a grace only cats could manage, the signs of her passage seen only in the tremble of branches and the foliage that still clung stubbornly to almost barren branches. Even without the faint physical evidence, he would have tracked her by scent alone. Despite the incongruity of a wolf lusting after a feline, her delectable aroma called him.

Trotting out into a clearing, a very empty clearing, Chris whipped his head from side to side, muzzle held high as he sniffed the air. Where had she gone? As if washed away by a heavy rain, the perfume he followed disappeared. Dissipated into thin air along with her.

Nose to the ground, he weaved through the grass, searching for a trace. Needing to find a clue. Needing to find her.

A whisper of sound and the change in air pressure warned him. He managed to partially turn, but didn't move out of the way. She hit him and they tumbled, bodies rolling through the long, dry grass and fallen leaves. They landed in a heap of *limbs. She batted him playfully and he nuzzled her. But cats and dogs couldn't mix, in their animal form at least.*

Shifting shapes, he enjoyed a brief sensation of silky fur against his skin before she too morphed into her human form. Skin to skin, he could have drooled in pleasure. Even better, he ended up on his back with her straddling him — naked.

Sweet, freakn' hell. If Chris still wore his tail, he would have wagged it.

Lips curved in a teasing smile, she regarded him with dark eyes. Her long dark hair hung over her shoulders, a tempting curtain over her breasts. But he could imagine them; small handfuls, high and perky topped with succulent berries. Lower, her smooth skin tempted as far as he could see. He longed to see all of her. To know if she shaved like a human girl, or, like most shifters, kept the fur between her legs. Short of craning, he could only see her smooth belly with its dimpled naval.

Flattening her hands on his chest, she leaned forward. "Caught you," she murmured, a mirthful lilt in her claim.

"Did you?" he queried back as he placed his hands on her hips. The feel of her flesh, warm and pliant under his fingers, made his simmering hunger flare, and his cock grew hard where it butted up against her ass. Oh how he longed to bury it inside her. To fill her with his essence. Watch her face as he stroked her to ecstasy. Claim her as his.

Why wait?

Quicker than she could reply, or taunt him more, Chris flipped them, cradling her body as he turned so she didn't hit the ground hard. He rested atop her, pinning her with his weight. Not that she did anything to protest his maneuver. Laughter spilled forth and her sharp white teeth gleamed in the moonlight while her eyes crinkled at the corners.

"I do believe you've turned the tables. But what do you intend to do now, sir wolf?"

31

Do? Why only what he'd dreamt of since first meeting her. As a cloud passed over the moon, plunging them into deep darkness, he lowered his head, intent on capturing her mouth and finally tasting the lips of the woman who haunted his every waking thought and dream since the day he'd met her.

Before they could touch, sharp claws raked his back and a heavy body tumbled him aside. Rolling to his feet, four of them as he changed back to his wolf, he wasn't quite quick enough to avoid another swipe of claws. Lucky him, he faced a very angry cat, a male cat who took offense at Chris seducing his woman. Couldn't really blame him, but it didn't mean Chris would roll over and bare his belly. Not if he wanted to win the woman who haunted him. He assessed his opponent, the little he could see.

Dark as the night cloaking him, only the glowing eyes and the scent of pissed feline helped him gauge where the enemy stood. The one thing that stood between him and his mate. Between Chris and …

"Hey, numb nuts, wake up!"

The rough shaking and name calling by his brother, Stu, yanked Chris from his dream into reality. "Screw off, jerk face," he mumbled, still groggy from sleep.

"I get better results when I screw on. And I wouldn't talk about faces. You look like you hit the front end of a truck and lost."

Patting his visage, Chris frowned. "What are you talking about? I don't feel anything wrong." The damage from the lacrosse ball to his face a few days ago was already gone. Thank God for his enhanced healing ability, an awesome shifter trait.

"Unlucky bastard. That's just your natural look I guess."

The punch he aimed his brother's way missed, unfortunately. But Stu achieved his aim. Chris, willing or not, was awake. "Any reason you woke me? Or did you just miss my witty conversation?"

"I have a better time talking with Naomi's babies."

"Probably because you're just about their age level," Chris retorted.

"Nothing wrong with being young at heart."

"Is that the line you use when you tell girls you still live at home?"

Stu's reply involved yanking the covers off and letting Chris, who slept in the buff, shiver, not from cold so much as the loss of his cozy dream. "If you're done being a douche bag, go away."

"I will, but the real reason I came up was to mention you have a phone call."

"And you couldn't take a message?"

"Do I look like your secretary? Besides, dude insisted on talking to you. Said it was important."

"Did he give you a name?" Chris asked as he rolled out of bed and yanked on some track pants left in a muddle on the floor. Screw the shirt. He'd hit the basement gym for a few minutes after he got rid of whoever was on the phone.

"No. But he's got a heavy duty accent. You know the kind most often heard in a corner store."

"Don't let mom hear you telling racist jokes. You know how she feels about them."

Flicking a worried look at the door, Stu didn't reply.

Chris snickered. "Look at the big bad wolf. Scared of his mama. I should tell."

"If you do, I'll tell dad about the television you put on layaway."

"I wish I was adopted," Chris growled. He'd thought his recent purchase a secret. He needed something to cheer him up when flashes of the Asian woman kept haunting him. How he'd explain an enormous, big screen TV to his dad when it showed up at the house he'd yet to figure out but surely something would come to mind. He hoped.

Of more interest was Stu's claim the guy on the phone sounded Asian. Could it be?

Heart thumping with excitement, Chris bounded down the stairs to the corded phone in the kitchen. His mother tossed all their wireless home phones out after claiming she was tired of hunting for the damned things throughout the house. Personally, Chris thought she liked the idea of having the phone stuck in the kitchen so she could eavesdrop. His mama made no bones that she liked to know what went on in their lives – and often meddled.

As for his cell phone … It probably died. Again. Stupid thing. Who remembered to charge it nightly? Not him, that was for sure.

Putting the thick plastic receiver to his ear, Chris pulled the handset connected to the base via a springy coil with him as he headed for the coffee maker. "Hello."

"Mr. Grayson?"

"Yup." Chris fought the elation bubbling up as he recognized the speaker.

"I'm afraid we might have gotten off on the wrong foot the other day."

Wrong foot? Understatement of the year. "Yeah. We did." He wasn't letting the guy off the hook too easy, even if he salivated at the thought of seeing the woman again.

"I-um-that is. Ow. Damn it all." The guy let out a curse and the scratchy sound of a hand covering a mouthpiece didn't completely mute the dull murmur of voices. The douchebag came back. "I'm sorry I acted like an ass." Oh, how grudgingly he said it.

"That's okay. It happens to all of us at one point in our lives." Oh yeah, Chris was the bigger man. "So, was there something I can help you with?" *Say like removing your wife's clothes and doing really dirty things to her while you're out somewhere.* Because despite his usual creed that married women or girlfriends were off limits, he felt no compunction about ignoring it in this case. Buddy deserved it. And she deserved better.

"I'd like you to come back and give me a quote on doing the basement renovation."

Yes! "No more slammed doors?"

"No," the Asian dude growled.

"In that case, sure. I'll swing by after lunch sometime, if that's okay."

"Fine. I have the day off, so anytime is good. Bye." Before the dude hung up, Chris heard him say a terse, "Happy now?"

Well. Well. It seemed his Asian friend wasn't too keen on calling him back. Of even more interest, it seemed the exotic lady haunting his dreams made him.

I'm coming back to see you, baby. This time, married or not, Chris intended to figure out if she was his mate because if he had to jack off one more time in the shower, he'd probably kill his brother. Stupid jerk kept knocking right at the crucial moment.

Whistling, he bounded up the stairs and ran into said brother in the hallway.

"What's got you grinning from ear to ear?" Stu asked blocking him from going into the bathroom.

"None of your business. Now move. I've got to get ready for work."

"Wait a second, little bro. Not so fast. You were just talking to that Asian dude on the phone. And now you're smiling. I get it. Someone's in love. I'm surprised. I didn't take you for a dick lover. Ah well, more ladies for the rest of us." Stu smirked.

Chris growled. "For the last time, I am not gay. Or have you conveniently ignored the fact I spend more nights out of the house than you?"

"And? It's not like you've ever brought a girl home. I think your stories about spreading the love with the ladies is a cover for an oral appreciation of sausage."

Oh, he did not just say that. "For your information, pencil dick, I was smiling because buddy's hot wife has a thing for me."

"Oh my freakn' god. You're going to have a threesome." Stu's eyes bugged out of his head. "And to think you made fun of Mitchell."

"I am not having a threesome. No way. No how. Over my dead body."

"Is that a comment on my lifestyle choice?" growled Mitchell's familiar voice.

Uh-oh. Chris turned and plastered a bright smile on his face "Mitchell. My favorite brother. I didn't know you were here."

"Obviously. I came to grab my bins of winter clothes. But I'm more interested in your views on polygamous relationships."

"Gee, I'd love to sit and discuss the merits with you, but I really need to shower. And shave. Important meeting with a client you know." One he preferred not to arrive to sporting a shiner. Chris healed fast because of his shifter heritage, but not that fast.

"Don't forget to shave down there," Stu remarked, gesturing to his groin. "Nothing worse than getting hot and heavy with a girl and her dude and having the pubes tangle."

Lucky for Chris, he didn't need to answer Stu's crude advice because Mitchell took offense and dove on their mouthy brother, the two of them ricocheting off the walls. With them busy pounding each other, Chris slipped into the bathroom to get ready. He wanted to look and smell his best, but for one person only. Despite what Stu implied, and how Mitchell chose to live, Chris wasn't about to be a third wheel in any relationship.

One dick. One hole. And that was final no matter how much his blood raced and his cock swelled at the thought of seeing her again. If things looked like they were heading into freaky threesome land, he had a backup plan. He'd move to Antarctica and freeze his balls off. Or kill the guy, whatever worked better.

*

Nervous, Jiao took more time getting ready than usual. She and Sheng shared the same weekday off. Unusual given they both worked at different places, she at a childcare center, and he at a car dealership. She still couldn't believe she'd convinced Sheng to call Chris and apologize, although, the concession only comprised part of the battle. Sheng still insisted that only the best quote would win. How crazy was it for her to cross her fingers and hope Chris came in first? Thankfully, Sheng didn't notice anything amiss, accepting at face value when questioned on her jumpiness that she was excited to finally see the gym plan moving forward.

Although Jiao expected it, the ringing of the doorbell still took her by surprise. Having hovered nearby on ridiculous pretexts, like dusting the spotless living room, organizing the front hall closet, washing light switches, she made sure she stayed close, wanting to see Chris for a moment alone before Sheng stepped in.

Lucky for her, when Chris arrived, Sheng was nowhere in sight. Wiping her hands on her jeans, an unusual giddiness flooded her. She hurried to the door and took a deep – not very calming breath – before opening it.

Awareness smacked her like a ton of bricks, followed by a heat wave, then a wet tsunami. How could Chris look even more perfect than before? Just who could wear a t-shirt reading 'Need Money For Beer Research' and still look sexy? Chris did, and his slow, sensual smile just made it worse.

Cheeks flushed. Nipples tingling. Cleft wet and aching. Jiao questioned her decision to get him back, even as she applauded it. As for her cat, you'd think the feline was given the biggest batch of catnip, she spun so happily in her mind.

"Hi," he said in a low rumble.

"Hi." The word barely whispered from her lips. How unlike her. She usually had a retort for everything. Confidence should have been her middle name. But, faced with an overwhelming attraction for the man before her, her body awash with sexual need, she doubted she could speak coherently.

Good and bad for her, Sheng chose that moment to arrive. Pushing her aside, features tight, Sheng stared up at the bigger man. Forget pleasantries or more apologies. Sheng did as she demanded, and no more.

"You're here." Sheng sounded so disappointed. "Follow me."

Jiao stepped to the side as Sheng whirled around and led Chris into their home. The handyman's fingers brushed hers in passing – intentionally she'd wager – and she sucked in a breath at the electric zing which shot through her. Her startled eyes met Chris' gaze as he swiveled his head, his expression equally shocked. A slow, sexy smile crossed his lips, unseen by the still moving Sheng, and her heart pitter pattered in her chest.

What was the reason for this insane attraction? Why did she have the biggest urge to throw herself in his arms and run her hands over his body?

Only one answer came to mind. *He's my mate.*

Oh dear. Sheng wouldn't like that at all. Jiao dropped her gaze and stared at her feet as the sexy contractor and her husband walked deeper into the house, heading for the door to the basement. A part of her yearned to follow, to stalk behind and watch. She didn't give in to her cat's curiosity, though. Instead, she did the smart – boring – thing and busied herself in the kitchen preparing dinner, even if it wasn't needed for hours.

Despite the fact she worked alone and forced her mind away from the handsome shifter, whose scent reminded her of the wolves she used to know in captivity, her body refused to quell, every nerve tingling. Anticipating what, she couldn't have said.

And somehow she doubted Sheng would like the answer if she decided to find out. As if that would stop her.

Chapter Five

Bad as it made him, Chris wanted to ditch the serious Asian dude and follow the hot female. Wrong move. He knew that. Doubly wrong, given she was already freakn' married, but dammit, having gotten a second whiff and then a brief touch, everything in him clamored – and howled – for him to hunt her down and make her his. The whining of his wolf in his head wasn't necessary for him to know for a fact she belonged with him. *Ours.* His wolf seemed happy he'd finally gotten the memo.

Finding his mate should have resulted in a celebratory moment, a naked sweaty moment, but somehow he didn't think her husband would approve, and Chris couldn't blame him. He wouldn't want to share her either. The possessive sort, Chris didn't want anyone touching his woman. Of course, that might be hard to enforce, given her husband had more rights than him.

Damn.

Surely destiny wasn't so cruel as to make him yearn for a woman already claimed? He didn't want to get involved in a polyamorous mating. He didn't want another man touching her silky soft skin. Making her pant. Or keen. Or …

Jealousy burned and his fists clenched at his side as he followed that other guy. How crazy was this? He wanted to beat the hell out of the dude for touching his own wife.

Perhaps he was mistaken. Maybe she wasn't Chris's mate after all. He'd not gotten any horizontal – cowgirl, or doggy style – action in a while, so perhaps he just reacted to her attractiveness. Yeah, right, and his uncle Hector didn't eat that tourist the year the deer were scarce.

Still though, what could he do? If she was truly his mate, then married or not, now that he'd met her, the mating urge, the fierce fever that caught his kind and brought on a sexual frenzy, would start. He feared it had already happened given all of his fantasies and dreams featured her – minus the husband. Whether the Asian dude liked it or not, and despite the fact Chris wasn't about to get involved in a ménage, simple hormones might force him into a situation not of his choosing.

Bloody freakn' hell.

But perhaps he jumped the gun. Just because she was married didn't mean she needed to stay that way. Not all marriages meant a true mating. He needed to find out more about her, and her marital situation, such as, was she happy? Did she and the uptight dude love each other? Were they actually mated, marked and everything, or just together? If Chris 'accidentally' killed her mate, would she forgive him and visit him in jail?

Important questions, and the best way to get some of those answers was to make sure he got this job and an opportunity to return, which, given the scowl on buddy's face, seemed less and less likely.

I'd better get my head in the game. The big one on top, not the massive one in my pants.

"So this is the space?" Chris said, gesturing to the unfinished basement. Empty of even a cobweb, the area was a blank palette waiting for his touch.

"What do you think?" was the sarcastic retort.

I think you're a douchebag. Easy. Calm. This wasn't a brother Chris could punch, but a client, a client whose wife he hoped to steal. "I think we can make an awesome gym." Turning on his contractor mode, Chris whipped out his measuring tape and got to work. He asked questions. Took notes. Made suggestions. Did everything he would normally do on a new job, and bit by bit, the dude relaxed, which meant the stick up his ass withdrew a few inches.

Crouched on one knee, finishing a sketch, Chris made small talk. "I never got your name by the way."

"Jack. Jack Smith."

Talk about a totally Anglophone name, unexpected given buddy's accent and obvious Asian parentage.

"You seem young for marriage," Chris blithely remarked as he packed up his tools.

"Jill and I have known each other all our lives."

Jack and Jill? Seriously? There went his wolf sense screaming something was hinky. But what? He doubted Jack would tell him. And there went his hope that he could steal Jill easily. Childhood sweethearts meant they shared some kind of bond. Even if they weren't officially mated, as a married couple, it meant to get Jill away from Jack, they'd need at the very least, a divorce, which made him think of something else. "Any kids?"

"No."

One small blessing. Chris would hate to wreck a family home. "So where are you and the wife from?"

"West."

The art of small talk seemed more than Jack could handle, but Chris didn't let up. "I've always wanted to see the coast. I hear its real pretty. So what brought you guys to town? Family? Work?"

"Is my life history necessary for you to do your job?" Jack rudely queried.

Clipping his pencil to his notepad, Chris stood up, and stared down at the shorter fellow. It took a lot to swallow his annoyance at Jack's continued rudeness. He'd be doing his Asian honey a favor when he took her away from this dude. "I didn't mean to pry. Just curious. I don't know how it worked back west, but out here, the shifters tend to stick together, like one big family."

"My wife and I prefer our privacy."

Gee, what a surprise, but like it or not, Jack and Jill would end up getting swallowed into the community, because it was what they did. His mama was all about being neighborly, whether a person liked it or not.

"Well, I'm done here. I'll email you the quote tonight after I get a chance to type it up. I can start as soon as you want."

"I'm getting other contractors in as well. For comparison, of course."

For a replacement you mean. Imagine that, Jack didn't trust him. Good thing he couldn't read Chris's mind and see the things he planned to do to his wife. Jack would really have a problem then.

The client saw him to the door, without a glimpse of the beautiful Jill. But Chris would return soon enough, even if he had to pay out of his own pocket to make sure he won the job.

When worried about getting a contract, there was one sure fire way to beat the rest. Make it so freakn' cheap, they couldn't pass it up. Or sabotage the competition. Chris wouldn't leave anything to chance, not with his future at stake.

*

Sheng did not look happy when he stalked into the kitchen.

"Was his quote that horrible?" Jiao asked as she dropped the chicken into the pan. It sizzled in the melted butter.

"No idea. He's going to email it to me later."

"If it's not the price, then why do you look like you swallowed a lemon?"

"There's something about him I don't like."

"You don't like anyone," she retorted, flipping the chicken she precooked for the casserole so it could brown on the other side.

"I'm just being careful. I won't do anything to jeopardize us."

"And how is a handyman going to manage that? Or do you think everyone works for Kaleb?" The man who'd held them captive from a young age. Their parents too, until they died. For a long time she and Sheng believed he ran the world, and he did in a sense, the compound in the mountains its own world outside reality.

"I am not paranoid. Just cautious."

"No, you're paranoid. Not quite tin hat crazy, but close. But I love you anyway." She grasped Sheng's hand. "Seriously though, isn't it time we stopped living like frightened animals? It's been six years Sheng. Surely Kaleb has stopped looking."

He sighed heavily. "I wish I could believe that."

"We have to put down our guard eventually. Why not here? I like it. It's nice. We finally have our own house. A yard. I met some of the neighbors. One even invited me over for coffee."

"This place is still too new. Unknown. Let's give it a while. Make sure it's safe. Then, maybe, just maybe," he repeated sternly, probably to counteract the smile crossing her lips, "we'll think about dropping the charade."

"Yay!" Jiao hugged her brother, the only family she had left. She loved him, but at twenty-two, their fake marriage was really starting to grate. Especially since she'd met a wolf who made her want a fake divorce.

"Don't thank me so quick. I said we needed to wait still. So don't get your hopes up yet."

His admonishment didn't stop Jiao from grinning the rest of the afternoon, doing hand sprints down the hall to appease her caged kitty, and singing to herself in the shower the following morning after a night spent dreaming of chocolate brown eyes and a sexy smile.

Imagine a life where she could go back to using her real name instead of her newest one of Jill Smith. A life where she could date, maybe kiss a man and plan for a future. True freedom instead of a hidden existence where no one could know the truth.

Only one thing marred her reverie. While she suspected Chris was her mate, he thought her married to her brother. If she told him they weren't, Sheng would kill her. If she said nothing, then Chris would walk away, or worse, find another woman.

The partially folded t-shirt in her fist shredded under the claws that popped out. Oops. Seemed her cat had jealousy issues. Well, so did Jiao. How to let Chris know she was interested? An honorable man wouldn't intentionally seduce a married woman. *But I could drop hints that ours isn't a match made in heaven. Maybe let him know I am open to cheating on my husband.* However, she'd have to keep it a careful secret. If Sheng thought for a minute she jeopardized them, he'd have Patricia relocate them faster than she could beg for forgiveness.

And I can't let that happen. Not when I might have finally met my mate. She needed to find a way to distract Sheng while she explored her reaction to the wolf. First though, she'd have to convince him to hire Chris for the basement project without letting on she rooted for him. How? She didn't know, but she'd figure something out. Hopefully.

Chapter Six

Chris bounded into his house with only one goal in mind. Winning. Consumed with thoughts of the woman he'd met, he whipped up a quote, then worked the numbers, massaging them into something only an idiot could refuse. Given Jack's mental deficiencies, he then worked it some more, just to be sure.

Intent on his task, he ignored the pokes from his brother Stu, cajoling him to come outside and toss a pigskin. He ignored his bellowing father demanding to know who made the great big mess in the living room. Chris had, but as he was busy, he didn't take the blame and instead pointed outside to his brother bouncing a ball off the house. The ensuing outdoor shouting match reached wicked decibel levels. Those distractions he ignored, but he moved his ass quick as a pup on the trail of prey when his mother quietly asked for a set of hands to help dry the dishes.

Only a stupid wolf got on his mama's bad side. Five foot nothing, she looked sweet on the outside, but she ruled the roost with an iron fist. His mother beat all other mothers hands down. Literally. Didn't believe his mother was tough? Just ask Katie Johnson. It took her weeks to grow back her front teeth. No one picked on Meredith Grayson's babies. Except for her, of course. Not that she resorted to violence with her pups. Often. Chris knew only too well the agony of an ear in an unrelenting grip. But worse were her subtle punishments. Starch in his underpants. Oh, and the laxative the time he didn't make it for Sunday dinner and came home stinking of booze looking for leftovers. The worst though, her sad sigh of disappointment, the one designed to make a misbehaving wolf tuck his tail and duck his head in shame.

Damn he loved her. Best mother ever!

Grabbing a dishtowel, he dried by rote as his mama washed. Sunk in his thoughts, he tried to figure out what to do about his dilemma. Killing the competition? A little too drastic. Kidnapping his mate? Might freak her out. He could …

"Why is your mind churning a mile a minute?" his mother asked.

Should he keep the news to himself? Nah, he was too giddy, and he could use her opinion. "I met my mate today." Well technically a few days ago, but seeing her again, he could now state it with certainty.

Crash. The plate hit the floor as his mother gaped at him. Chris ran for the broom and dustpan. As he knelt to clean up the mess, she asked, "Who? I thought you went through all the ladies in town. Or so their mothers have complained. Not my fault their daughters gave away the *milk* for free."

Chris grinned. He'd sowed quite a few oats with the ladies. In some cases, twice. "She's new to the area."

"Have I met her yet? What's her name?"

"Jill."

"And?" His mother tapped her foot as she waited for more information.

"Oh, you want details." He laughed at his mother's arched brow. "She's short like you, Asian heritage, cute as hell, oh, and married."

Chris should have known better than to drop another bombshell so quickly.

"Come here." Words quietly spoken, his mother crooked a finger beckoning him close.

Sighing, Chris crouched down and tried not to wince as his mother cuffed him upside the head. "Christopher Phineas Grayson. You'd better not have seduced a married woman!"

"I haven't. Yet."

He managed to avoid her next swing, but he caught the full brunt of her glare.

"I raised you better than this."

"But, Ma. She's my mate. I swear it. It's just like dad said it would be. My wolf went nuts. I got a shock when we touched. I can't stop thinking of her. The whole nine yards."

His mother frowned. "But she's married. So does that mean you're going to be in a polyamorous relationship like your brother?"

"Hell no. Not me." Chris wanted only one dick in bed. *Why couldn't she have been married to a girl?* That he could have handled.

"Well, exactly what do you plan to do if he's not just her husband, but her mate? Matings are for life."

"I guess killing him is out of the question?"

"Christopher!"

He grinned. "Just kidding." Mostly.

"Perhaps, you're mistaken. It's been a while since you came home smelling like a bottle of cheap perfume. Maybe someone needs to get laid."

A grimace crossed his face. "Ma!"

"Don't *ma* me. You're a grown man, and like all males, you need sexual intercourse to keep your brain functioning."

"We are not having this discussion," Chris growled.

"Hey, you were the one who wanted to talk."

He gaped at her. "I did not. You made me tell you."

She blew a raspberry. "Oh please. Any idiot with half a brain could see you had exciting news."

"Dad didn't notice. Or Kendrick. Or Stu."

"I said an idiot with half a brain, not empty space."

They both snickered.

"So you think I should try dating someone else?"

"Date. Screw. Whatever you want to call it. And avoid this woman. If you manage to stay away, then chances are it's not the mating fever."

"Yeah, staying away is not a likely option given I just sent her husband an awesome quote to do a job. He's sure to accept."

His mother shook her head. "You're playing with fire, my son. Even if she is your mate, if you start flirting, or more, with this man's wife ..." His mother shook her head with a woeful expression. "Don't come crying if you get hurt. A husband is well within his right to kick the ass of an interloper, possible mate or not."

"Don't worry. I've got a plan to keep him distracted while I see what's up with Jill."

Actually, he didn't have any ideas as to what to do other than the fact he intended to get to know Jill better. Naked preferably so he could mark her. Then once she was his, well, then he'd deal with the repercussions.

*

Several days later, Sheng balled up yet another quote and tossed it at the garbage can. Six contractors other than the wolf he'd had in. Five gave him exorbitantly high quotes, much higher than expected, and one didn't contact him back at all. He expected it from the humans, damned crooked thieves looking to make a heap of money, but the second and third shifter he called for numbers came in even higher. Only one quote shone amidst the rest.

One problem. He didn't like the wolf behind it.

The moment he met Chris, Sheng smelled trouble. He'd not missed how his sister and Chris looked at each other with moonstruck eyes. Talk about a complication he didn't want or need.

He knew Jiao thought them safe, his fault really because he'd done his job as protector too well. Sheng and Patricia, the RCMP shifter with connections who'd helped them disappear when they escaped the mountains, had helped him hide the evidence of Kaleb's continued interest in their whereabouts. She noted inquiries made into their identities, and if too frequent, changed their name and moved them. She monitored reports of suspicious shifter activity. When she moved from one RCMP office to another, Sheng and Jiao moved with her, using the change of scenery as another chance to further muddy their trail with a new name and life. However, despite the fact they appeared safe, Sheng knew with a certainty that often woke him with sweating, heart pounding nightmares, that Kaleb would never let them go. He'd never give up looking, not when Sheng and Jiao were so valuable as the last two of their kind, shifter kind at any rate.

Their pretend marriage kept them safe. Or so Patricia thought. Kaleb was looking for a brother and sister, not a married couple. By sticking together they protected each other. At least that was the plan, however, only an idiot wouldn't notice his little sister chafed at their false marriage. Truthfully, Sheng chafed too.

As a man, it wasn't easy to take care of his sexual needs when he had to do so in a manner that wouldn't come back to bite him. Playing the role of married man meant acting the part, and not getting caught cheating. It sucked. A lot. What Sheng wouldn't give to be able to have a real girlfriend that he could see on a regular basis. One night stands, all he could indulge in for the moment, left him feeling more alone sometimes, and dirty. What did those poor women think when he never called them back?

But despite how he felt, Sheng would do anything to keep Jiao safe. He'd promised his father, and he would keep his word.

"Lee! No!" his mother's cry of panic almost had Sheng dropping his sister as they practiced their routine on the practice rope strung only two feet from the ground. Without speaking a word, Sheng and Jiao raced out of the gymnasium to the courtyard. The harsh sobs of their mother slowed their steps, but it was the coppery stench of blood, which halted Sheng. Not so Jiao.

With a cry, she flew to their mother and dropped to her knees, her tears falling as freely as her sobs. Throat tight, Sheng clenched his fists at his side, warring with an urge to run away, to deny what happened in front of him. But his father didn't raise a coward.

Stiff legged, his back ramrod straight, he stalked to the huddled group, ignoring the indifferent gazes of the guards milling around. *Show no weakness*, he could almost hear his father say the words. He'd heard them so often, he knew better than to display any emotion. He wouldn't give the guards or Kaleb the satisfaction. But damn, it was hard.

His mother and sister made room for him as he arrived. The shock of seeing his father's face, pale and covered in blood, obviously dying, sent Sheng to his knees.

"No." He whispered the word, tried to deny the evidence of his father's impending mortality.

Hearing him, his father turned his head, and caught his gaze. A wan smile crossed his face. "My son."

"What happened? I thought you were out leading a hunt. Did someone mistake you for the prey?"

"No mistake. I was the prey. My punishment for getting old."

Shock sent Sheng rocking back on his heels. "Kaleb did this to you?"

"In a sense. But it's not important. I'm dying, Sheng." The words made his mother and sister wail louder. His father winced and beckoned him closer. Sheng bent down to hear.

"Promise me. Promise me you will take care of your sister and mother. Do not let Kaleb hurt them. Find a way to escape. Find the courage I lost to regain your freedom."

"But how? He's too strong. I need your help. You'll heal. You always do."

A cough wracked his father's body, a violent spasm that once completed left his father's lips sprinkled with bright red. "They used silver buckshot. I won't be healing. Once I die – "

"No. You can't die!"

"Too late," his father stated, his certainty firm, sending Sheng's mother into hysterics. "You need to escape. Have to. You're smarter than I, Sheng. You'll find a way. You must. Promise me."

Death lingered close by, the chill of the grave already reaching for his father. Tears hot in his eyes, Sheng nodded, what else could he do? He whispered. "I promise." Eyes closed shut in an attempt to stem the pooling moisture, Sheng didn't need to look to know when his father died. He heard it. Heard the last rattle of breath leaving is body. Heard the heart wrenching screams of his mother. The soft sobs of his sister.

The weight of his promise hung heavy on his young, narrow shoulders, but at the same time, they gave him strength. His father believed in him. He'd live up to that promise.

If only he could have given some of that will to survive to his mother.

Shaking his head to dispel the sad memories, Sheng hardened his heart. So what if Chris was possibly Jiao's mate? Sheng didn't believe in the mating fever and Jiao's safety would always come first, whether she appreciated it or not.

Despite the spark he'd sensed between his sister and the wolf, despite the fact she might resent his actions, Sheng would keep them apart. Keep them from destroying the charade that protected them. Even if it meant dishing out more money and working longer hours for the home gym he'd promised her, a safe place for her cat to exercise away from prying eyes. *I will protect her from herself.*

Problem was, when he tried to call the overpriced contractors, not a single one could take the job. One cited a full workload, despite previously claiming he could start within a day. Another had a family emergency. No answer for the third or fourth.

As for the fifth, the only other shifter who'd bothered to send in a price? He claimed he'd under quoted and wanted to double the money.

Fuming, Sheng stared at the only remaining quote on his desk.

"Why are you trying to set the paper on fire with your eyes?" his sister asked, as she came to stand behind him.

"I have to go with the wolf if you want the gym by the next full moon."

"I want the gym."

"Maybe we should wait. One of the guys says he'll have time in about six to eight weeks."

"Two months? No way. You promised me somewhere I could let my cat out. Unless you've changed your mind about the woods?"

"You know we can't be seen."

"Then the answer is easy. Hire the wolf. Get me my gym."

"I don't think hiring him is a good idea." Every instinct for preservation he owned screamed no.

"Why not? What's the problem?"

"I don't like him." Didn't like the feeling he got that letting Chris into their life would introduce chaos and disruption.

"So you've said. Numerous times and I'm still not sure why. I thought he was rather nice."

"Therein lies the problem," Sheng snapped. He whirled his chair around and glared at her. "I'm not blind Jiao. I saw how you stared at him."

Turning away, his sister toyed with the books on the shelf and shrugged before she replied. "He's attractive. Who wouldn't look?"

"You're married. It's not seemly for you to notice."

"It's a fake marriage to my brother," she growled back. "Can you really blame me for admiring a handsome man? Not only do I have eyes, I'm twenty two years old and a virgin."

"As is proper for an unwed woman." Actually, he'd prefer she remained that way permanently. Some things a brother just didn't want to think of.

"But that's just it! How can I get married if I can't even look at a man?"

"It's to keep you safe."

"Maybe I'm tired of being safe. Maybe I'm ready to do something dangerous. What was the point of escaping for our freedom if you've got me chained up just as tight?"

Sheng's lips tightened. Did she really compare his careful protection of her to the monster that held them prisoner? "Well excuse me for everything. If I'd known you'd prefer staying behind and playing brood mare so Kaleb could sell your cubs, then I would have left you to rot in his prison." No he wouldn't, but in the heat of anger, the words slipped out. The immediate fear in her eyes slapped him with chagrin. "I'm sorry, jiĕ zĭ. I didn't mean that. I'm just worried."

"I'm sorry too, Sheng." Jiao knelt beside his chair and laid her head against him. "I know what you've sacrificed. I'm just impatient. I think it will help when I can let my cat out to exercise."

Such a small request, one he could give her, appease her with so she'd forget the rest for a while longer. "I'm chafing to let my feline out too. Which is why, despite my better judgment, I'll hire the wolf.

But," he held up a finger. "Promise me you'll stay away from him."

When Jiao didn't reply, Sheng wanted to grab a hold and shake her. He could tell she planned to do something. A part of him couldn't really blame her. Given this insight, he realized he'd have to do his best to keep them apart. If the wolf had any honor, then perhaps he'd stay away from a married woman.

If not, then it wouldn't be the first time Sheng did something drastic for his sister. Something for her own good.

*

Jiao left her brother with her heart heavy with sorrow and, at the same time, bursting with joy. On the one hand, Jiao would get to explore the feelings Chris evoked. Discover if he was her mate as she suspected. Indulge in things she'd yet to experience like flirting and maybe even a kiss.

But, on the other hand, Jiao hated going against her brother's wishes. Sure Jiao didn't reply when Sheng asked her for a promise to stay away, didn't lie to Sheng's face, but only because she knew she couldn't stop herself from finding out more about this Chris. From seeing him. Touching him.

Hugging her brother's stiff body, Jiao bit her lip at the realization Sheng already guessed her plan.

How she wished she could find her brother a mate of his own so he'd agree once and for all to drop the charade. Or, if that proved impossible, at least help him get laid so he'd lose some of his uptight attitude. Some relationship doctor on a late night show claimed sex cured everything. It wasn't just her cat's curious nature that wanted to test that theory out. Perhaps a good screw would fix her brother's inability to laugh and smile.

How she missed that side of him.

Only seventeen when they escaped, Jiao barely sixteen, he'd taken the role of protector seriously. He'd kept his promise to their father made less than a year before, getting them out of that freezing river before a fish ate them or they drowned. He'd held her head above water when her leaden arms would have given up. Despite their captivity and inexperience with the outside world, he'd persevered and found them a way through the wilderness to civilization. A frightening time she'd never forget, where hunger seemed their constant companion, and terror haunted their footsteps. Lucky for them, they'd run into a grizzled bear of a man who knew who to call for help.

Even when Patricia took them under her wing, spiriting them across half a continent, Sheng didn't relax. Didn't let down his guard. Didn't smile.

In an odd twist, freedom lay more heavily on him than captivity. He trusted no one. Constantly looked over his shoulder. Jumped at every shadow. How she wished she could change that. The only way she could think of involved taking herself out from under his protective thumb, leaving him free to live his life without having to worry about her.

He'd never agree to that unless he thought her safe, which meant she couldn't just move out on her own. But, if she found her soul mate, a strong male who could take over the role of protector, then perhaps Sheng would finally let go. Say, someone like a big, strong wolf?

Just the idea made her giddy. Yet, she got ahead of herself. First, she needed to find a way to get to know the wolf without having her brother freak. Then she needed to ascertain if what she felt truly was the mating bond and not just a delayed hormonal reaction to an attractive male.

Either way, Jiao wouldn't let life and this opportunity pass her by. She just hoped – and she crossed her fingers tight – that she didn't end up inadvertently alerting Kaleb, the very thing Sheng feared. She'd hate to have to listen to his 'I told you so' for the rest of her – possibly short – life.

Chapter Seven

Chris got the phone call late in the afternoon telling him he got the job and to show up the next day at nine a.m. Letting out a whoop of victory, Chris grabbed his mother and swung her around.

Sighing, she tsked him when he set her on her feet. "Calm down. What did I tell you about taking it easy? And what happened to showing a girl a good time first before chasing after the married one?"

"You want me to cheat on my mate?" He drew himself up with an indignant huff.

"You're sure she's your mate?"

"Absolutely. I can't stop thinking about her, Ma. It's all I can do to stop myself from marching over there and claiming her."

"My baby boy is in lust."

"Love."

"It's too soon to call it that," his mother admonished. "You don't even know this girl. She could be a right bitch for all you know. Just because fate wants to tie you together doesn't mean it's a match made in heaven."

"Pessimist." Her words of caution couldn't penetrate his bubble of excitement.

"Realist. While it's rare, not all matings work out. Yes, our heritage ensures the sexual spark and need to claim the other person is there, but sometimes, despite the attraction, personalities just don't mesh."

"Not in this case. Wait until you meet her."
Sure, he'd only exchanged the barest of greetings, but
his gut – and his wolf – told him this girl would exceed
his expectations.

"Why wait? I want to meet this girl who's got
you in such a tizzy. Invite them over for Thanksgiving
dinner on Sunday. I've got more than enough turkey
for a few extra mouths."

"Them?" Chris frowned.

"I can't exactly invite her without her husband.
Despite what you hope, there's a strong chance he'll
be a part of your life if you claim this girl. We can't
leave him out."

"How am I supposed to get to know her, like
you said I should, if he's hanging around? Dude is a
serious stick in the mud."

"*Dude* is her husband. She must have seen
something redeeming in him or she wouldn't have
married him."

Actually, Chris preferred to think she'd not had
a choice in the matter. While uncommon, some shifter
groups still believed in arranged marriages, and also,
how many childhood sweethearts got together young
only to realize later what a mistake they made? Jack
and Jill as a couple were a mistake, an unfortunate
pairing he intended to split up. Damn, that sounded
cold even when not spoken aloud. But still, what else
could he do? Jill was his mate. Once his mother saw
that, maybe she'd think of a way to help him claim her.

"Fine. You win. I'll invite them both to dinner
on Sunday."

"No. I will. If the husband already dislikes you,
then it's best if I do it. Besides, I'd like to meet this
paragon who's managed to snare your interest."

"No baby pictures," Chris warned.

"Aw. No fun, my son. And here I had a whole slide presentation ready of your most embarrassing moments."

"You're kidding? Right?"

Her serene smile didn't reassure.

*

Jack let Chris into the house when he returned the Friday before Thanksgiving. Not catching sight of Jill, Chris couldn't help asking, "Where's the wife?"

"Work. You won't be running into her much. I got a key made for you. I want you to restrict your work hours to between nine and four thirty when we're both at work."

How devious of Jack. Did he suspect Chris's interest? "It will take a lot longer to get the job done," Chris warned. "I don't mind staring early and finishing late."

Baring his teeth in a smile that didn't reach his eyes, Jack replied. "Take as long as you need. I don't mind paying a little extra to ensure my wife and I retain our *privacy*."

Chris didn't miss the emphasis and jealousy reared its head. However, punching his employer on day one probably wouldn't go over well. He gnashed his teeth as he followed Jack to the basement. He needed to find a way to change the husband's mind about his work hours. The whole point of getting the job was to run into Jill. Flirt a little. Touch her a few times innocently and see what happened. He'd have a hard time convincing her of their destiny as a mated couple if he never saw her.

As Chris worked, getting his job site setup and some of the basics started, he pondered the problem. Stewed over it all day as a matter of fact and when four thirty hit, he was tempted to ignore Jacks' request and stay late. He could have pled losing track of time. But, just as he pondered the wisdom of pissing off his new boss on the first day, he got an idea.

Returning Saturday at nine a.m. – because Jack didn't specify what days, just the time – Chris knocked. No one answered and he noted the lack of vehicle in the driveway. Damn. He'd hoped his decision to work weekends would allow him to run into Jill. However, just because they weren't there now didn't mean they wouldn't return soon. Perhaps they went out for breakfast, or to run some errands. *Maybe they're having sex?*

Chris growled at the thought until he reminded himself the car was gone from the driveway. They weren't home, but if he was lucky, they would probably return while he worked. Desperate, he knew, but unable to get her out of his mind, he'd take whatever thin chance he could. Chris let himself in with the key Jack gave him.

As soon as he stepped in, her scent enveloped him. Clinging to the walls, the furniture, it surrounded him and while it roused his wolf, at the same time, it calmed him. Breathing deep, he allowed himself to enjoy the fragrance for a moment before heading to work. He'd almost made it to the basement stairwell, when something whacked him on the back of the head. Stunned, he didn't initially react, so the person hit him again.

Chapter Eight

Jiao heard someone knocking at the door but ignored it. House rule number one when Jack went out was 'don't answer the door'. So she didn't and nearly peed her pants when someone opened the front door. Worse, she couldn't smell them because she'd caught a cold and with her nose stuffy – red too, from blowing, ick – she didn't know if friend or foe entered. Although, considering they had no friends, foe seemed more likely.

Grabbing a hold of the rolling pin she was using to make a pie crust for the quiche she'd planned for lunch, she vetoed the hallway which would have meant a direct confrontation with the intruder and instead, slunk through the dining and living room area coming up behind the stranger in the front hall. Wearing a plaid shirt, jeans, and a baseball cap, he seemed really large and imposing.

Shutting her eyes tight, she swung. The object of her whack, grunted, and she opened her eyes to see him still standing, so she swung again.

Down he went in a sprawled mess. Rolling pin held to the side, she approached him on silent feet, ready to hit him again if he moved. Up close, she noticed a few things. How the jeans molded a taut ass and the seams of the shirt strained. Oh, and the fact that lying prone on her floor, face turned to the side, eyes closed, was Chris, the wolf and object of her fantasies the last few days.

Oops.

Chagrined, she dropped her weapon of baking destruction, and knelt beside him. Before she could touch him and see if he lived, she found herself flat on her back, a heavy body pinning hers to the floor. Startled she could only squeak in surprise. While her tongue lost its ability to speak for a moment, her body had no problem feeling, though. She noted how his calloused fingers gripped her wrists above her head. How his lower body nestled against hers, igniting a heat that crept through her limbs. Her lips parted as he caught her gaze with his intense brown one. She wondered what he planned in retaliation for his injury. Was it bad to hope for a kiss? A punishing one of course.

"Good morning," he said, in a rumbly voice which did nothing to ease the agitation of her body, but rather increased it. "Do you always greet visitors with possible concussions?"

"Visitor? How was I supposed to know it was you? I thought you were a robber!" She tried to hide her rapid pulse and flushed cheeks behind a partial truth. Yes, she'd initially thought him a bad guy, but the truth was, the reaction of her body owed less to fear and more to excitement that he pinned her.

"I'm sorry. I didn't mean to frighten you."

"Apology accepted," and then because she did feel a twinge of remorse, she asked. "Did I hurt you?" But she bit her tongue before she could also say, *Do you need me to kiss you better?*

"Does my pride count?" he asked, his lips quirking in a grin.

Okay, so a small flicker of pride lit inside at the admission she'd snuck up on him. Feline one, canine zero. "Perhaps you shouldn't sneak into houses?"

"It's not sneaking if I have a key. And, I might add, I did knock first."

Hmm. So he had. But she couldn't admit the rule forbidding her from answering. It sounded crazy and super controlling when spoken aloud. "I was busy."

"Cooking I would assume? I guess I should count myself lucky you didn't choose something more dangerous, like a spatula, or a fork."

She couldn't help smiling. "I did think of using the frying pan."

"Ouch. I'll consider myself warned. Next time, I'll be sure to call out when I enter."

"But what if I'm in the shower? I wouldn't hear you then." Why she tossed that out there, she couldn't have said. The reaction proved interesting though. His gaze practically smoldered, and he shifted his hips against her, a hardness pressing against the vee of her thighs in a most delicious fashion.

"I should be so lucky," he murmured.

Flustered at his innuendo, she pulled her hands free from his loose grip and pushed at his shoulders. Rock hard, and unyielding, she clenched her fingers into fists attempting to resist temptation. It didn't work and her hands flattened on his shoulders.

"You should let me go."

"And if I don't want to," he replied, dipping his head lower.

This close to him, the insanity of before returned in spades. Even without a scent, her cat made a fuss and her claws popped out of her fingers, wanting to dig into his flesh. Knead him and purrrrrr…

It wasn't just her cat that was going nuts. She couldn't stop her body from reacting, her core temperature rising while her heart pounded a mile a minute. She wanted to kiss the lips so close to hers. Remove Chris's hat and run her fingers through his thick hair. Wanted to …

A tickle in her nose warned her. "Oh no. I have to sneeze," she gasped. He reared back, but not far enough. She achooed with gale wind force right on to the front of his shirt.

It wasn't pretty.

"Oh my god. I'm so sorry," she babbled, the heat in her body gone because it bolted to her cheeks.

Getting off her, Chris stood and couldn't quite mask the incredulity on his face as he stared at his shirt front. "It's okay. Not your fault. I should have moved faster. Quite the cold you got there."

Embarrassed, she nodded. "I'm really sorry. Usually, I can't catch a thing, but the seniors home I work at is overrun with sick people this week. And, well my body hasn't quite fought it off yet and … " She trailed off as he grinned, his eyes twinkling.

"No big deal. My niece and nephew have done worse to me."

"You're an uncle?"

"Yup. My sister had twins. Cute little suckers too. But gooey. I don't think that much drool is normal, but my sister insists it is."

"Better than spit up," she replied recalling the few babies she'd encountered growing up.

He shuddered. "Don't remind me."

The humor in his tone, laced with an obvious strong affection for his family, made her drop her eyes. She once again noticed his chest and the mess she made on it. "If you're planning to work here for a bit, then maybe I could wash your shirt out for you?" She said it, not really thinking through what it meant.

"If you don't mind, that would be great."

Quicker than she made the offer, the shirt came flying off. Holding the bundled fabric out, Chris waited when she didn't immediately grasp it. Um, she knew she should grab it and run, but she couldn't. She couldn't move at all actually, not with so much skin in front of her. And not just skin, but muscle. Corded arms led to the impossibly wide shoulders she'd admired before. His chest rippled with definition, from his pecs to his washboard abs. A dusting of hair on his upper torso led down to his navel, to a lean waist under which his jeans hung low, indecently so.

Swallowing hard, she forced her gaze up to his amused one. Cheeks burning at having been caught staring – and by a woman he thought married, no less – she grabbed his dirty shirt and practically ran away. But she couldn't escape the low rumble of his chuckle, or the heat burning through her body.

Maybe having him so close wasn't a good idea after all. Because now she didn't have a single doubt. Either that wolf was her mate, or at twenty-two, her body was going into a sudden sexual revolt and was ready to jump anyone not related to her. Given she'd not had an urge to kiss the pizza delivery guy the night before, or maul the gas attendant, it made the first option most likely.

And frightening. Not only was she in a fake marriage, hiding from a criminal who wanted her back, she'd sneezed chunks on her mate. Way to go.

I'm doomed to be single forever.

Or not. Chris didn't seem all that perturbed she'd used him as a Kleenex. Good looking and with a sense of humor? She should end up so lucky. Given the seriousness of her life, a little laughter sounded awfully nice. Not to mention, he came with a built in family, one he appeared close to. What she wouldn't give to belong somewhere again. To have babies to hold, and other women to talk to.

Dream or possibility? Of more importance, did he feel the same connection?

Dumping his shirt into the washer along with some soap, Jiao recalled the brief moment before the untimely sneeze. That one unforgettable second in time where he almost kissed her. Despite her inexperience, she'd watched enough movies to know they'd come close.

A frown creased her brow. *He almost kissed a married woman.* For some reason, it bothered her. It was one thing for her to plan to drop subtle – or not so subtle – hints at her availability, another for him to manhandle her and take liberties when, for all intents and purposes, she was taken. *Just what kind of wolf is he?* Did she truly want to get with a man who would do such a thing as seduce another man's wife?

Much as it pained her to admit, perhaps Sheng was right. Maybe Chris was bad news. Perhaps he wasn't her mate but a man whose physical appearance appealed to her.

Or …

Could Chris, like her, feel so drawn that it didn't matter if she appeared taken? Did he know or sense they were mates? Was he unable to stop himself?

Jiao recalled her mother saying when a shifter met the 'one', all common sense, all reason went out the window. Need, a pure need to mark and claim, drove the fated pair.

In that case, could she hold his inability to keep himself at arm's-length, as was proper, against him?

Look at her. Knowing the danger, and how her brother would freak, did she not do her best to ensure Sheng would hire Chris? Going so far as to shred one quote and bribe others to pretend unavailability. She did that, and would have done more to see Chris again. And yet, she took offence at his actions?

Oh the confusion. More than ever, she wished she had someone to talk to. How she missed the wisdom of her mother. Would have loved to have a friend, a female friend, someone who would listen and give advice. But Sheng thought it too dangerous. The fewer people who knew their secret, the better. Yet, Jiao wondered if perhaps Sheng's paranoia was too extreme. Kaleb and his goons lived so far away. *And not everyone we meet is a spy.*

However, did she dare take that chance? It wasn't only her life at stake, but her brother's. Despite her need for change, she would never do anything to harm him.

Back to square one. What to do?

The shirt washed on a quick rinse cycle, all Jiao dared given her brother wouldn't stay out running errands forever, she tossed it in the dryer. As it tumbled around and around, she couldn't help thinking of the wolf in her basement, the shirtless wolf. The very handsome, deliciously sexy, half-naked man.

Right or wrong, she couldn't help herself.

Minutes later, she headed downstairs, her arms loaded with a tray carrying a steaming decanter of coffee and a plate of pastries she'd bought a few days back. A little stale, they at least provided a plausible cover for when she went to corner the wolf, and hopefully figure out some things. *Like will he try to kiss me again?* Was it wrong for her to fervently hope yes?

*

Perturbed at what happened upstairs – *I almost kissed a married woman!* – Chris took up where he left off the day before, letting the calming monotony of work – hold nail, hammer, hold nail, hammer – bring his frenzied state of mind down a notch.

His mate attacked him. A fact his brothers would think was hilarious. In his defense, Chris didn't smell her approach, not with the scent of her all over the house. And she'd not actually hurt him. Surprised him yes, but as soon as she got the first hit in, he'd guessed who wielded the weapon. Not wanting to frighten her, he'd let her get in a second lick and feigned falling to the floor unconscious. His ploy gave him a great excuse to touch her and he'd almost gotten to kiss her. Almost got to taste the lips haunting his dreams.

Her ill-timed sneeze ruined it, and in a sense saved him from himself. What would she think of a man, a virtual stranger, manhandling her and stealing a kiss? She'd think him a right jerk especially considering he knew she was married.

Still, though, in the heat of the moment, that simple tidbit of sanity fled him. So much for seducing her slowly. Forget discovering more about her situation. One touch of her body against his, and boom, he turned into an idiot.

An idiot who turned her on though. Yeah, baby. He'd noted the way she admired his bare chest. *But what about my mind?* Chris snickered to himself. In the past, he'd used his body to get women, counted on his physique actually to do the work. Yet, now that he'd met his mate, was it enough? He couldn't help recalling his mother's words about attraction not meaning they'd have anything in common. Did it truly matter? Since when did he care if a female just wanted him because he was hot?

He cared a lot, he realized. He'd met the woman he'd spend his life with, a woman he hoped to convince to leave her husband. He'd need more than good abs and excellent technique if he wanted to claim her.

A clatter of feet on the stairs saw him putting his hammer down. He didn't need to sniff, or have his wolf yip, to know she came to see him. It was his lucky day. He'd have to remember to buy a lottery ticket when he finished work.

Balancing a tray, Jill wouldn't look him in the eye as she approached, but her awareness of him showed in the blush on her cheeks. Cuter and cuter.

"I was making myself some coffee and wondered if you'd like some."

"I'd take it intravenously if I could."

She set the tray on the worktable he'd set up the day before and busied herself pouring, still not meeting his eyes, nor speaking. Funny, because he'd not taken her for the super shy type.

He broke the silence. "Sorry about what happened before. I think I might have still been groggy from the blow to the head. I usually don't molest the wives of clients."

Big brown eyes met his. She looked startled at his boldness. "Oh. No worries. I shouldn't have hit you in the first place."

"And I should have knocked longer or harder."

"Yes, you should have." Her mischievous smile stole his breath, lighting up her whole face. "Now that we've ascertained you've won the blame game, how do you like your coffee?"

Cute and sarcastic. He liked her more and more. "Hot. Dark. And in my mouth." Okay, so he imbued the harmless words with a little more meaning than he should. Totally worth it. The pink in her cheeks heightened, and taut nipples poked through the fabric of her shirt. Damn, but she knew how to tempt a man, even if inadvertently.

"Here you go." She didn't reply to his innuendo as she handed him the cup.

He intentionally touched her hand as he grasped it, watching her closely for a reaction. He got one. Her breathing hitched, and her fingers trembled before she yanked them away.

Chris hid a grin by taking a large sip. Damned coffee just about turned him into a furry wolf. Strong didn't come close to describing it. Something of his shock must have shown because her lips twitched.

"I guess I should have warned you that my coffee sucks. I'm a much better cook than I am a coffeemaker."

"No, this is great," he lied taking another gulp. Oh yeah. Strong enough to wake the dead. With the amount of caffeine already coursing through his body, he'd probably have to do a few hundred laps before going to bed in like fourteen hours.

"So how's it coming?" she asked as she wandered around peering at the two by fours he'd gotten in place against the exterior concrete walls.

So the hot kitty wanted to talk? Excellent. "I'm just getting the framework up first. Then, the insulation followed by drywall. Once that's done and approved by the city inspectors, I'll get started on the actual gym itself."

"Will it take long to build?"

"Depends. I've been told I can only work from nine to four thirty."

A small laugh left her. "Ah yes. My husband wants to make sure you don't impact our home life, and yet, here you are on a Saturday."

Time to play dumb. "Was I not supposed to work on weekends? He didn't mention any specific days, just times."

Turning to face him, he could see the mirth in her gaze, a look that clearly said she didn't believe him. "How remiss of him."

"Indeed. I take it he's not home?" Chris asked casually as he picked up his tape measure and marked out the next pieces to cut.

"Nope. But he's coming back soon," she warned.

"He seems rather protective." With good reason given Chris wanted his woman.

She shrugged. "I guess. But he has his reasons. What about you? Do you have a wife or girlfriend waiting for you to finish work?"

He ducked his head lest she see his grin at her casual foray into his personal life. "Nah. I'm a single guy. Just waiting to meet the right woman."

"And when you find her?"

Chris raised his eyes until he caught her gaze, and held it. "When I find my mate, nothing will keep me away. I will seduce her. Mark her. And claim her."

"What if she's not available?" she asked in a low voice.

"I won't let anything stand in my way."

Caught in a staring match, he could hear her heart pounding. Smell her lust. Craved to clasp her in his arms and show her the truth of his words.

The phone rang and broke the spell. Like a skittish cat, she bounded up the stairs, away from him. But while she could run for now, he'd catch her in the end. *And make her mine.*

Of course, that task got harder when Jack, the annoying husband came home, exchanged words with his wife, and then came barreling down the stairs. Thankfully, Jill had tossed down his clean and dry shirt a while before, so at least the husband didn't have to wonder why a half dressed handyman came in on a Saturday.

"What are you doing here?" Jack barked.

"Working." Chris powered up the saw and zipped through another piece of wood.

"I see that. But why?"

Chris hefted the cut piece of wood and headed for the wall. "You said to work between nine am and four thirty. It's currently only just after noon."

"But it's Saturday."

"And?"

"You're supposed to come Monday to Friday."

"Well, you never explicitly said that," Chris replied playing dumb. Something his brother Stu would have claimed he did all too easily.

"I am now."

"Are you sure? Because, given I can't start early or work late, that's going to add at least two weeks to the job. Maybe three."

Before Jack could yell something, probably to the effect of 'So what!', he got saved in an unexpected way.

"Let the man do his work," Jill admonished coming down the steps.

"This doesn't concern you," Jack growled, a tone which put all of Chris's hackles up.

No one talks to my woman that way.

Forget springing to her defense though, Jill did that all on her own. "Doesn't concern me?" she snapped, eyes flashing and chin tilted stubbornly. "You promised me this gym before the next full moon. And now I find out you're sabotaging that by forcing our contractor to work restricted hours."

"I have my reasons," Jack muttered.

"I know your reasons and I'm telling you right now, to stuff them. I want this gym. The quicker the better." Hands on her hip, she glared at her husband, and Chris stifled a grin. Damn but she looked hot when she was irked. Even better, not all was rosy between the couple.

"But —"

"Don't you but me, *husband.* Or else."

What the or else was, Chris didn't know, but Jack and Jill exchanged a look, and the Asian man scowled.

"Very well. You win. He can work whatever days and hours he likes." The smile of triumph on her face just made Jack's glower deepen.

Singing inside, Chris pretended to ignore their marital spat as he measured out another crosspiece. His wolf quieted as her footsteps receded. Drawing a line on his next length of wood, he ignored the stare of the man still standing across from him.

"So, am I to expect you tomorrow as well?" Jack finally growled.

Sunday? Hmm. Not this week. "No, actually. It's Thanksgiving and my mother would shave me bald if I missed the family supper. You got any plans?"

"No." With his terse reply uttered, Jack spun on his heel and stalked off.

Only then did Chris grin. Married or not, either Jill just gave him the opening he needed, or she truly wanted that gym. According to his ego, and his wolf, it was the former.

Freakn' awesome.

Chapter Nine

When Jiao answered the door later that day, just after dinner time, a woman about her height with graying hair pulled into a pony tail, stood there. A familiar scent washed over her. The stranger smelled an awful lot like Chris, which meant...

"Hi. You must be Jill. I'm Meredith Grayson, Chris's mother, also head of the Shifter Welcome Committee for the Ottawa area. Nice to meet you."

Jiao clasped the outstretched hand and shook it, wondering at the woman's presence. *Did she come to warn me away from her son?* Oh please, no. If Sheng heard anything of the sort, he'd have them packed and gone by the morning. "It's nice to meet you, ma'am."

"Oh goodness. Call me Meredith. We don't stand on formalities around here."

Remembering her manners Jiao opened the door wider. "Would you like to come in for a cup of tea or coffee?"

"Perhaps another time. I'm in full prep mode for Thanksgiving dinner, but I thought I'd take a little break and pop on over to introduce myself and invite you to come tomorrow for supper if you don't have plans."

"Oh, I couldn't impose." Even if the thought of seeing Chris and meeting his family intrigued.

"But I insist."

"My husband –"

"Should come along, too." Meredith's smile turned almost predatory. "I'd love to meet him as would my husband Geoffrey."

"He's not the most social of people," Jiao admitted.

"Perhaps we can cure him of that."

Good luck. She'd not had any success. "I'll ask him."

"Ask me what?" Sheng asked coming into the room.

"Jack, this is Meredith, head of the Shifter Welcome Committee. She's invited us to come for Thanksgiving dinner."

"How kind, but I'm afraid we must decline," he answered politely. Gee, like she couldn't have guessed his response on her own. And usually, she would back him, but ...

"Why can't we go?" she asked, pinning him with a stare. "We don't have any plans, and I've yet to master making a turkey."

"My family is very friendly, as are our friends and neighbors," Meredith added. "The more the merrier."

"We wouldn't want to create more work," Sheng replied throwing Jiao a warning look.

"What work? I always make a ton of food. It would be a great way for you to meet some of the other shifters in the community."

Before Sheng could refuse again, Jiao answered, ignoring his wishes. "You know what? We will come. It sounds delightful. Can I bring anything?"

"Just an empty stomach. Say around four-ish? Or earlier if your husband likes to watch football.

Geoffrey insists on having it blaring the entire day on every television in the house."

Sheng would hate that. Too bad. "We'll be there," Jiao replied brightly, elbowing her brother in the midsection hard enough to make him gasp before he could contradict her.

Jiao saw Meredith to the door and held it open long enough to wave goodbye as she drove away before turning to face a simmering Sheng.

"Exactly what do you think you are doing?" he asked tightly.

"Fitting in. It is what we're supposed to do so we don't draw attention to ourselves. Right?"

"By accepting an invitation to a dinner with what sounds like a lot of shifters?"

"What better way to meet the people we live among? Oh come on, Sheng. It's not like I'm going to change into my cat and announce we're fugitives from a rich sicko who likes to collect shifters. Stop being so paranoid."

"I'm not paranoid."

"Cautious. Paranoid. There's a fine line, brother. Besides, I want to go. I think it might be fun to meet other people." To see Chris, but she didn't mention that for obvious reasons, just like she'd omitted who Meredith was in conjunction to their handyman. Sheng would have never agreed, even reluctantly, if he knew.

"We'll go, but no alcohol, or staying too late."

"I am not leaving before dessert."

"Fine. But if this shindig ends up backfiring –"

"Yeah. Yeah. You can say I told you so. Thanks, Sheng." Jiao flung her arms around her brother and hugged him tight. Excitement at the coming dinner warred with anxiety. She didn't fear discovery by Kaleb, or one of his supposed spies. No her fear bore different roots.

What if Chris has a date?

Could she handle the wolf she already thought of as her own, paying attention to another woman? Judging by the claws popping out from her fingertips, no. But she didn't let it sway her mind from attending the dinner. She sure did hope, though, that Sheng's attitude would adjust so he didn't look like he swallowed a crate full of lemons. He took antisocial to a whole new level.

*

Sheng, despite the nagging doubt in his gut, didn't cancel their dinner plans the next day. He could see how much Jiao wanted to go. How she chafed at their boring existence and he understood how she felt, because their hiding tired him, too. But he preferred a stale existence to captivity.

A part of him understood their chances of discovery were slim despite their unique heritage, after all, Asians were in evidence all over Canada. Heck, he'd even spotted a few shifter ones in this very neighborhood, not clouded leopards of course, but still rare breeds for the climate. On the surface, he and his sister would pass muster. However, he feared them relaxing their guard. Getting too comfortable. Letting the wrong person know or see who they were inside.

One wrong word or observation to someone related to Kaleb and it could all end. One harmless Facebook picture, or Twitter and poof, they could end up back in their cage in the mountains, prized pets brought out to perform, earning their keep lest they lose their usefulness to the man who controlled their lives.

Sweat beaded Sheng's brow as he slid his bare foot along the corded rope suspended so high in the air.

"Don't look down," his father advised from the platform behind him. "Keep your eyes in front of you and pretend it's the balance beam just like we practiced."

Sure, except the balance beam stood only inches from the floor, not a few stories. His gaze flicked down, far, far down, and he swallowed hard. He should listen to his father. He brought his gaze back up and pointed it straight ahead. At the other end of the rope, standing on a small platform, he saw Jiao watching him, her teeth gnawing her lower lip in worry. Dammit. He couldn't act afraid. Not with his little sister watching. Not when her turn was next. They needed to get this right or Kaleb would punish them – if the fall didn't kill them first.

One foot moved forward on the tautly strung rope, his toes curling for grip, while his arms hovered outstretched for balance. With slow steps, he made it to the middle.

"Good. Now, remember how we did it in practice. Bounce, leap, change, and land." His father's words emerged smooth and encouraging, but he couldn't completely hide the worry in his instructions.

Jiao didn't even try. She clasped her hands to her chest and watched him with wide eyes.

Sheng could do this. Just like they'd practiced. He tried not to think of the plunge if he failed, or the lack of a net to catch him if he slipped. At least his mother wasn't here to watch, her services required elsewhere. He just wished she'd taken Jiao with her, just in case …

No. He would not fail. Couldn't.

One deep breath. Two. He pushed his weight down, and then sprang up, calling his cat. In midair, his body contorted, the pain of the change still so new. But he couldn't focus on that. Couldn't focus on anything but the fact he descended, gravity gripping his lithe form. He hit the rope, but his front paws slipped. His sister gasped as he heaved forward, face first. The floor, so far below, mocked him with its hard surface as his body followed his flailing paws, and he toppled. But didn't fall.

Hind feet hooked around the rope, he hung upside down, swaying slightly. It was times likes these he thanked the fates his animal had a rare agility.

Muttered, but still audible to a shifter with keen ears, Sheng heard his father's quick prayer of thanks. "Good job, son. But next time, try and land on your feet instead of giving me a heart attack," his father joked.

It took lots of practice, and a few more scares, but Sheng did manage that. Plus hand stands, swings, pirouettes and other acrobatic feats meant to please a crowd who came to see the cat-boy and his sister perform.

The worst part? They weren't the biggest freaks in the show, and while it wasn't a great life, they survived. Until the day Sheng overhead Kaleb discussing his plans to breed his sister to the highest bidder. Even without his promise to his father, Sheng would have done anything to get her out of there, and he did.

If only Patricia could have found the compound they escaped from and stopped Kaleb for good. While the shifters didn't really have an army per se, they did have a governing body that would have put a stop to Kaleb's crimes if they could find him. However, despite their searches, they came up empty handed. The Rockies they'd fled, too vast for a proper search.

What a shame, because a dead or incarcerated Kaleb would have solved their problem. Sheng knew there weren't many sickos like him who got off on capturing their kind and using them for his perverse performances, both inside the ring and in the wild for the hunt. Sheng often dreamed of killing the fat bastard himself. A massive bear of a man, and one hundred percent human, Kaleb went nowhere without guards. Guards or not, though, if given a chance, Sheng would try to kill him.

I'd do anything to end this limbo we're living in. Anything to stop the nightmares that we might end up back in that sicko's clutches.

Jiao was right. Something had to change. Running forever wasn't an option. But damn, it was so hard letting go of the fear and the paranoia, to relax his guard. Did he want to go to this stupid Thanksgiving dinner? No, but did he need to? Yes. And not just for his sister, but himself.

Sheng needed to meet other people. Adjust his thinking that the whole world was out to screw him and his only remaining family over. He needed to learn to trust others, maybe make a friend. A girlfriend.

Well into his twenties, he desired the last most of all. At least he wasn't a virgin like his sister. He'd taken care of that curiosity while still in captivity. And, despite his stand offish attitude, he never had a problem finding a partner for a bit of between the sheets action. However, those quick, impersonal couplings left him feeling incomplete. Sometimes even lonelier than before. At the same time though, it was all he could allow himself because until he could ascertain the danger was gone, he couldn't drag another person in to possible danger.

And if I can't have a woman in my life, then neither can Jiao, a man that was, no matter how petty it sounded.

Chapter Ten

Late Sunday afternoon, the doorbell rang, but Chris didn't pay it any attention. Despite the packed living room and family room, it seemed more people had arrived, his mother's fault for being such a good cook. Who could blame so many of his family, friends and neighbors for showing up? No sane person could resist the mouthwatering smells coming from the kitchen – and the slap on his hand was well worth the taste.

The glimpse he'd gotten of the pumpkin pie, with whipped cream on top, made him want to do battle so he wouldn't have to share. He restrained himself though from rescuing the pie. The last time he did that – trying to sneak off with it to the woods with a single fork – the pie got destroyed when his brothers caught him. '*No, not my precious,*' he'd cried as it soared in the air and hit the floor upside down. Pissed, his mother had him and his brothers doing slave chores for weeks afterward. Years later, he still mourned the loss of the pie no one got to taste.

Over the din of the crowd, he could hear his mother speaking with the new arrivals, her enthusiastic greeting carrying. Years of practice with so many boys left her with an ability to have herself heard that most army sergeants would envy. However, as he and his brothers well knew, it wasn't her loud tone they needed to fear, but the quiet one.

Something tickled his senses, a prickling awareness dancing across his skin. Suddenly awake, his wolf raised a shaggy head in Chris's mind, ears perked with interest. Chris didn't need to turn around to know his mother did exactly what she threatened. She'd invited his mate. And – he took another whiff to be sure – her damned husband.

Angling around, he positioned himself by the bookcase, making it hard for them to spot him, but giving him a perfect view of Jack and Jill – without their buckets. Curious glances were sent the Asian couple's way, and a couple of admiring ones from his single male cousins, and his brother Stu. Jill looked too damned cute in her clinging silk blouse and form fitting slacks. It didn't please him or his wolf at all to see the interest she attracted.

Mine. The growled thought almost left his lips. Acting on his possessive impulse though wouldn't go over well. But he couldn't let his brother's slobbering look go unpunished. He made a mental note to do something evil to Stu later.

A soft touch on his arm had him peering down, way down. Gina, his favorite female cousin, and the shortest at a ridiculously small five foot nothing, stood at his side. A hoyden in her youth, she grew up to look like every man's wet dream until she opened her mouth and turned into a foul mouthed, raspy voiced trucker. God, the trouble they'd gotten into as kids.

"What's got you looking like a dog who just got his nuts chopped and is looking to kill the man responsible?" she asked, in her usual delicate fashion.

"What's got you looking like a cheap penny whore in need of some quick cash?" he retorted, pointing to her skin tight, strapless ruby red top, and micro mini.

She snapped her gum and grinned. "Like it? The big man down at the precinct has me working the downtown strip. We've got a john who's been preying on the women coming out of the clubs. I volunteered myself as bait."

"You'll use any excuse to wear your everyday out clothes instead of a uniform." Chris shook his head.

"Can you blame me? Those damned things are uncomfortable. Not to mention they make my ass look fat."

"Maybe if you stayed away from the obligatory doughnuts …" He expected the punch to his arm.

"Jerk. Just for that, I'm going to give you some parking tickets."

Chris grinned at her threat, knowing she wouldn't – he hoped. "What are you doing here? Doesn't your mom usually make you eat at your grandma's?" he asked, an eye on Jill, who under the firm hand of his mother, met his family, whether she wanted to or not. Her husband – his usual pissy expression in place – followed along behind.

"Grandma's on a cruise so Ma's gone to Florida early this year because she's planning to make it to Christmas dinner for once."

"I thought she hated celebrating Christmas." Chris returned his focus to his cousin, his attention diverted for a moment at the news. Keeping his aunt Carolyn away from family functions was something everyone strived for. A wonderful woman, most of the time, when she got around his mother, who happened to be her older sister, sparks flew, and sometimes hair.

Sibling rivalry at its most violent. They almost made him and his brothers look tame.

"Oh, she still hates Christmas. Says she can't stand all the fakeness of the holidays. But your brother Stu, who I swear I'm going to shave bald one day, said what a shame she couldn't come since your mom makes the best cranberry sauce ever."

"Uh-oh." How like Stu to throw a gauntlet at their aunt for his entertainment. Awesome. He'd have to make sure to get some popcorn for the main event. Oh, and save the sugar pie from the battle. His second favorite dessert, after pumpkin pie.

"Yeah, uh-oh. So now my mother is determined to stay and prove she makes the best cranberry sauce in the family."

A snort escaped Chris. "So in other words, I shouldn't buy my mother anything fragile or likely to stain this Christmas. Gift card it is."

"I heard that," his mother hollered.

"Love you, Ma," he yelled back. Not that anyone really noticed with the usual family gathering cacophony going on. Correction. Two people did. One, with a tilt to her lips met his gaze and inclined her head in greeting. The other, peered from his mother to Chris, then tightened his lips as understanding dawned. It seemed his mother hadn't quite explained exactly whose house Jack was coming to. *Sucker!*

God love his mother. Chris knew he could count on her to help him win his mate. Now, how to get Jill alone? In other words, away from the old ball and chain.

"You've got smoke coming out of your ears," Gina retorted.

"Do not."

"You're right you don't, but your face is all squinched up like you're thinking too hard, which in turn means you're up to no good. I want in. Spill."

"Can you keep a secret?"

Gina smirked and flicked the room and its occupants a glance.

He frowned. Duh. If he spoke, even in a hushed whisper, everyone here would hear what he had to say, including a husband he preferred to remain oblivious. Inclining his head, he indicated she should follow him. Slinking out of the crowded house – a skill wolves excelled at, along with howling at the moon and chasing pesky squirrels – they headed out to the backyard, Gina's curiosity evident. Chris didn't speak, though, until they'd entered the woods and he was sure they were alone. Even then, he kept his voice low.

"Promise you won't say a word."

"Seriously? What are we in, like grade school? Afraid our moms are going to catch us?" Gina rolled her eyes.

"It's not my mom I'm worried about. Swear or I won't tell you."

"Loser." Disparaging insult or not, she spit in her hand and held it out.

Chris made a moue of distaste. "Gross."

"What? You didn't have a problem with it when we were kids."

"Yeah, back then I also wore the same underwear for three days. A simple 'I promise' would suffice."

"Oh fine then. I, Gina, hottest wolf around and best cousin ever, promise not to tell a freakn' soul about the secret you're about to impart."

"Or else you have to dress like a Mormon for a month."

"That's just cruel!" she exclaimed.

"Then don't break the vow."

"I swear, but this better be good, or I will lock you in a cell with a hairy, horny inmate," she growled.

Slightly disturbing as promises went, but satisfied his cousin would keep her lips sealed, he leaned in and said in a low tone. "I'm pretty sure I've met my mate."

Eyes wide, Gina gaped at him. "No freakn' way. You're screwing with me."

"Nope. God's honest truth."

"Holy cow. And here I thought Stu was going to go down next."

"Why my brother? He's a pig."

She grinned. "Exactly. I'm looking forward to seeing him fall and turn into a respectable family man so I can make fun of him."

A snicker turned into a laugh. "You and me both."

"So, who is the lucky, or should I say, cursed girl?"

"Are you implying I won't make good mate material?" he huffed, only slightly offended. Gina, after all, was privy to some of his antics when it came to girls. Heck, she'd played the part of jealous girlfriend more than once when he needed to rid himself of a cling-on.

"Well, you do have a nice set of teeth and hair. No signs of balding. Yet."

"Ha. You are so funny short stuff. Still shopping in the little girls section at Wal-Mart?"

"Do you still watch cartoons in the morning while eating Fruit Loops?"

"It's Captain Crunch now, and Sportsnet, thank you very much."

"Oh, yeah, that will just totally make your potential mate fall over herself to snag you."

"I'm really starting to dislike you," he grumbled as Gina pointed out some of his habits.

"Poor Chris. Are we feeling unloved? I'm sure she'll look past your less than endearing qualities. At least you have a decent job, which I guess counts for something."

"Gee. Thanks for the vote of confidence."

"Anytime. But seriously, Captain Crunch aside, who's the lady? Do I know her?"

"Did you see that Asian girl inside?"

"Yeah. She's the one hanging with the hot dude who looks like he's getting his testicles squeezed in a vise, right?"

A chuckle escaped him. "That's the one. Well, I'm pretty sure she's meant to be mine, problem is, she's kind of married to the dude."

"She's married?" Gina cackled. "Ha. Ha. Ha. And to think you made fun of Mitchell because he had to share his woman with another man."

A scowl creased Chris's countenance. "Who says I'm sharing? I said they were married, it doesn't mean they're truly mated. Or that I plan to share her."

"So what are you going to do? Kidnap her and run away? Kill the guy?"

"I would, but Ma won't let me." At her shocked look, he snickered. "Just kidding. I don't suppose you could arrest him and throw his ass in jail? Maybe forget he's there for a while?"

"If I could, I would have done that with my cheating ex. I had to settle for having him rectally searched when the boys downtown pulled him in for a drug charge."

Chris winced. "Ouch. That's cold. And I don't think I could ask you to do that, even to win my mate."

"So what is your plan then?"

"I thought it might be a good idea to get to know Jill first, have her fall for me and decide on her own to divorce the guy. But, I'm having a bit of a problem with that plan because her husband is always around."

"Gee, could it have to do with the fact they're married?" Sarcasm thick, Gina rolled her eyes for added emphasis.

Annoyed at the reminder, and Gina's evident lack of sympathy, he scowled. "You know what. Forget we talked."

"What do you mean forget? This is way too juicy, Christopher Phineas. I want to know what you intend to do next."

"Well I had planned on getting her alone to get to know her." And kiss. "But I'm not sure how."

"You need a diversion." Nodding sagely, Gina adjusted her boobs in her top, plumping them up until they threatened so spill out. "Got it, partner. Good thing I'm already dressed for the part."

Unease gripped him at the anticipation on her face. "What are you planning to do?"

"Oh please. I have yet to meet a man who can resist these babies when I've got them in his face."

"You're going to seduce him?"

"Hey, this is a family function. Give me a little credit. I'm just going to reroute the blood in dude's brain for a little bit while you slip away with his wife and smear her with your version of charm."

A grimace twisted his lips. "You make it sound so tawdry."

"Isn't it?"

Hmmm. She did have a point. "You don't mind?"

"Mind? I deal with dirty John's all day long. Trying to seduce a husband sounds like fun."

"You don't have to go that far."

Blinking her eyes, Gina smiled slowly, a smile that would send most normal men running for cover. Jack didn't stand a chance. "Oh, but I do. Because then you'll owe me a favor."

"G-i-n-a." Chris stretched out her name.

Her smile widened. "Nothing too awful, just a custom organizer in my closet."

"How big is it?"

"Put it this way, my three bedroom condo is going down to two."

Chris groaned.

"Do we have a deal? I distract the hubby, you give me shelf and hanger heaven."

"What if I need you for more than one time?"

"How long we talking about?"

"Maybe a couple of weekends as my assistant at their house?"

"You making my new closet with real wood?"

Sigh. "Yes."

"Deal, partner." And yes, she did spit in her palm again and made him shake it. Nasty wench. God he loved her like another sister though. Even better, he now had backup in his quest to win his mate. Hopefully it wouldn't backfire.

*

Jiao couldn't help but note the cute female leaving the room with Chris – her cat didn't like it at all. It was her worst fear come true. Chris had a girlfriend, or someone he liked enough to bring to a family function. *So much for thinking he felt the same connection*, she thought somewhat morosely. She hoped none of her dejection showed but had to wonder when Meredith said, "Oh dear, you've just missed Chris and his cousin, Gina."

"Cousin?" Well that eased her mind, but did the woman sense her interest in Chris? God, she hoped not. What would she think of Jiao, who was supposedly married, chasing after her son?

"Yes. They're the same age and have been best friends since they were in diapers. I'll introduce her to you later if you'd like."

"Okay." What else could Jiao say? She'd already met a ton of family members and people. She doubted she'd remember even a quarter of their names by morning.

"Oh dear. If you'll excuse me for a moment, I hear the door again." Off Meredith went leaving Jiao with an uncomfortable appearing Sheng.

"Why didn't you mention she was the handyman's mother?" her brother hissed in her ear.

She shrugged in reply lest their conversation become common knowledge. Already she wondered if her decision to come was a bad one given the attention they kept drawing. It seemed Sheng's paranoia was contagious. "I'm thirsty. Let's go find a drink."

Not waiting to see if her brother followed, Jiao weaved her way through the crowd, most of the bodies towering over her more petite frame. They sure bred them big around here, and clumsy. A man stumbled into her, and she might have fallen if a pair of strong hands – replete with a tingle – hadn't caught her. She didn't need to look up to know Chris held her.

"Thanks," she muttered, trying to pull free before Sheng saw.

However, Chris didn't immediately let go, leaving one hand on her waist and guiding her through the crowd, his large body clearing the way.

"Where are we going?" she asked, peering anxiously over her shoulder, expecting to see a glowering Sheng at their heels. To her surprise, her brother, usually glued to her side, was nowhere in sight.

"You looked kind of overwhelmed, so I thought I'd take us somewhere a little quieter."

"But what about Sh—Jack?"

"He's busy right now with my cousin Gina."

Turning her head again, Jiao scanned the crowd until she spotted her brother's stiff back. Then she bit her lip, just imagining his consternation when the voluptuous Gina draped an arm around him and whispered something in his ear. Coincidence or planned? *Did Chris just use his cousin as a distraction so he could spirit me elsewhere?*

Eyeing Chris, who led her away from the crowd with purpose, she could honestly say she didn't care. The simple touch of his fingers on her waist teased her, and rendered her hyper aware of him by her side. She ignored the looks they got. Forgot her brother. Under a spell of curiosity, she let him lead her somewhere private. Somewhere hopefully alone.

Opening a door to the kitchen, which immediately immersed her in heavenly smells, he then opened a second door and flicked on a switch. At his urging she headed down the stairs first. *Where are we going? His bedroom?* Oh how her pulse quickened at the thought. She got the destination wrong, though.

As they reached the bottom step, she noted a basement gym. And what a space. Momentarily entranced, she stepped away from Chris and eyed the professionally finished space. She ran her fingers over the padded walls. Noted the vinyl, cushioned floor. The hemp wrapped posts. The monkey bars going up the wall and across the ceiling. The pegs on the wall, and so much more.

"Did you build this?" she asked in wonder, now able to finally picture what her own basement gym might look like once done. Although, she also planned to add some plants to give it a more of a jungle feel.

"Yes, with a little help from my dad. Our original gym got wrecked. My brothers and I can get kind of unruly."

Judging by the twinkle in his eyes, he understated. "How many brothers do you have?"

"Four and one pesky sister who's worse than them all. What about you?"

"Me?" She bit her lip. What to admit? "One brother."

"Older? Younger? Prettier?"

"Older and bossy," she answered with a laugh.

"I'm familiar with the type," he remarked dryly. "What about the rest of your family? Do they live nearby?"

The question killed her mirth. "I have no one else. Only my brother."

"I'm sorry." Softly spoken, she could hear the regret in the tone. "That must be hard. I can't imagine not having a horde of family members. Although, it would probably be quieter." They both peered at the ceiling as the muted thumps of the ongoing celebration managed to penetrate the soundproofed basement.

"I would love to have a big family." She couldn't hide the wistful tone. "But at least I have Sheng." Too late, she realized she slipped with her brother's name. *Oh shoot. He's going to kill me.*

But Chris had no idea she'd made a grave booboo. "I'd like to meet him sometime. Find out your deep dark childhood secrets." He waggled his brows and grinned.

"Oh, I doubt they'd interest you." Although, some of her upbringing would probably shock. Captured before her tenth birthday along with her brother and parents, she spent most of her teenage years training to entertain Kaleb's guests.

"Somehow I don't think anything about you is boring." His words, mixed with his intense gaze, left her no wiggle room to misconstrue his meaning.

But she did her best. "So why rebuild the gym with you and your brothers all grown up? Who uses it?"

"We might be grown up, but some of us still live at home while we save up for a house. Me, my brothers, Stu and Kendrick, haven't left the nest yet and use it quite often. Dad still comes down here sometimes too. Soon, it will also accommodate my niece and nephew, once they pass the slobbering stage into the walking one. Then, there are kids of my own one day. Young shifters need a safe place to explore their animal side. What better than a jungle gym made for them? We've got climbing bars and a wall. Hemp covered poles and even some distressed wooden panels for them to rub their nails. And if you look in that bin over there, you'll find knotted ropes and balls for playing. Pups can have a lot of energy, and with my sister popping out two at once, we got this place finished just in time."

"Family is important to you?"

"Family is everything. We all stick together, no matter what."

"That sounds great." She envied him that. Once, she'd at least had her mother and father to count on, now, it was just her and Sheng against the world. Or against Kaleb, at any rate.

"Yeah, it's great, until they stick their nose in your business," he muttered darkly before grinning.

His frankness and love for his family just cranked her liking of him up another notch, however, it was his smile that sent heat shooting through her veins. She needed to turn the conversation to something less intimate. More boring. "Will my gym look like this when done?" she asked, turning to feign interest in the setup again.

"If you want. Or nicer. Anything you want, let me know. I'll give it to you."

She whirled at the sound of his voice behind her. He stood so close she needed to crane to look him in the face. Just a half step forward and she would have hit his chest. The small space separating them might as well have not existed seeing as how her entire body tingled. "Is this why you brought me down here? To show me an example of your work?" Did she wrongly assume he'd wanted to get her alone for another reason?

"Honestly? No. I have an ulterior motive. But first let me ask you something. Are you feeling an urge to sneeze?"

His question surprised her. "What? No. My cold is gone. My healing ability finally kicked in and got rid of it. Why?"

"I'd rather show you."

With wide eyes, she gazed up at him as he encroached her space further. Mouth dry, tummy full of butterflies and her heart beating too loudly, she whispered. "Why did you bring me here?"

"So I could get you alone and do this." A large hand cupped the back of her head and drew her closer, but he was still too tall. With a growl, his free arm wrapped around her waist and he lifted her smaller frame until her face was level with his. "Say something now if you want me to stop."

As if. Lips clamped tight, she didn't say a word. Wasn't even sure she could have if she wanted to. She'd dreamt of this moment for days. She wanted this kiss more than she'd ever wanted anything.

Relief replaced the worry in his eyes as she gave him her silent assent, followed quickly by a smoldering gaze. Her eyes fluttered shut as he leaned in and kissed her, a firm embrace like nothing she'd imagined.

Good thing he held her, because she would have surely sunk to the ground in a boneless, melted – but very happy – puddle.

*

As soon as his lips touched hers, Chris questioned the wisdom of the kiss even as he reveled in it. One taste. One delicious, cock hardening, toe tingling taste and he was lost. And in lust. Possibly, deaf. Definitely dumb because he didn't care that anyone could come down and spot them. Didn't give a damn a party was going on upstairs, or that Jill's husband probably looked for her.

One simple embrace, just lips sliding sensuously across each other, and his whole world tilted. *Mine.*

He could have shouted for joy when instead of pushing him away, her hands curled around his neck, holding him close. Soft, full lips parted for him, and he took full advantage, slipping his tongue past the barrier of her teeth, groaning at her sweet surrender.

How could such a petite woman, still almost a stranger, feel so right in his arms? Make him want to go against his own personal rules? Tempt him into doing bad things. Bad, bad, arousing things.

Whirling and still holding her off the floor in his arms, he strode a few paces and pressed her against the padded wall. Using it as a support, he freed his hands to skim the length of her body, cupping her pert ass cheeks, nudging her thighs apart until she got the hint and wrapped her legs around his waist.

Sweet, freakn' heaven. The core of her, so hot even through her slacks, burned against him. He couldn't help rubbing himself against her. Only a thin thread of sanity kept him from removing the clothing keeping them apart. *Anyone could come down. And do I really want our first time to happen fast and furious in a gym?*

No. She deserved better. A bed. Roses. A slow languorous exploration. A chance to come so often, she'd end up hoarse from screaming. Wanting to make their first time special was one thing. Caught in an electrifying embrace, he couldn't make himself stop. Couldn't halt the fire raging through his veins. Didn't want to stop touching or kissing her. Ever.

It seemed the same mad passion gripped her, too. She panted in his mouth and small sounds of pleasure escaped her. He caught them all, and gloried in them. Reveled in the fact she wanted him.

A shrill giggle, from way too close had him muttering a soundless 'Shit'. *What is Gina doing?* Because, if he wasn't mistaken, he heard her on the steps to the basement.

Quickly, he put Jill down, but looking at her face – her expression dreamy, her lips swollen – he realized any idiot would immediately guess they'd spent the last few minutes kissing.

Much as he hated to do it, he needed her to snap out of it. "Jill. I think your husband is coming." He whispered it as Gina let out one of her infamous belly laughs.

"My who? What? Oh no." Panic lit in Jill's eyes and Chris cursed the untimely interruption.

Her fingers flew to her lips and he could see the plea in her eyes for help. Despite the fact her husband catching his wife making out with the handyman would provide a great excuse for Jack to exit the picture, leaving Chris to scoop her up, he couldn't do that to Jill. Bending down, he picked up a medicine ball and showed it to her.

Immediate understanding dawned, and she nodded her head. Taking a breath, inwardly wincing, Chris then threw the ball at her head, just as an angry Jack said, "What are you two doing down here?"

Smack.

Chris winced, unseen by all but a staggering Jill, as the heavy ball hit his mate in the face, not truly hard enough to do damage, but convincingly enough to account for flushed cheeks and swollen lips.

What a way to end their first kiss.

Chapter Eleven

One minute, Sheng followed Jiao through the crowd, looking for a drink, the next, a curly haired brunette wearing an outfit more appropriate for a bordello, stepped in his path and slung an arm around him.

Not one for any kind of touching, even the friendly kind, he shrugged her arm off. She didn't seem to care that he rebuffed her because instead of leaving, she moved to stand in front of him.

"Hey, cutie. I don't think we've met. I'm Gina."

The words, 'I'm not interested,' hovered on the tip of his tongue, but somehow got wedged. Maybe because his cat swallowed them before he could lie.

Standing a little shorter than him, everything about this Gina girl embodied what he disliked in modern culture. Buxom, and not afraid to flaunt it in a corset type top, wearing a short skirt revealing rounded thighs encased in fishnet stockings, she wore too much makeup and not enough clothes. Despite his preference for a sleeker more decently covered female, something twitched down below and his cat purred.

What. The. Hell. No. No way was he attracted to this - this outrageous woman. *Tell that to my cock.* Despite his repugnance, it continued to swell.

He must have silently stared for too long because Gina snapped fingers, tipped in absurdly long nails, in front of his face. "Let's try looking up here, pussycat. Eyes on my face, if you please, while we talk, not my tits."

"I wasn't–"

"Sure you weren't," she interrupted with a wink. "Not that I can blame you. I'm pretty proud of these babies myself. One hundred percent God given, and sensitive too." And yes, she said that while cupping them and holding them up higher, enough they almost spilled out of her top.

Yes, he stared at the offered cleavage despite her admonition not to. He was a man after all. A poor, lonely man who'd not gotten laid in months at this point. His dick got harder and his cat practically fell off the shelf of his mind rolling around in pleasure.

What would it feel like to bury his face in that soft haven? To slide his dick …

Startled at his unusually dirty thoughts, he recoiled and forced his gaze up to her amused one. Thought she was funny, eh? He'd solve that. "Shouldn't you put some clothes on? This is after all a family function."

The insult didn't work as planned. A short laugh left her. "Oh please. My family wouldn't recognize me if I came all covered up. You must be new around here."

"I am."

"So what's your name, pussycat?"

It occurred to him to take offense at her nickname, but that would indicate he cared what she thought of him. And he didn't. "My name is Jack. And my wife's name is Jill," he added pointedly.

"Ooh, a man not afraid of commitment. I like it," she exclaimed.

"Good for you. Now if you'll excuse me, I should go find her."

Before he could edge around the busty brunette, Gina clasped his arm, in a grip he doubted he could pry off with a crowbar. "Forget your wife. You'll have more fun if you stick with me."

He probably would. But that wasn't the point. "Listen Gina, I'm married and not into what I think you're suggesting."

"Suggesting?" She laughed, a boisterous sound that drew a few more gazes than he liked, mostly centered on her jiggling chest. Where was a tablecloth or a cardigan when a man needed to cover up some breasts? And no, despite his mind's opinion on the matter, his hands would not work.

"Can you tone it down?" he whispered harshly, and not just because of the attention she drew to him. For some reason, he didn't like the admiring glances shot her way. Someone needed to step up and keep this she-wolf out of trouble, starting with a wardrobe makeover.

"Oh, pussycat. This is just how I am. Loud, outspoken and hot."

"It's not proper for a young lady," he replied stiffly.

"Maybe where you come from. But around here, I'm pretty normal. You'll see. It seems you've got a lot to learn about me and this family."

"I'd prefer not."

"Too bad. Now that you're part of our community, you will be assimilated." Gina giggled. "Assimilated? Get it? As in Star Trek and the Borg?"

Lips tight, he didn't answer.

"Hmm. Not a Trekkie fan? No problem. We can fix that with a sci-fi marathon sometime. But of greater urgency is the need to do something about your uptightness."

"I am not uptight."

"Really?" She arched a brow and he wanted to bluster and explain he only acted like this because of necessity, that if given a choice he'd happily live more carefree. Or not.

Sheng's parents raised him and his sister to act a certain way. The proper way. Sure, it seemed old fashioned to some, but given the decay in morality nowadays, Sheng preferred it. Uptight indeed. He opened his mouth to refute her claim, then stopped. Despite her insult, and his urge to show her the contrary, he didn't defend himself. *Because I don't care. Much.*

"Wow, pussycat. You really are new. Most shifters around here would take those as fighting words."

"Some of us have more control."

"I would have said more like you've got cold blood. Surprising, given most cats I know are hot blooded creatures."

And just how did she know this? None of his business, and he was most certainly not jealous. Sheng repeated that a few times in his head in an attempt to calm his cat, which really took offense at the idea that Gina knew about other felines because of an intimate experience. "Having a grip on my emotions does not make me cold."

"If you say so." Her smirk said she thought otherwise. "I know what will help you find your pulse and your balls. A drink."

"No, thank you. I don't partake of alcohol."

As if she'd start paying attention to his wishes now. "What do you mean you don't drink alcohol? How boring, even if it explains a lot. Well, there's no time like the present to start." She pulled him, and short of making a scene to disengage her, Sheng had no choice but to follow. But first chance he got, hard dick or not, giddy internal kitty or not, he would escape and find Jiao. It was time to end this failed experiment in socialization and past time he escaped this woman, who against all odds, made him want to do things. Naked things. Very improper things. *But enjoyable, I'd bet.*

His chance to slip her grip arrived when a huge thug of a man swept her off her feet into a hug of spine cracking proportions. Inside his mind, his cat spit and hissed, demanding he rip her away from the offending giant. Sheng clenched his fists. Nope, not jealous. Not one teensy tiny bit. He reminded himself of this as he stalked around the embracing couple and went on the hunt for his sister.

He'd just managed to make it to a door in the kitchen, where Jiao's perfume faintly lingered, when a plush body scooted in front of him prevent him from going down the stairs.

"And just where do you think you're going, pussycat? I thought we were getting a drink."

"No we weren't."

"Lighten up. You're too young to frown all the time."

"Exactly why do you care?" he snapped back. "Don't you have better things to do with your boyfriend?" Yeah, he sounded catty.

She laughed. "Kendrick? My boyfriend. Gross. He's my cousin. You know, family? I don't know about your family, but in mine, we don't screw first cousins. We had to stop that centuries ago. Too many three eyed, slack jawed children."

He didn't mean to. Truly he didn't, but a snort of amusement left him.

Surprised, she gaped at him, then grinned, way too pleased with herself. "You should smile more often, pussycat. It suits you."

The compliment pleased him, which in turn annoyed him. "Maybe some of us don't have much to smile about."

"Or, maybe someone just takes everything too seriously."

"You know nothing of me. Or my reasons."

"Does anyone?"

He couldn't reply to her astute query because he feared she'd spot the lie. Feared she'd see too much. Grasping her around the waist, the soft skin he brushed in his attempt to move her, scorched him. She took in a breath too, a sharp one, as he lifted her aside. Despite himself, his fingers lingered, and he spent a moment looking down at Gina, her height just perfect for a man who never went past five foot six. His gazed locked with hers and his heart stuttered to a stop.

What's happening? Why did it feel like he stood on the threshold of something momentous? Something life changing that involved the blowsy she-wolf? Flustered, he dropped his hands from her waist, and turned away, but not before seeing the disappointment in her eyes.

He went down the first step. Gina squeezed by him and stood on the next, arms braced across the way, blocking him.

"What are you doing?"

"Annoying the pants off you?" she asked, her lips curved in a mocking smile.

"And succeeding," he snapped. Just not in the way his body would prefer. An actual removal of pants so he could bury a certain rigid part of himself into her, an easy task with the short skirt she wore, would have worked better.

"Oh, pussycat. You are so easy to rile. It's making me hot. Wanna screw?"

"No," he sputtered, only stopping himself at the last moment from saying yes.

A rich chuckle emerged from her and wrapped around him, leaving him harder than before. "Liar."

"I'm married."

"I'm open to a threesome," she said with a wink.

Oh, gross, that was his sister she imagined in a three way. Not that she knew. But still. "Not happening."

"Don't tell me you'd prefer another guy in the bedroom? Seems to be happening a lot more often these days," she mused aloud.

"Like hell. Now would you get out of the way. I need to find my wife." So he could use Jiao as an excuse to escape the woman who set every nerve tingling and frustrated every ounce of patience he owned.

They did a little dance on the stairs, her sidestepping at the same time as him, before with a growl he made it past her. Hitting the floor of the basement, he saw Jiao's back to him and in front of her the damned handyman, Chris.

"What are you two doing down here?"

His barked question made Jiao startle and thus she missed the ball Chris threw at her. It smacked her in the face. She reeled only slightly from the impact. Jack hurried to her side, but she waved him away before he could check on her.

"I'm fine. Next time though, mind waiting until after I catch the ball before shouting." She rubbed her swollen mouth and Jack felt chagrin, but only for a second as he sniffed the air.

"What were you doing?" he asked, already having a suspicious idea.

"I was showing her the gym I built down here to give her an idea of what to expect at your place," Chris said, jumping in.

"Isn't it marvelous?" Jiao added a tad too brightly.

"Great. But –"

"Get moving everybody. That's the dinner bell, and you don't want to be last in line for food," Gina exclaimed, hovering nearby. "Coming, cousin?" she asked with a pointed stare at Chris. Brows knit, Chris nodded. The two wolves left, but before Sheng could give his sister hell for coming down here alone with the wolf, she whirled and pointed an accusing finger.

"What is wrong with you?" she snapped.

"I was looking for you."

"Obviously. Why?"

"Because we're supposed to be a married couple and yet you're wandering off with a strange man somewhere alone."

He didn't miss the pink flush in her cheeks or the way her eyes wouldn't meet his. "Jiao!"

"Nothing happened."

She lied to him. He could tell. "We need to leave. Now."

Spine straightening, shoulders back, she met his gaze. "No. I want to stay for dinner."

"After what you did?"

"Oh please. And you behaved so appropriately?" She reached forward and pulled a dark hair from his shirt. A long curly one.

"It's not what you think."

"Ditto. So, if you're done being over protective and over bearing, then let's go eat."

Short of throwing her over his shoulder, and making a scene Sheng wanted to avoid, Jiao gave him no choice but to follow.

He just hoped he could sit far away from Gina and her melons. Far, far away even if he feared there was no distance far enough.

*

Almost caught kissing the handyman, Jiao found she couldn't muster enough emotion to care. How could she when her whole being still burned? Wanted to say to hell with her cover as Jill, the married woman. One taste. One touch, and she was ready to risk it all.

Jiao's thoughts were chaotic. Fragmented. Ever since her kiss with Chris, she couldn't seem to gather her wits. The arrival of her brother should have thrown an immediate damper on her feelings when the ball in the face as a cover didn't. Nope. Nothing it seemed could extinguish the fire burning inside her.

Totally, utterly insane. Yet exciting. She could no longer deny Chris was her mate. *Mine. Mine. Mine.* A wonderful revelation, but one she couldn't act on.

That freakn' sucked.

Sitting at a table, one of the many set up outside in the backyard under a white tent for the Thanksgiving feast, she locked her feet under her chair and fisted the tablecloth lest she stand up and go to where she belonged. Chris's lap. Or arms. Or bed. She didn't seem to care at this point.

Only a thin thread of sanity and self-preservation kept her glued to her seat, that and her glowering brother beside her. Any wrong move on her part and he'd have them packed up and gone before the day was through. It behooved her to behave. Yes, she might have won the battle to stay and enjoy the meal, but she'd hear about it later, and despite the clamor of her cat, she wouldn't escape Sheng's sharp eyes or presence any more this day.

It made her want to scream in frustration.

So unfair. I finally find my mate, the man meant for me, but I can't have him because my brother, who is my husband, says I have to stay a virgin. It sounded like a topic for Jerry Springer.

Annoyed, she would have eaten in sullen silence, unwilling to talk to her brother unless it was to beg him to end the charade, but Chris didn't exaggerate about his family. They didn't have any boundaries when it came to personal space and privacy. They also owned as much curiosity as her cat.

A good looking, long haired brunette sat down across from Jiao flanked by an extremely large man carrying a baby dressed in pink on one side, and a tanned Latino type holding another baby on the other.

Sharp eyes took her in. "Hello. I don't think we've met," the brunette said. "I'm Naomi. Daughter of the folks hosting this thing and these are my mates, Ethan and Javier. And their precious bundles are Mark and Melanie."

Two mates? How fascinating. Exactly how did that work? Maybe not the best question to ask of a stranger. "I'm Jill, and this is Jack." Yeah, Jiao omitted the husband part. She didn't think she could say it aloud without sounding ready to file for divorce.

"You're the couple Chris is working for."

"He spoke of us?" Jack asked sharply as he tuned into the conversation.

"Not exactly. I'm his accountant, so he sends me all his contracts and receipts so I can keep his taxes and business stuff in order."

"Oh. I see." The tension in Sheng's body eased.

"Best money woman around," Gina announced flouncing into the seat across from Sheng. "I trust her with all my finances."

"It's an easy job since Gina doesn't have any money, just a gift for spending," Naomi remarked dryly.

"It's a family trait," Javier confided with a grin, not even flinching when his mate elbowed him in the ribs.

"Says the man who keeps buying stuffed animals every time he sees one," Ethan rumbled.

"So shoot me for spoiling my babies."

"Does anyone have a gun?" Naomi asked, a smile hovering on her lips.

The only one who didn't laugh was – guess who – Sheng. The look of confusion on his face as he followed the playful banter made something ache inside Jiao. Had their captivity and subsequent hiding damaged him so much that he no longer recalled how families acted with each other? Did he not recognize happiness when he saw it?

"So what brings you to town?" Naomi asked.

Using the answer they'd rehearsed, her brother replied. "We decided on a change of scenery."

"And weather." Jiao jumped in, improvising as Sheng's short answer seemed to leave them with more questions in their eyes. "We used to live out west on the coast where it rarely snows. I can't wait to experience my first real winter." A lie. She knew exactly what snow felt like. Loved playing in it. But, having lived in Vancouver for a while where the season went from warm and wet to cold and wet, the lie wasn't too far from the truth. She had missed the fluffy ice crystals.

"You came to the right place then. Ottawa gets its fair share of the white stuff," Gina said with a shudder.

"You'll love it. When the canal freezes over, you get to skate on it, which is a total blast," Naomi replied.

"She doesn't skate."

No one paid attention to Sheng. Babbling and talking about the things they could show her, and Sheng, if he ever stopped scowling long enough to let anyone get close to him.

From time to time, as the conversation and laughter flowed, she'd peek over at Chris who sat with a redhead and a few men, both of whom seemed somehow familiar. Was one of them Chris's brother? They seemed to share some of the same facial features. While Chris didn't come over to join them, his intense gaze whenever their eyes met screamed how much he wanted to. She didn't know whether to thank him for his tact in not actively pursuing her in front of her husband, or to take him to task for not even trying. As for herself? She hated that he kept himself so far away.

But only for now. Starting tonight, she'd work on Sheng, and his obstinate stance. Convince him it was time to get on with their lives. Once she got her brother to drop the ruse once and for all, the wolf wouldn't stand a chance. Her cat would make sure of it. Meow!

Chapter Twelve

Hours later, dinner over and done with, most of the family departed for their own homes, his mate whisked away by her cold fish of a husband, Chris could finally relax and think back on the magical moment in the basement.

She kissed me!

And he finally understood why some romance novels said it was like fireworks going off. He'd never expected the tumultuous reaction, the wild, almost untamed urgency of the embrace, but damn, what a rush. Only one problem though. Now, he wanted Jill more than ever, but the same problem stood in his way. Jack. The husband that even Jill seemed to barely tolerate. A guy who brought new definition to the term antisocial. A man who got to go home with the woman Chris wanted.

Yeah, that freakn' sucked. He couldn't help wondering what happened when the pair got home. Did Jack exert his rights as the husband? Did he even now touch the body Chris thought of as his? Did Jill close her eyes and pretend it was Chris?

Why couldn't he stop torturing himself? As if sensing his inner turmoil, his mother gave him a clean-up task.

Stuck with kitchen duty, Chris washed while Naomi dried. Odd, because of late she usually used the excuse that she needed to care for her babies as her reason not to help. More annoying, their mother let her get away with it.

Women! They were always in cahoots.

Take earlier, during dinner for example. His sister took Jill in hand, stealing her from her dullard of a husband and tugged her around, talking animatedly. The occasional tinkle of laughter by Jill, a mirth he'd not yet inspired, rang out. Each time Jill giggled, Chris sported a boner, which really sucked when he got caught by his Aunt Matilda who unfortunately noticed and smirked, saying, 'Randy pup.'

Still though, while torturous, he'd enjoyed seeing his woman – *yes mine*, despite whose ring she wore – getting to know his family, and even better, the instant way she blended in. Even his cousin Gina seemed to like her, her ribald laughter ringing out loud and often, which brought an amusing wince to Jack's face, each and every time.

Someone should give the guy some Mary Jane laced brownies. Anything to lighten him up.

Mind whirling with thoughts of his mate – and ways to rid himself of the obstacle in his way – he'd not noted the heavy silence between him and his sister as they did the dishes. But Naomi did.

"What's got you so quiet?"

Startled from his musings, he shot her a quick glance. "Me? Nothing. Just, um, tired. Yeah. It was a long day, you know, helping Ma clean. And stuff." It sounded lame, even to him.

Judging by Naomi's snort, maybe he should have omitted the last part. "Here I thought Stu was the comedian in the family. So are you going to tell me what's up?"

"I have no idea what you mean."

"Oh please. I'm not blind and if it's any consolation, I don't think she's happily married,"

The dish slipped from Chris's grip and splashed in the soapy water. "Excuse me? What are you talking about?"

"Jill, of course. I don't think she and that Jack fellow are mated or all that happy with each other. I think you should go for it."

"I don't have a thing for Jill," he lied.

"Oh please. Mom already told me."

Dammit! "She what? I thought it was a secret."

Naomi shook her head. "You have met our mother, right? Born a meddler. Or have you forgotten she got my mates to drug me so they could slip under my guard and seduce me, the jerks."

"I heard that," Javier yelled.

"Love you too," she hollered back. A glare in Chris's direction made him halt the gagging noise.

"Someone kill me now," he joked. In truth, he thought it great his prickly sister found a pair of men to love, even if Chris couldn't beat them in a sport, the pricks.

"The husband might put you out of your misery if he catches you putting the moves on his wife."

"She's my mate though."

"So you'd better get him to start liking you if you intend to be part of their lives. Or are you going to be like Mitchell and fight the other man in her life and make her miserable?"

A violent shake of his head accompanied his horrified. "No way. You seem to have gotten the wrong idea. I am not getting into a threesome. It's not my thing. At all. I just have to find a way to get her to leave the asshat."

"You know it would be a lot easier if you just unwound your morals long enough to accept she already has a man in her life and joined in."

"I don't share."

"And yet sharing is so much fun," Ethan rumbled as he came into the kitchen with steps more silent than a man his size should have managed.

"It is," Naomi giggled, tilting her head back for a kiss.

"Oh gag me with a spoon. Just because you and your jocks like to get your freak on in a naked pretzel, which I really prefer not to think about lest I get nightmares, doesn't mean all of us do."

"Want me to hold him so you can hit him?" Ethan asked his mate.

"Nah. I may be younger than him but I can still kick his ass if I need to without any help."

"You wish," Chris taunted.

Of course, the problem with daring his sister was she usually acted, which was how he ended up on his ass on the floor while Ethan shook with laughter.

"If you weren't a girl …" Chris growled.

"I'd hurt you even more," she sassed back. "Now stop avoiding the question. You want this Jill girl. Who by the way, I can't believe is married to a Jack. What did they meet tumbling down a hill?"

"So I'm not the only one that thinks it's weird?" Chris asked picking himself up off the floor.

"What's weird?" Gina asked wandering into the kitchen and hopping up onto the island.

"Jack and Jill."

"Went up the hill."

Naomi laughed. "We know that part. What we want to know is, what are the odds of them being married?"

Gina popped a cherry tomato in her mouth from the remnants of a vegetable tray before answering. "It does seem kind of odd. I mean, here you have two obviously Asian folks, with accents, bearing extremely English names, and not just any names, but a pair from a nursery rhyme."

"What are you implying?" Chris asked, hackles up in defense of the woman he wanted as mate.

A shrug lifted Gina's shoulders. "Nothing. It's just odd. Do we know anything about them?"

"They're new to the area."

"From Vancouver," Ethan added. "Or so she said."

"Do you know anything else? Did the guy drop anything about their past when he hired you?"

It was Chris's turn to shrug. "Nope. He's as tightlipped as they come. But I do know she has a brother, Sheng, I think she called him." Which was decidedly Asian in origin. Odder and odder.

"It's a start."

"Start to what? What are you going to do?" Chris asked.

"Me? What makes you think I'm going to do anything?" Gina asked with patently false wide eyes.

"G-i-n-a!" Before he could go after her and make her promise to stay out of Jill's affairs, which in turn were his affairs, his mother hollered, "I don't hear the sound of dishes being washed!" The mild observation in itself wouldn't have stopped him from putting Gina in a headlock, but the following announcement did. "If you guys are done washing, then there is a pair of poopy diapers looking for a change."

Despite the crowded conditions, Chris, Gina, Naomi and Ethan squeezed and jostled to grab a dish to scrub or dry. Wrinkly fingers were a much better prospect than the smell that came out of his niece and nephews bottoms.

"Someone has rotten breast milk," Chris hissed, just to annoy his sister.

"And someone might need to invest in lube," she replied.

Yeah, his sphincter tightened in response. "Delicate freakn' flower my ass," he muttered darkly.

Chapter Thirteen

Sheng no sooner slammed the front door shut than he let loose his frustration – most of it not caused by his sister but a certain dark haired temptress. But since he couldn't give Gina what she deserved – a naked tongue lashing – he ranted at Jiao instead for getting him in to his current emotional mess.

"What the hell were you thinking?"

"You'll have to explain because I'm sure I don't know what you mean," Jiao calmly stated as she kicked off her shoes.

"Going off with that wolf. Do you know how that looked?"

"Yeah, it looked like the son of the host, who happens to work for us, wanted to show me an example of his work."

"Alone? Without your husband? It was completely inappropriate and you know it."

"Maybe in medieval times," she shouted back, losing her temper in the face of his own.

"People won't believe we're married if you act like a she-cat in heat."

"Oh, you did not just say that," she growled. "Especially considering you're covered in the scent of that wolf, Gina. What did you do? Roll yourself all over her?"

No, but he sure as hell wanted to. "She's the one who was all over me."

"So it's okay for you to socialize with a woman and let her mark you with her scent, but I'm not allowed? I'm sorry, did you want me to start bowing and scraping too while we're in public? Maybe following you three feet behind like a good little geisha?"

He blew out a noisy sigh. "That's not what I'm saying."

"Funny, it's what I hear. Do as I say Jiao and not as I do. God, I am so tired of this charade."

"We need –"

Eyes flashing, she held up her hand to stop him. "Don't you dare say it one more time. I really don't freakn' care anymore whether this fake marriage is for my own good or not. For the first time in a long time, I had fun tonight. Do you hear me? Fun. I made friends. It felt great. Despite your constant scowl, they want to have lunch with me and maybe go shopping."

"I don't think that's wise."

"How did I know you'd say that? Gee, what a surprise, you're already trying to ruin my new friendships. Trying to make me feel guilty for acting normal. Did it ever occur to you that your behavior is what sets us apart and gets us noticed? Because it's so normal for married couples to ignore their neighbors and shun attempts to get to know them. Why not stick a big sign on our house that screams this couple wants to be left alone because they have a secret? Better yet, get your forehead tattooed with something to the effect that your antisocial behavior is a ploy to hide your true identity. Your attitude is what's making us stick out like sore thumbs."

"You're wrong. I ..." Sheng trailed off, because he realized he didn't have an answer for her accusation. For some reason, her observation struck him. In his quest to keep them under radar, had he inadvertently brought them more attention? In a close-knit community of shifters, would a pair who rejected contact and friendship stand out? The answer deflated him. "I'm sorry, ji☐ zǐ. Much as it pains me to admit, you might be right. It's so hard for me to trust. I worry that we will be discovered. Worry that we will befriend the wrong person."

"But wouldn't knowing the people around us help instead of hinder? If we had friends, people we could count on, wouldn't they help keep us safe? You can't do it alone forever, Sheng."

"I know. But what if we choose wrong? What if the person we confide in betrays us?" What if he let down his guard and Jiao got hurt?

"What if I cross the street and get hit by bus? Or the sky falls? Risk is all around us, Sheng, and yet, people still manage to live and have fun."

"But those people don't have a madman determined to get them back."

"Or so you assume. Come on, Sheng. Kaleb won't look forever, so you're going to have to lose that excuse eventually. What's the real reason? Is it because you're scared? Have we hidden from the real world so long that you fear it?"

Sinking onto the sofa, Sheng cradled his face in hands. Had Jiao stumbled on something? Did he fear losing the safety of the small world he'd created with Jiao? He'd lost everything – his old life, his parents, his naïve belief that everything would turn out all right. Could he stand to lose the one thing, the one person, he had left to love? He'd die if that happened. But it seemed cowardly to admit it aloud. "I don't know.

Maybe. It's been so long since I've allowed myself to trust anyone other than you and Patricia." And it took him a while before he believed the shifter who offered them her aide had their best interest at heart.

"What's it going to take for you to let go of the past? To believe we can live our lives in freedom. I'm not willing to wait forever."

And neither was he, but did he dare risk Jiao's life because she chafed at their fake marriage? "I'm meeting with Patricia on Thursday. Let me talk to her and see if she's heard anything about Kaleb, or seen anything suspicious pop up on her reports for the area." He'd also get her to run background checks on the Grayson family who seemed to have too much interest in his sister.

"Thank you. I promise it will be okay. We'll be okay." Jiao hugged him, squeezing him tight, and he closed his eyes.

I want to end this constant fear too, jǐ zǐ. And not just because of the dark haired wolf in a short skirt who made his cat rumble. It was time to face the future instead of running from their past. Jiao said it best: *It's time to live.*

Chapter Fourteen

Chris went to work on Tuesday, Jack having made it abundantly clear that Monday was a holiday. The house stood silent when he entered, Jack and Jill already gone to their respective jobs. The lingering scent of his mate tickled him, reminded him of their aborted embrace and he wanted to pound something in frustration.

How to win her when Chris couldn't even see her? He'd yet to find an answer to that question even though he'd pondered it incessantly since his kiss with Jill.

Forty hours and sixteen minutes since he'd seen her, and he couldn't forget the taste of her. The torrid embrace also ramped up his dreams a notch, taking him from fantasy flirtation to full blown erotic feast. But his mind wrought fantasies, fun as they were, didn't compare to the real thing. Not to mention the consequences of his wet dreams. He'd now washed his sheets for five days in a row to his brother's amusement. He hated it, but at the same time, as soon as his head hit the pillow, he craved the dreams featuring his beautiful Jill, because for now, it was the only way he could have his mate.

Why did the claiming of his woman have to be so freakn' complicated? And frustrating. Ball aching, fist clenching, frustrating.

Entering the basement area, Chris dropped his toolbox with a loud thud on the floor. If he couldn't have Jill in his bed, he could at least give her the home gym of her dreams. He'd seen the way she wistfully admired his. He didn't understand why she needed it so bad, after all, her place abutted the forest, but no matter her reason, he'd give it to her.

About to start work, he noted his stack of wood seemed to have changed. A small piece, a scrap one he'd tossed into a corner for clean up later, sat on top. Curious, he picked it up and wanted to shout for joy when he saw the piece of paper tucked under.

Unfolding it, a looping scrawl greeted his eyes along with the distinct scent of his mate. She'd penned him a note. He held his breath hoping it wasn't the Dear John type.

Chris, I want to see you, but we must be discreet. I'm going to do groceries tonight at the Sobey's around the corner. Sevenish. Will you meet me? J.

Oh, he'd be there. But this time, before they kissed – because he was so going for another taste – he'd also have to ask some questions, like 'Where is this going?' and 'Want a number for a divorce lawyer?' Hmm. Maybe too forward, but he did need to find out more about her relationship with Jack before things went any further. Needed to know where he stood in her affections and her future plans, plans he really hoped didn't include her dour husband.

The day seemed to drag as Chris worked, his mind consumed with his upcoming meeting with Jill. What would he say? *Hey baby. How you doing?* Too creepy and overdone. But hello seemed too simple. And 'Wanna rent a motel room?' just a tad too pushy.

Why did one little woman completely mess with his confidence? Chris never had problems communicating with women. Then again, in the past he mostly dealt with women he wanted to screw, not keep as his mate forever. He needed more than just attraction and sex with Jill. He wanted a deeper connection like his parents had. An ability to converse and understand each other, a life of laughter like his sister shared with her mates.

But how to get from where he was now – third wheel looking to steal his mate from her husband – to his happy ending – where she fell in love with him and they lived in a four bedroom house, with a two car garage, a white picket fence and a theatre room with a bar all his buddies could envy?

Yeah, he'd spent a lot of time thinking about his future with a woman he couldn't yet claim. He'd even canceled the big screen television in case he needed the cash for a down payment on a home, a home he'd share with Jill. He had to wonder if the same questions ran through her mind. They'd not spoken since their interrupted kiss. Would their meeting tonight end up awkward? Would she chicken out? Would she …

With a million questions, and not a single answer, he packed up at four thirty, despite Jack's new instructions to work whenever he wanted, and headed home for a shower and dinner, stalling tactics to waste time until their appointed meeting. At six thirty, he gave up the battle to wait and stalked the Sobey's aisles, pushing a cart laden with a few items so as to not look suspicious while he waited for Jill to arrive. To his delight, like him, she arrived early, looking delectable in a pair of worn jeans, her hair tied up in a high ponytail and a windbreaker. He angled his cart up alongside hers.

"Hi." He went with a simple greeting and bit his tongue lest he ruin the moment with some of his insecurities. Real men didn't admit to fear.

"I wasn't sure you'd come," she said, casting him a brief sideways glance.

"Funny, I was going to say the same thing." Oops. He'd admitted to being unsure. He'd have to do something manly to counteract. He tossed some Frank's Hot Sauce in his cart. Nothing said I-am-a-man like shit that burned you inside and out.

"Thanks for covering for me on Sunday."

"Don't thank me. It was my fault you needed a cover in the first place." He'd dragged her off and kissed her, the least he could do to keep her from getting caught up in something ugly. Damned altruistic side. Had he done nothing, perhaps he could have met her somewhere a little nicer than like a star crossed lover in the grocery store. She ducked her head again, cheeks blushing as she – or so he hoped – remembered their kiss. He never found out for sure because she changed the subject.

"The dinner was really good. Your mother is a great cook."

"Yes she is. Wait until you taste her Christmas dinner. It's almost as good as her Thanksgiving one." There went his runaway mouth. Nothing like jumping the gun and making plans weeks down the road and before they'd even ironed some of the more pressing issues in their budding relationship.

She didn't let him off the hook. "Is that an invitation, or a statement?" she asked. "Seems kind of early to be planning that far ahead. October isn't even finished yet." Unlike their American counterparts, Canadians celebrated their Thanksgiving in October.

But forget the timing of holidays, she was waiting for an answer. He brazened ahead. In for a pound and all that. "Holiday suppers are just the tip of the iceberg. You'll probably be expected to come for Sunday dinner too."

"I will? And why is that?" Jill halted her cart in the middle of the aisle and stared at him.

"You're going to make me say it, aren't you?" Her eyes shone with mirth, and expectation. Chris groaned. Well, here went nothing. "As my mate, you'll be expected to attend all family functions."

"Your mate?"

"Yes, my mate. I've known we were meant to be together since the first moment we met."

Pleasure lit her eyes for a moment, before dejection set it. "Somehow I don't think Jack will approve."

"This has nothing to do with Jack."

Her lips pursed. "Have you forgotten something?"

"No," he growled. "I know you're married to the guy. I just don't understand why you haven't divorced. I thought my sister was moody, but he really gives the word new definition."

"He's got his reasons – good ones – for the way he is."

How could she defend him? And what reason could Jack have for the stick up his ass? Chris didn't really care because he hoped to use Jack's attitude against him. "I want you to leave him." Yeah, he said it boldly. Forget seducing her slowly, or easing her into his life. He just couldn't stand the thought of her going home to another guy.

"I can't."

Okay, not exactly the answer he hoped for. "Why not? Do you love him?" Waiting for an answer just about killed him, especially, when she sighed and met his gaze, sadness on her face. *Uh-oh. Why do I get the feeling I won't like the answer?*

*

How did Jiao end up in the grocery store, slowly walking the aisles with the man fated as her mate, having the most intense conversation of her life? He asked if she loved her husband. Waited for a reply. But how to answer?

"Yes, I love him." But not in the way Chris thought. Oh how she hated the pain in his eyes. However, she couldn't lie. She did love Sheng and would never willingly hurt him. What she did now was such a betrayal of his trust, but necessary. She needed to make some things clear with Chris. Get him to give her some time without revealing her secret, time enough that things could turn out right for everyone. She should have known better. Her impatient wolf wanted direct answers.

"Is he your mate?" Strong hand clutching a box of cereal, she noted how the cardboard bent as Chris squeezed it tight, waiting for a reply.

She shook her head. "No, he's not. I think we both know who my true mate is." How she wished she could tell him everything, right here and now. Stop the sham and be with the man destined as hers.

"I don't understand. You know we're mates. You know what's happening between us is just going to get stronger. Why can't you leave him? I know we haven't known each other long, and I'm not asking you to move right in with me, but the fact you're living with him is killing me."

It killed her too. "It's not what you think. And I can't explain. Trust me when I say I want to be with you. More than you can imagine. But my marriage is complicated."

"So explain it to me."

God, she hated the lying. When would it end? "I can't. Please. You mustn't push me on this. I am working on a way for us to be together. But you need to give me time."

"You can't expect me to keep letting you go home to him. To his bed," he said, his tone low, angry and frustrated. "I want you, but I also won't be screwed around. I have some pride."

"If there's one thing I can promise you, it's that Jack and I aren't sleeping together. We –" Her phone rang.

"Don't answer it," he growled.

Glancing at the screen's caller id as she pulled the phone from her pocket, she bit her lip. "I have to or he'll get worried."

Snarling something she couldn't quite decipher, Chris stalked away and headed for the check out. Teeth gnawing her lower lip, she ignored her phone and raced her cart after him. He didn't say anything as he paid for his purchases and neither did she. Their silence lasted only until they reached the parking lot.

"I thought you had to answer the phone," he finally muttered, not quite over his sulk. She couldn't blame him. The whole situation was frustrating.

"I should have. But I can't stand to see you mad."

"And I can't stand to see you married to someone else. So I guess we're at an impasse."

Halting her cart again, she turned and grabbed his arm, his very muscled and tense arm. "Don't be angry."

Chris wouldn't look at her. He stared up at the night sky. A heavy sigh left him. "I'm not mad at you. Just frustrated. Can you promise me one thing?" He dropped his gaze from his perusal of the stars until he met hers. "Please promise I don't have to get in a threesome with your husband to claim you."

A threesome? With Sheng. Eeew. She couldn't help making a face and laughing. "I promise you will never, ever have to share me with someone. Especially not Jack."

"Swear?"

"On my life."

"Thank freakn' God." His bags rustled as they thumped to the ground, leaving his hands free to scoop her up for a kiss that stole her breath. Clasped in his arms, Jiao could understand his frustration. Felt it as well because if it weren't for the ruse Sheng wanted her to keep, she could indulge in this anytime. Anywhere. Naked.

*

Devouring her lips, lost in sensation heaven, Chris would have promised Jill anything, especially after hearing he wouldn't have to share her. His elation over that small fact, though, couldn't completely stem his annoyance in other matters. For example, her reluctance to split from Jack. She didn't love the guy. He wasn't her mate. So why did she hesitate? What wasn't she telling him?

All questions he should have demanded answers to, however, animal need drove him. With his passion overtaking his common sense, all he wanted was to taste her. Touch her. Imprint himself on her so that she would know who she truly belonged to. *Me. And only me.*

Figured the damned phone would interrupt again. To his immense male satisfaction, when he broke the kiss and leaned back, she stood with her eyes closed, lips parted, completely lost in the moment.

"Shouldn't you answer that?" he teased.

Cheeks flushing from pink to red, she fumbled her phone out. "Give me a second." Back turned, she answered the phone and a rapid fire conversation ensued in a language he couldn't make heads or tails of. Her eyes flashed with annoyance when she ended the call and turned back to face him.

"I have to go. I stayed too long."

"When will I see you again?"

"Thursday. He has a meeting and I am supposed to go to a yoga class, but I'll get out of it and stay home."

"That's two days from now." Two days of not seeing or touching her. Yanking her to him, he kissed her again, a hard embrace that probably relayed some of his frustration. She kissed him back, her embrace just as fierce and hot. A rude shout about getting a room broke them apart, panting.

"See me tomorrow?" he asked.

She bit her lip. "I can't."

"And I can't wait until Thursday."

"I doubt I can either." She sighed. "I'll figure something out and leave you a note."

"Why does it feel like I'm back in high school?" he grumbled.

She laughed. "I've always wondered what it would be like to meet a boy under the bleachers."

Not very comfortable. But he didn't say it aloud. This wolf knew better than to talk about past conquests with the woman he hoped to win for life. Chris stroked her cheek with a calloused thumb. "I'll miss you."

"Me too. I'll work something out." She rubbed against the palm of his hand, a small rumble of pleasure vibrating against his skin.

"I won't hide what I feel for you forever," he warned.

Her eyes flashed. "Don't threaten me. You don't understand what's at stake. "

"Because you won't tell me. So get whatever's keeping us apart taken care of or I will do it for you. That's a promise."

"If I didn't feel the same way, I'd probably be really annoyed with you right now," she snapped. Then softened. "But I understand. I promise to do what I can to be your mate in every way possible as soon as I can," she added in a husky voice. Before he could grab again for another kiss – and grope – she fled, pert ass swaying, and he forced himself not to chase her.

She wanted time. He'd give her time, but not much because she was his, and she belonged in his arms. His bed. His life.

Chapter Fifteen

Jiao parked a block before the house, relishing the scent of Chris on her skin. On her lips. The taste of him on her tongue. It seemed a sacrilege to erase it when all she wanted was to revel in the aroma of her mate. But Sheng would notice. Then he'd yell – loudly. Things would get ugly and, cowardly or not, she wasn't ready yet to deal with it.

She wanted, hoped really, that her brother would come around on his own and end their fake marriage. Let her go free. Hopefully sooner rather than later, because like Chris – *my impatient and very sexy, wolf mate* – she didn't think she could go a day without seeing or touching him. *I need him.*

How did it happen so quickly? Who cared? The mating instinct drove her at this point, cajoled her to give in to the inevitable. To be with her mate.

Given her strong feelings, and desires, she knew she wouldn't be able to hide her affair with the handyman for long. But she could for tonight. Licking her lips one last time – damn he tasted so good – she implemented her plan to ensure Sheng suspected nothing. She exited her car and pulled a bag from the trunk. With a flick of her wrist, she broke the jar of pickles by dropping the bag that held it on the pavement, then tossed it back in her car. She'd ensured at the checkout that the rest of the items in the bag were waterproof. However, nothing could stop the smell. The pungent aroma of garlic pickles in vinegar filled the car, covered her in a miasma that overrode Chris's, while a piece of gum took care of her mouth.

Sheng wrinkled his nose when she walked in.

"Did you bathe in a vat of brine?" he asked, as he entered the front hall to give her a hand with the bags.

"Stupid jar broke when I put it in the car," she grumbled. "Can you take care of it while I shower the stench off?"

"Can it wait until I make myself a sandwich? I suddenly have an overwhelming urge for deli."

"Ha. Ha. Look who's a comedian. Not!" Shoving the bags in his direction, Jiao fled to the safety of her bathroom before she was forced to lie even more. God, she hated this. She could only hope when Sheng visited Patricia on Thursday, she would sound an all clear. And if she didn't …

Then Jiao didn't know what she'd do, but she knew Sheng wouldn't like whatever she decided. Safe or not, with or without the blessing of her brother, Jiao would act. Would claim. Would live. And love.

Despite the danger, Jiao gave in to temptation the following day, despite all the arguments she made in her mind to the contrary. Knowing Chris was at the house, hoping to see her, it turned her into someone she wasn't sure she liked. Someone capable of lying to the one person who trusted her.

She kept her eyes shut tight as she spoke to her brother on her cellphone, already seated in a cab on the way to the house.

"I'm going home early. I have a headache."

"I'll come get you and drive you home," Sheng replied, and she heard him shuffle the phone then rifle through some papers, probably to check the schedule to see if he could call someone in early to take over his shift at the car dealership.

"I'll be fine. I already called a cab. I just want to lie down."

"The contractor is there."

She knew, and looked forward to seeing him. "I know. I'll close my bedroom door. I won't even see him. Don't make me sing you Paranoia again."

"You're a brat."

"You raised me," she sassed.

"I should have grounded you more often," he said in a mocking growl. "But seriously, are you sure, you'll be okay?"

The concern in his voice tightened her throat. "I'm sure."

"I'll be home soon."

"Don't hurry on my account, I'll probably be sleeping." Or at least have her eyes closed while she indulged a lip lock.

I am such a horrible sister. Fibbing so blatantly. Worse, she'd do it again in a heartbeat if it meant spending time with Chris.

Thankfully, Sheng bought it. Minutes later, she entered the house, dropped her bag by the door, yanked the deadbolt, and then headed downstairs. Forget primping or talking herself out of it. It wasn't just her cat's yeowling insistence making her frantic. *I need him.*

Chris met her before she even reached the middle of her descent, swinging her into his arms, his joy at seeing her worth the subterfuge.

"You made it!"

"I said I would,' she replied twining her arms around his neck.

"I was afraid you wouldn't. I mean, yeah, whatever. It's not like I was waiting or something."

She snorted. "Is that your macho way of saving face?"

A grin lit his whole face, a boyish smile that made her all warm inside. "Needs work, huh? I always said I wouldn't be one of those pussy whipped guys who lives for the moments he's with his mate."

"And now?"

"I met the right pussy." He waggled his brows, and she laughed. Laughed so hard her cheeks hurt and she gasped for breath.

It seemed to please him, if his tight hug was any indication. Sitting cross-legged on the floor, he tucked her into his lap, turning her slightly so he could see her face. She lifted a hand to stroke the rough edge of his jaw. She gave in to temptation and slid her lips along it before touching his lips. The embrace lasted only a moment before he pulled away.

"What? No kisses today," she murmured, only partially shocked at her own risqué words.

"Not because I don't want to," he growled. "But, I thought maybe we should talk. Get to know each other."

"Talk?" She arched a brow. "About?"

"I want to know more about you. What makes you tick? Your roots. Your family. Your favorite television show and color."

"Can't we kiss instead?" Because his reasonable queries treaded into dangerous territory. How much did she dare reveal without giving away too much? She didn't want to lie, but she also owed it to her brother to at least attempt to keep their cover story.

"We'll have a lifetime for kisses. I want to get to know the woman that's got me going crazy."

How unexpected and cute. Yet, at the same time, dangerous. "I'm boring." *Well, boring if I omit the part of my life where I was kidnapped along with my family by a psycho who used us as attractions in his perverted version of a circus. Oh, and by the way, I escaped just before he could breed me to the highest bidder.* Yeah, she'd keep that part of her past to herself.

"I doubt anything about you is boring. What do you do for work?"

Easy. "I work in a seniors home as a group counselor and personal aide."

"Why? I mean it seems an odd job for someone your age."

Why do I do it? Not for the pay that's for sure. She did it because they needed her. Or was it more like she needed them? So young when captured and selfishly concerned with herself, Jiao wasn't able to give her mother what she needed when her father died. She still felt the sting of shame that she didn't try harder. Didn't find the right words or actions to convince her mother life was worth living.

I failed. But she kept trying to atone.

The seniors, while not her mother, just wanted someone to care enough to give them that extra urge to fight. "I like old people. They're interesting. Your turn. Why do you work as a contractor?"

"Because I'm great with my hands?" He lifted them from her long enough to wiggle his fingers. "In all honesty though, I like to build things. As I told you before, I grew up in a house with lots of siblings. We were a little rambunctious."

"A little?" she teased.

He laughed. "Okay, a lot. Things had a tendency of getting broken around our place. My dad spent a lot of weekends fixing our accidental catastrophes for my mom. From an early age, I helped. Not that my dad appreciated it at first. Apparently having a three year old wave a hammer around makes the process a little longer and more difficult. Thankfully, I got better with age."

Too easily, she could picture a miniature version of Chris, tousle haired and grinning from ear to ear as he whacked things. Would their future end up with a similar memory involving children of their own? The thought warmed her. *Oh to start my own family and pass on the traditions I learned from my mother.* A dream she could now realize, even picture since she'd met Chris. "I'd say your lessons from your father turned out pretty darned good, given you now have your own business. You came highly recommended."

"Aw, shucks. Make a guy blush why don't you? Enough about me and my greatness, it's your turn again. I get the impression not everything was rosy with your upbringing. What happened to your parents? Why don't you see your brother?"

Talk about a double whammy. She looked away, trying to gather her thoughts and come up with an answer, but he didn't give her time. He gripped her chin and turned her face back to him. "What's wrong? Why did you get the saddest look on your face? Is it that bad?"

Yes! "My parents died and I don't like to talk about it."

"You were close?"

"Very much, and their death was very hard on me. And even harder on my brother. He took care of me afterward. He was still just a kid himself, and we were all alone." Her voice dropped to a low whisper as the memories came unbidden of that time. Alone, and frightened, they lived under the control of a man who treated them little better than animals. Freaks of nature, not worth the basic courtesies, because in Kaleb's mind, despite their human shape, Jiao, Sheng and all shifters were animals. The only thing Kaleb drew the line at was starvation and physical abuse. He needed his pets to look good for the crowd. But, he punished them in other ways if they didn't toe the line.

Refuse to perform? Their mother got sent to the hole, a literal hole, alone with no means of contact. Talk back? Try sleeping on the concrete floor without a stitch of clothing or blanket.

The only time Kaleb broke his own rules was when someone lost their use, like Jiao's father. Injured after an accidental fall during a practice, his age and the poorly set break left him limping and unable to walk the rope. Not one to waste resources, instead of feeding a lame cat, Kaleb sold him as a prize in a hunt. A fatal hunt, because no matter how agile and stealthy, a cat couldn't outrun a bullet. And in the end, her mother couldn't escape her grief.

Even if Jiao didn't need to keep her identity secret, how could she explain something like that to someone who'd grown up in a community where they lived freely, or as free as shifters could be amongst humans?

Chris and his family never knew the terror of wondering when they might be called to perform. Worrying they'd fall or fail. And when her menses finally hit in her sixteenth year, well, Kaleb's plans for her went from horrible straight into I'd-rather-die.

Jiao's pride would never have allowed her to whore herself to the highest bidder and Sheng would have died trying to save her.

But they'd escaped and now had a chance to live again, if Kaleb didn't find them. The reminder almost saw her fleeing the comfort of Chris's lap, but tired of running, wanting the safety he somehow managed to impart, she didn't move.

"Where is your brother now? I'd like to meet him?" Chris said softly, his hands stroking her as if trying to ease the pain of her memories.

"He's close by." Closer than Chris guessed. "And I'm hoping you can meet him soon. Although, I doubt he'll like you."

"Why not?" Her future mate reared back with an indignant expression.

"Because he doesn't like anyone."

"Kind of sounds like your husband."

If he only knew. "Can we talk about something else? Something happier than my past and family? What do you do for fun?"

"I like to play sports. Video games. Race miniature gas powered cars."

She wrinkled her nose. "Classic guy stuff, I see."

"Oh really? Well, what do you do for fun in your spare time?"

"I sew. I made all the drapes for this house."

"Boring. I said for fun."

"I cook."

"Chore."

Hmm, she probably shouldn't mention she stripped and varnished the old dining room set she bought at a garage sale. What did she do for fun?

"Don't tell me you don't have a hobby that's pure pleasure? Reading?"

"I read." Hot and dirty contemporary romances of normal people falling in love.

"That's better. What about active stuff? Do you run? Like to take walks? Skinny dip in the moonlight?"

Run, she'd love to, but Sheng drew the line at her performing solitary activities. Shopping with a crowd was fine. A stroll through the woods for exercise wasn't. She shook her head. "You don't really swim naked, do you?" Oh how she'd love to watch. The thought of moonlight, gleaming on his bare, muscled skin warmed her, but the thought of him wet and slick, roused her.

"Naked as the day I was born, baby. If it weren't getting too chilly at night, I'd take you to my secret place."

Mmm, something to look forward to, if all went well. The reminder that their time together could get cut short at any time made her bold. She cupped his cheeks. "Enough talk. We don't have much time. Jack will come home soon."

His brow creased. "I could have done without the reminder."

"Soon, my wolf," she whispered, leaning close. "Soon, we won't have to hide." Soon, she'd experience fully what her body desired and she'd mark him. Mark him, scratch him, and never let him go. Crazy and quick as it seemed, she was falling in love, and she didn't think she could hide it for long.

Screw hiding it. She'd done that for long enough. When the time came, maybe she'd shout it from the rooftops. Carve it in a tree. Hold onto it with all her strength and never let go.

Speaking of holding on ... She drew his face back down and caught his mouth with her own. How she loved the taste of him. Minty because of the gum he liked to chew, his lips hard and commanding, his tongue sinuous and electrifying. Under her ass cheeks, she could feel him, a hard bulge that rubbed against her, blatant evidence of his desire. As if she needed such an obvious clue when he kissed her with such passion. Such hunger.

He manipulated her so she sat astride him, her legs parted around his waist, a position which seated her more fully on him. The new arrangement and his erection put pressure on her mound, more specifically her clit. Jiao couldn't help the small sound that escaped her when his hands, spanning her waist, rubbed her back and forth against him.

"This would work much better naked," he growled.

Mmm, skin to skin sounded yummy. However, it also reminded her of one crucial fact. She was a virgin – and still technically undercover. *How do I explain that when I'm supposed to be married?*

"I'm not ready yet," she lied, her head tilting back as his lips devoured the skin of her neck.

"And you deserve better than a quickie in the basement," he murmured against her flesh. "But you make it hard when you're just so freakn' tempting. Ignore me. I'll take what I can for now."

Arching her even further back, one of his hands supported her upper body as he nuzzled his face between her breasts, rubbing his bristled jaw against her small mounds, the drag of fabric across her sensitized skin making her gasp. However, it was the continuous friction of his groin against her cleft, a subtle yet steady pressure that had her tightening her fingers on his forearms. Claws dug into his skin. Her eyes closed and breathing turned erratic as her body coiled.

Fully clothed, sitting on a basement floor, and from just touching and kissing, she still came, the rush of her climax making her cry out.

After she came down from her high, panting, heart racing, a languorous heat controlling her limbs, she lay cuddled against Chris's chest, unable to stop herself from purring as his arms wrapped tightly around her. Intimate. Loving. Perfect. She wished the moment could last forever, but knew it couldn't. Not yet. How though to break the spell of perfection before she completely lost herself and said to hell with waiting for what Patricia had to say?

"I think I've found a hobby we can both enjoy together," she whispered against his skin. A rumble of laughter shook him, and made her smile. If only tomorrow could hurry up, so she could begin her new life of love and laughter – and finally experience everything her mate had to offer.

Chapter Sixteen

Sleep. What a concept, Sheng thought as he said goodbye and hung up with his ailing sister who intended to go straight home for some shut eye. He'd barely gotten any since the disastrous Thanksgiving dinner. He couldn't have explained why, but the she-wolf, Gina, just wouldn't leave his thoughts. Worse, she kept invading them with an inviting smile and no clothes.

No amount of masturbation, self-castigation, or chastising speeches to himself seemed to help. His obsession for the wolf wouldn't abate. And it was frankly really starting to piss him off.

How dare Gina turn his carefully controlled world into chaos? Why did he lust after her too curvy body barely covered in her scanty clothes? And her speech? Vulgar, outrageous, husky and sexy.

Thank God he wouldn't have to worry about running into her again. It wasn't like he'd go back for another dinner at the Grayson house, no matter how much Jiao begged. Out of sight, eventually out of mind. Or that was the theory he counted on.

The buzzer for the front door of the showroom went off, and given his two other coworkers on the sales team were out getting coffee, Sheng stood and straightened his tie. Time to make a sale. Sure, some people attached a stigma to car salesmen, but Sheng didn't care since his knack for selling brought home a nice paycheck. As in all things he took on, he excelled at his profession.

Most of his colleagues adopted a jovial, best-friend persona for potential clients. Sheng didn't. He gave it to them straight. Found out what the buyer needed, and didn't try to upsell them on features they didn't want. He gave them solid numbers, which in turn, brought him steady sales.

Striding out to the front, he didn't immediately see the client, a short stature hiding the person behind a car, but when he came around the corner, he stopped dead and said, "You!"

Dressed in a black uniform, a hat tucked under her arm, her hair pinned back in a severe bun, stood his annoying fantasy girl. And damn him if he didn't already know tonight's feature dream attraction would have Gina dressed in her sexy police girl garb with him handcuffed to a bed while she frisked him. Damn her for messing up his plan to forget she existed.

On a side note, he'd better get more hand lotion because he could see where the evening was heading – again. His poor hand never had to work so hard.

Worse, though, he couldn't understand why her, and why now? Eying her up and down, her lush curves still apparent despite her rigid dress, he still couldn't figure out the attraction. Sure, she bore a fresh faced complexion now as opposed to the thick makeup one of the dinner. But her lips were still too full, too pouty, like that of a porn star who sucked …

No. He was not going there. He'd been there last night. Twice. No way was he letting his mind wander down that dirty avenue again. Now if only his cock, swelling once again, would get the damned message.

"What do you want?" he snapped. *Because I know what I'd like. You naked, on your knees.* And then to please his possessive cat, flip her before she was done with her oral tease to her knees so he could take her from behind.

Damn his raunchy thoughts. Would she notice if he grabbed her gun and shot himself? Or would she wrestle him into submission? And why oh why did he hope for the latter?

*

Well wasn't it her lucky day, Gina thought, eyeing the handsome Asian dude she'd met at her aunt's party. The one married to Chris's mate. Jack, the unforgettable hunk who did such naughty things in her dreams. But then again, she did even dirtier things right back, things that wiped the snarl off his face.

Gina couldn't deny a hot spurt of pleasure – and moisture — at seeing him again, and this in spite of the fact he looked less than happy to see her. Too bad.

"If it isn't my pussycat. I didn't know you worked here."

"And I didn't know you were a cop," he replied, with way more astonishment than she liked. "Or is that just your stripper costume?"

Oh, zinger. The man sucker punched her with words, and she grinned at his temerity. "Sorry, pussycat. This uniform is one hundred percent real. You're looking at one of Ottawa's finest. Although, if you want to come back to my place, a stripping could be arranged if you don't mind the lack of a pole." She lightly smacked her forehead. "Wait a second. What am I saying? I'll just borrow your pole for dancing."

How interesting. His cheeks turned bright red, but his eyes smoldered with lust, and as for below his belt, yup, definite tenting. What a shame. She had more interest in him when he acted the part of self-righteous married man. She should have known he was a pig like every other guy she knew. But still, it wasn't like she planned to marry him – even if her wolf kept getting excited when he was around. Nope, her only motive in flirting wasn't to appease the ache between her legs, but to help out her cousin Chris.

Always willing to give a helping hand, she'd take one for the team. Sacrifice her virtue – snicker – so her cousin could snag his mate.

Sauntering close to Jack, she kept going, passing him to run a finger over the cherry red paint of the convertible in the showroom. "Nice car."

"You looking to buy?" He didn't seem convinced.

"Yes, actually. My car died on Monday. On the highway too, the piece of crap. The garage wants more money than the hunk of junk is worth, so I thought I'd look into replacing it instead."

Straightening, his expression smoothed out into that of a sales-shark who caught a scent of blood. "What are you in the market for?"

A hot Asian male, wearing nothing but her, naked, on his dick? Hmmm. He probably wouldn't go for that. So she'd stick to something he could handle. "I'm thinking something compact since I work in the city. But with seats I can fold into the floor in case I need to fit a body in the trunk."

"Excuse me? Did you say a body in the trunk?"

Oh how she loved his wide-eyed expression. She smiled. "Yes. Yes I did. Mine, and maybe someone else's. I like to go camping, but I seem to have the misfortune of always picking days when the weatherman is wrong. In other words, despite the clear skies, it always freakn' rains. So, I need a dry spot I can climb into, maybe with a friend. Got something that fits the bill?"

"Crazy wolf." Or so she thought he muttered, as he wandered off, leading her to another vehicle.

Gina only half listened as he recited a flawless spiel about the compact, four door car he showed her. Honestly she didn't pay much attention, checking out his ass instead as he walked around the vehicle, his hands pointing out features.

She interrupted him before he'd completed his speech. "You know what, that all sounds good. Can we take one for a test drive? I'd like to get a *feel* for the ride." Yeah, she teased him a little bit, loving how his eyes flashed and his lips tightened. Did the guy ever relax? Would he wear that same pinched expression as he came? It made a she-wolf want to handcuff him to a bed and find out.

"If you leave a copy of your license, you can go by yourself. I've got one out back with a full tank."

"Alone? Oh no. I insist you come with me. My previous car was old and didn't have all those doohickeys on the dash and stuff. I might need your help figuring things out."

Damn, but the sigh he let out as he acquiesced sounded begrudging .Way to stroke her ego. If it weren't for the fact she could spot the boner he kept trying to hide and the erratic race of his heart, she'd think he didn't like her. Thank goodness for her powers of observation. But the fact he wanted to blow her off raised him back in her estimation. He was trying, the poor guy. Trying to resist, but without a true mate bond with his wife, he didn't stand a chance, especially not if Gina put her mind to it.

She tried to tell herself she did this to help Chris, but honestly, something about Jack just pushed all the right buttons. She ignored her wolf's growling and snapping in her head. No way would she cave to her wolf's mistaken belief the uptight, Asian dude was her mate. When she settled down eventually, she'd do so on her terms, with a guy she chose, not her hormones. The past taught her well that once the passion faded, usually after a few rounds of hot sweaty sex, there was nothing left. Most men couldn't handle her job or her attitude. And the one went with the other. No one stepped all over Gina Greco. *I wear the boots that go walking.* Thigh high ones, with stupidly high heels. *Bet you he'd like those.*

Snagging some keys off a board, Jack led Gina outside through the parking lot where new vehicles sat waiting for owners. He'd chosen a gleaming black model for her to try. It would match her underwear perfectly. Not that she'd show him. As an officer of the law, a certain decorum was expected of her when she wore the uniform.

Oops, she almost laughed out loud at her inner thoughts. Okay so prim and proper, by the rules wasn't exactly her forte. That said, she did have the utmost respect for her job and the police force, so she wouldn't do anything to harm either. But, a stolen kiss, or two, never hurt anyone. And in the privacy of her home, so long as no one taped it, strip teasing, also known as changing into something more comfortable, after a long day's work, was totally allowed.

Somehow she doubted Mr. Jack Smith would agree to go home with her. Yet. But, it didn't mean she wouldn't give it her best shot. Dabbing on some cherry flavored lip gloss, she slid into the driver seat. Seated beside her in the passenger seat, Jack didn't look at her and kept his hands primly folded in his lap.

This is going to be so much fun.

"Hold on tight. I want to see what this baby's got," she warned only seconds before she pounded the gas and squealed out of the car lot. The disapproval radiating from him just widened her smile.

And gave her an idea.

*

Caught in the car, windows up, with a she-wolf whose scent teased him mercilessly, Sheng suffered the cruelest torment. *Why me? Why her?* Of all the places she chose to car shop, of all the people to walk in, it had to be her. He tried to find his composure, his cool attitude, but in the face of her taunts, grins and her damnable presence, he couldn't keep it for long. Wanting to get rid of her as soon as possible – screw the sale – he no longer touted the car's features. But she didn't seem to notice or care as she weaved in and out of traffic on highway four seventeen heading westbound. He assumed she knew where she went, and if she didn't, then the handy built in navigation system would.

Kilometers from the city, she exited on Carp Road, heading north, a barren stretch with few businesses and even fewer houses. Without pausing, she turned left at a side road, then right on an unpaved one before pulling over completely.

"Why are we stopping?"

"Time to test the trunk," she answered before hopping out.

Okay, he'd admit to a bit of nervousness. She owned a gun. Kaleb had money. Was this where the police officer, bribed by the rich criminal, shot Sheng dead then covered up the crime? And why did he suddenly hear the refrain from that song Paranoia again? Damn his sister. "Couldn't we test the whole space thing back at the dealership?"

"I'm in uniform. It wouldn't be seemly for the public to see my big ass bent over as I crawl into the trunk."

Big? Her ass was perfect, a rounded cushion meant for – "It's called a hatchback."

"Whatever. Are you coming, pussycat?"

Not at the moment, but probably later with your face as my incentive. "What do you need me for?"

"Lots of things, pussycat, but for now I'll settle for your body."

His what? "Excuse me?"

Gina laughed, a throaty chuckle that sent chills down his spine. "I want see if we both fit."

Eying the hatchback space, large, but not large enough for what she intended, not if he wanted to keep his sanity, he shook his head. "I'd rather not."

"Oh come on. I promise not to tell your wife. Get your sweet Asian cheeks into that trunk."

"You have a crass mouth." It was also lush and full, the perfect shape for … Yeah, he'd probably dream about that tonight too. While she wore the uniform.

"I prefer the term dirty, and trust me, that's a good thing. Or at least, my ex-boyfriends all thought so."

No. He wasn't going to ask for names and numbers so he could kill them because he most definitely didn't not feel a jealous rage coming on. Nope. Not him. He couldn't care less just who she screwed. Dammit! "This is a bad idea. We should go back," he snarled.

"Someone needs to learn to relax. I could help you with that." He glared. "Or not. Your loss. This will only take a minute. One minute of your time for a client with an already guaranteed bank loan for a new car. You want the sale? Then get in there and prove this trunk has enough space for two adults."

Why him? It wasn't the loss of a sale that bothered him so much as letting her win. She knew her antics drove him nuts, and she didn't care. Why couldn't he? He still tried to change her mind. "Shouldn't you be doing this with a bigger guy?" On second thought. No guy. His cat didn't like that idea.

"I don't date big dudes." No he wouldn't get excited. "They're too hard to kiss. Now stop arguing and get in here." She wiggled to the side and waited.

Lips tight, Jack crawled in beside her and lay stiff as a board on his back, hands folded over a certain part of him that refused to play dead. "Happy?" he snapped.

She rolled on top of him, straddling him, and oh yes, someone was definitely happy to see her. Sheng cursed his cock out silently.

"Almost," she replied. Staring down at him, her hair still caught in a tight bun making her features stand out in stark contrast – a ski slope nose, bright brown eyes, rounded cheeks – he found himself caught. Speechless. Expectant. And not one bit angry, or disappointed when she leaned down and kissed him.

On the contrary, for the first time in forever, everything felt just right.

Sheng forgot to breathe as the crazy she-wolf kissed him. Forgot he hated her brazen mouth, or her provocative way of dressing. Forgot all the reasons he should shove her away. Instead, he opened his mouth for her sinuous tongue, and happily stroked hers back.

Insane. Out of character. Dangerous. Hot. Erotic. The right thing to do – push her away – couldn't compete with the pleasurable one, which saw him meeting her kiss for kiss, tongue to tongue, hands on her ass, grinding her against him.

Lust, plus something more, rode him. A wild urge to mark this woman, to sink his teeth in her skin and claim her. *Mine. She's mine. My mate.*

No freakn' way.

Shock had him pulling his mouth away.

"Stop," he said weakly, desire riding him hard. He didn't sound convincing. Her teeth grazed the column of his neck, sending his cat into an ecstatic, tail thrashing spin. He managed a stronger, "Stop. No. We can't do this." Even though he wanted to. Wanted to flip Gina onto her back, tear the clothes from her and drive into her body as his teeth sank into her flesh, claiming her as his.

This couldn't be happening. Her lips came back to his as she ignored his request and for a crazy second, he let himself taste her again. Felt the need building.

Oh damn. He was in so much trouble. He needed to stop and get away from Gina. "No. This is wrong. We don't even like each other."

"I'd say your body thinks otherwise," she replied huskily as she rubbed herself against him.

"I'm married." And in so much trouble if Jiao found out, especially after all his lectures to her.

"Not happily. Any idiot could see that. Don't worry. I won't tell. I'm not looking for something permanent," she whispered against the lobe of his ear, before nibbling it.

He couldn't help the involuntary thrust of his hips at the sensation of her teeth on his flesh. What he wouldn't give to forget his role as a married man, and the danger courting him and his sister. How he wanted to give Gina what her scent so clearly desired.

However, Sheng hadn't survived that long by taking the easy route. He pushed her to the side, and slid from the hatchback. Standing in the crisp autumn air, he sucked in big breaths, attempting to calm his racing pulse, and his rock hard dick.

When he felt under control, without a glance at her – out of fear he'd temporarily go insane and do something he'd regret – he got back in the passenger seat and waited.

Moments later, Gina joined him on the driver side. She didn't say a word as she drove them back to the dealership. Sheng couldn't have said why that irritated the heck out of him.

Swinging into the car lot, she parked, but before he could escape, she placed her hand on his thigh and murmured in a husky voice. "I'll be seeing you soon, pussycat."

Sooner than she thought if the dreams of the previous nights were any indication. And wearing less clothing.

Chapter Seventeen

Less than two hours of talk, frantic kisses and the glorious moment she came apart for him didn't come close to satisfying Chris. On the contrary, he hungered for Jill more than ever. Worse, she burned just as hot for him, and Chris needed to act as the voice of reason, peeling his woman from his chest lest they get caught by her husband. *Don't mind me, dude, just making sweet love to your wife.* Somehow he couldn't see that scenario ending well.

"Meet me tonight," he asked. Leaning his forehead against hers, he waited for his racing heart to calm – not likely to happen while he remained in close proximity to her, but he pretended to try.

"I wish I could," she murmured wistfully. "But I can't. He'll know something's up."

"Something is," he growled, grabbing her hand and placing it over his groin.

Her eyes widened and her cheeks flushed bright. Damn, how could she appear so innocent? If he didn't know any better, he'd swear she was inexperienced. Impossible given she was married, but cute nonetheless, and utterly arousing.

"I don't work tomorrow and was planning to skip my yoga class. I was hoping we could spend some time together."

"What about your husband?" He could barely bite the word out. *I'm the one who deserves that title.*

"He has a meeting in the city. He should be gone for at least two hours or more."

"That's it?" Definitely not enough time to do half the things he planned.

"It's better than nothing."

"What happened to working on him so we could be together?" Because otherwise, Chris might have to revise his stance of no killing.

"I'm trying, but it's hard. There's so much I can't explain."

"You could try."

"I can't. I wish I could, but I can't."

"You don't trust me." He said it flatly, knowing his irritation showed, but unable to stem it. It didn't matter that he asked a lot of her, that he wanted her to turn her whole world upside down for him. He didn't care they'd first met just over a week ago. Ready to change his life – whip it inside out, turn over a new leaf, including getting rid of his black book – he expected the same of her. He trusted his gut when it told him she was the one and it hurt – not that he'd admit it aloud – that she didn't feel the same.

"I do trust you, and I want to tell you, but I can't betray Jack. I made a promise."

"You also made a promise to cherish and be faithful, yet you have no problem breaking that," he snapped, regretting the cruel words as soon as he tossed them out there.

The hurt on her face made him feel like the biggest jerk alive and when she struggled to get away from him, he hugged her tight. "I'm sorry. I don't mean that. I'm sure you never expected, neither of us did, to have the mating fever hit us. I'm just so frustrated. I need more than a few stolen moments, baby."

"And that's supposed to make it okay for you to call me a cheater when you're the one who seduced me first?"

"Me? You're the one who made me melt when we first met."

"Oh please. As if. I could barely even talk."

"Really?" He couldn't help the pleasure at her admission. "So you do think I'm hot." He said this with an arched brow and a wide smile.

"I would have said conceited, but –"

He dug his fingers into her ribs and tickled her until she squirmed and gasped for mercy. "Okay, you're cute," she cried. He didn't relent, loving her laughter. "I give in. You're superhot."

"That's better. Nothing like admitting the truth."

"Like you didn't know," she scoffed.

"A man enjoys hearing it though. Just like I'm sure you enjoy hearing you are the prettiest damned thing I've ever met."

"Now who's lying?"

"Hey, I resent that."

"I find it hard to believe I'm the prettiest girl you've met."

She denied his compliment, and yet, he couldn't help but hear the pleasure in her tone, and the sense she needed reassurance. "I've met good looking girls," he stated. And bedded most of them, a fact he kept to himself. "But none ever made me feel like the world stopped spinning the first time we met. None ever gave me sleepless nights." Or never ending hard-ons. "And none ever made me want forever. Or talk like some geeky freak in touch with his feelings." A moue of distaste curled his lips. God, he sounded like such a sappy idiot.

"If it's any consolation, you're the first man to ever make me regret my promise and marriage. I wish I could have met you before it all happened."

The sincerity in her tone humbled him and made him feel like an absolute ass for his earlier words. "I am truly sorry for what I said before. I'll try to be more patient."

She stroked his hair, sifting her fingers through the strands. "I'm going to tell Jack it's over. I can't wait any longer either. I need to stop the lying. "

"When?"

"After his meeting tomorrow."

Not the answer he wanted, not with a rock hard dick and another projected evening of whacking off alone, then beating his brother for ridiculing him. "Why after?"

"Because. Don't push me on this."

"Or?"

Her nose wrinkled. "Anyone tell you that you're stubborn?"

"All the time."

A soft smile graced her lips. "I need to go. Jack will be home soon and he mustn't find us like this."

"Fine." Chris sighed. "You know you're killing me, right?"

She kissed him softly. "It's hurting me just as much. Until tomorrow."

Away she scampered, leaving him hard and aching, pining for her presence, angry that she wouldn't give in to what they both wanted.

Worried he'd do or say something he shouldn't to Jack, Chris packed up and left just before four thirty. He wished he could figure out the deal between Jack and Jill. What was she so worried about? Did Jack have a temper? Did she worry for her safety?

If that prick laid one hand on her, he'd rearrange his face, gladly. Or did her concern stem from something else? If Chris could just figure out what kept them apart, he'd … what? Understand?

Probably not. But he also lacked the patience to wait like a good wolf on the sidelines while his jealousy and need grew.

Just one more day. She'd promised to broach it with Jack tomorrow. Surely he could wait one more day. He hoped so because otherwise he didn't know if he could stop himself from doing something rash that would require his cousin Gina pulling strings to spring him.

Stomping into his house, he ran into his mother carrying a baby on her hip.

"Thank goodness, you're here," she exclaimed, handing over his nephew Mark who looked ridiculously cute in his Redskins football jersey and mini blue jeans.

Juggling the baby, he eyed his mother. "What's up?"

"Naomi went to dinner with her mates."

"And?"

"Melanie's still napping upstairs."

"You still haven't explained how this concerns me," Chris replied, making a face at the long line of drool hanging from his nephew's lower lip.

"You need to babysit while I run to grab a few things."

"Why me?" he complained. Hmm, good thing Naomi wasn't here, she would have offered some cheese to go with his whine.

"Why you? You're about to settle down with a mate. It's time you learned what some of that entails."

"How does dumping Naomi's kids on me teach me anything?"

"Babies are the result of physical affection. You know, sex. The thing you're hankering to do with your lady friend."

"Ma!"

"Christopher," she aped back in a tone laced with mirth. "As I was saying, since you can pretty much expect your own little bundle of joy to arrive in nine months or so if you don't wear a rubber hat —" Chris moaned and covered his eyes. "— it's important for you to learn some of the basics so you're not useless to your mate when the time comes. Like feeding a baby. Or changing diapers."

He held up a hand. "Wait a second. I've heard dad brag about how he never had to change diapers when we were babies. If he didn't have to, why should I? Isn't the rule of thumb preach what you practice?"

Arms crossed, his mother pursed her lips. "No, it's do as I say and not as your father did. See, the reason Geoffrey didn't change diapers was because he puked on your brother, Stu, the three times he tried. It seems he has a low gag reflex."

"He puked on Stu?" Chris snickered, then howled. "Oh my god. The ammunition you just gave me. Priceless."

"Oh no you don't, Christopher, or else someone with loose gums might just find the pictures of himself playing with the big brown shark in the tub hitting Facebook."

"You wouldn't." Her gaze remained steady. He sputtered. "I was two!"

"Older than your brother when your father hurled on him. So do we understand each other?"

"Yes," he said it begrudgingly. But you had to hand it to his mom. She was the best mother ever – when it came to blackmail. In her defense, she needed an evil side to stay ahead of the chaos he, his brothers, sister, and father would otherwise cause.

"This is not what I had planned for the evening," he muttered, his fantasy of Jill doing a strip tease on the back of his eyelids fading fast.

"Thank goodness, I say. Some of us are tired of you moping about like a lovesick puppy."

"I do not mope," Chris retorted. "I pout." His lower lip jutted far enough to make his mother snicker. A chuckle shook him. "Sorry about the bad moods. It's just, since I've met her –"

"No need to explain. I went through it when I met your father. I understand how overwhelming it can seem. Hence, the distraction. You can thank me later."

"But …" Chris tried sticking out his bottom lip again, but his mother proved immune.

She shook a finger at him. "Don't you dare teach that face to the baby! Otherwise, he'll have his mama doing backflips and spoiling him rotten. Now, as for what you need to do. Listen for Melanie. She'll wake up soon. She's a better sleeper than her busy brother. They might get hungry. If so, there's breast milk in the fridge –" Chris made a face, "– and instructions for heating it on the counter. Have fun. I'll be back before you know it."

As his mother walked out the front door, Chris demoted her from best mother ever to ... dammit, still the best mother ever. She was right. He needed something to keep his mind occupied and teaching one little boy how to rule the world – through the use of cute puppy dog eyes – would fit the bill.

Setting the baby down on the floor, Chris then sat beside his nephew, watching him strain to push himself up on his forearms.

"Good job, little buddy," he said when his nephew regarded him with a drooling smile.

Piece of cake. Look at him, taking care of the baby. Who said he wasn't ready for parenthood? Wait a freakn' second. Once he and Jill hooked up, they could end up with kids of their own in nine months. His mom's words penetrated his thick skull finally.

Holy shit, I could be a dad. What once would have put him into a panic, now just made him grin. Funny how meeting the right person could change a man's mind.

An hour later, elbow deep in dirty diapers, screaming babies, and encased in a layer of baby powder, he decided that perhaps he should invest in a case of condoms. Maybe two.

And that was how Naomi found him, along with her tag along guest, Jill. The icing on the cake though? Melanie spat up the breast milk he'd managed to feed her, and it landed on his bare foot. Gross!

*

Stopping the giggle proved much too hard despite Chris's pleading look for help. How could Jiao not laugh until tears pricked her eyes at the sight of her big and strong wolf? He was the picture of a male out of his element and steps away from full-blown panic. He sported a half dressed baby on each hip, hair in a mussed tangle on his head, eyes wide through the layer of powder on his face, and as for the steaming layer of vomit on his foot? Funniest thing ever.

Laughter bubbled forth, a belly laugh like Jiao couldn't ever recall. She snorted and giggled so hard, her eyes watered and she hiccupped for breath.

"It's not that funny," Chris growled.

Risking a peek at him, while trying to stifle her mirth, she saw him wince as one baby drooled on his arm. It set her off again.

With a shake of her head, Naomi, grabbed a squealing baby, slapped a diaper on and handed the child back to Chris who'd just straightened after wiping his foot off with his filthy shirt.

"Hey!" he tried to protest.

"I'll tell Ethan you made Melanie cry."

Chris clamped his lips shut, but his eyes shot daggers as Naomi took care of the other bare bottomed tot. She shoved the second child – now thankfully diapered – at Jiao before taking off with the toxic waste her children created.

Shocked, Jiao gaped at the baby dressed in pink, who in turn regarded her with suspicion. What should she do with the little critter, um, girl? Jiao didn't exactly have much experience in the baby department and the unblinking gaze freaked her out. "Why is she staring at me?" She whispered the question, even if she couldn't have quite said why.

"Melanie is trying to decide whether to scream or drool."

"Maybe you should hold her then," she exclaimed, holding Melanie under her armpits and aiming her at Chris.

He shook his head, and gestured to his armful. "Nah. I'm good. You keep her. Me and my buddy Mark here are going to chill." Chris flopped onto the couch and balanced the baby on his lap. Content with the choice, chubby Mark stuffed a fist in his mouth and sucked noisily.

Jiao sat more gingerly, afraid she'd drop the child. Melanie didn't want to sit, though, and let out a yodel. Jiao shot up and the baby quieted – and Jiao could have sworn she smirked.

"Ha. Works every time. She's a true princess in training." Chris beamed at his niece and Jiao couldn't help but smile.

"I take it she's done it to you."

"Done it? Who do you think taught it to her? While my sister wasn't looking, of course," he confided in a low whisper. Then louder. "What are you doing here? I thought you couldn't get out tonight."

"Not without a good excuse. Your sister showed up and insisted I come over to her place for coffee. She wouldn't take no for an answer."

He frowned. "I thought she was going to supper with her jocks."

"She did, but they got called in for some kind of emergency team meeting, so she detoured to my place and insisted I come with her for a coffee over at her place. We just stopped in here to grab the babies first."

"Sorry you had to see me like this," he said ruefully.

A smile curved her lips. "Why? I thought you looked very cute."

"Well, I guess that's nicer than inept."

"If it's any consolation, I think you handled it better than me. I can't imagine taking care of two babies at once." Heck, she found it hard to picture even caring for one.

"You'll have lots of help when it happens to us." He stated the eventuality they'd have children together in a matter of fact tone.

"We will, will we? And have you decided on how many we're having?" She arched a brow.

"Lots." He laughed. "But not right away. I'd like to spend some alone time first with you before we get into the whole baby business."

"I like the sound of that." She liked the sound of any plan that included a future with Chris. Now, if only tomorrow would come faster so she could have her talk with Jack – not a pleasant one she could predict already – and start her life with her wolf.

"I'm back so you can stop making googly eyes at each other," Naomi announced. Two pairs of baby arms went up and Naomi scooped her children up, nuzzling them.

"I do not googly eye," Chris retorted. "I stare longingly."

Jill didn't say a word, though, too shocked by the fact Naomi guessed her interest in Chris.

"Don't look so panicked," Naomi admonished. "I know about your secret yen for each other. I won't tell a soul. Promise. However, you might want to do something about your I'm-married situation, because it's kind of obvious you both have a thing for each other."

"It is?" Jill's shoulders slumped.

"What does it matter?" Chris asked, moving from his spot on the couch to kneel at her feet. "After tomorrow, Jack will know the truth, you'll be free, and we can mate just like fate intended."

Or, her brother would knock Jiao out, kidnap her and not let her regain consciousness until they'd gotten far away with a new life and identity. However, she couldn't tell Chris her fear. God only knew what he'd do. "I just hope everything works out," she murmured in a low voice. *But I have a really bad feeling.* A sixth sense that things would not go as planned.

Chapter Eighteen

Only a few days since the Thanksgiving dinner, and just over twenty-four hours since Gina had driven her Asian pussycat to the edge of his control, Gina was no closer to forgetting him, no matter how many C batteries she went through riding her plastic substitute.

Where did the insane attraction stem from? Sure, Jack was freakn' hot with his short hair, smooth skin, and tight little bod, but she'd screwed better looking men than Jack. She'd walked away from cuter ones too. None ever had her masturbating like she'd die if she didn't come. None ever took up residence in her mind, got comfortable and refused to budge. And none, not even hot to trot, Frank Miller, ever got her wolf panting and drooling.

She really didn't like what she thought it meant. *Not my mate.* A dozen, a hundred, more times than she could count, she repeated that to herself. It ran through her head like a melody. Unfortunately, she found it harder and harder to believe. *Not my mate. Oh yes he is. No he's not. Stop fighting destiny.* God she hated arguing with herself. As for her wolf, she'd swear it mocked her.

Stupid dog had no sympathy for the human half that wasn't ready to get tied down, and to such a stick in the mud. Although, according to her research, Mr. Jack Smith might not be as pristine as he appeared.

Gina drummed her fingers on her desk at the precinct as she hit another dead end on her latest query. Despite all her searches, through public, and some private, databases, for all intents and purposes, Jack and Jill Smith didn't exist until a few months ago. A check of their previous address showed a home still under construction. Their previous employers were both businesses that suddenly went under with no one to reach. No arrests. No parking tickets. Not even a Facebook or twitter profile. In this day of technology and accessible online records, they were virtually nonexistent.

Impossible. And probably illegal. The most obvious reason for their lack of paper or electronic trail was they must have arrived as immigrants. Wanting to skip the laborious citizen application process, they instead acquired themselves new identities. Gina could call the immigration department on them, if she chose. But she wouldn't. Jack and Jill – who didn't live on a hill – seemed like an upstanding couple if you ignored their false identity. Were they even truly married? Damn her heart for racing as it suddenly hoped her pussycat wasn't.

Single or not, Jack was not meant for her. Well, not permanently at any rate. A test drive, though, just to get him out of her system? Whole other matter.

Of more immediate interest, what did Jack and Jill's pretend existence bode for Chris and his quest to win his mate? Who knew? But it did mean Jack, the uptight Asian fellow whom she couldn't seem to forget, was possibly a criminal.

As an officer sworn to uphold the law, she needed to think twice before associating herself – A.K.A. knocking boots – with someone involved in a crime. Even if he made her panties wet enough to wring, and had her inner bitch panting like he was the juiciest steak bone ever.

Or, did she examine the evidence, more like lack of, from the wrong angle? What if the couple she snooped on hid from something other than immigration, say like their past? In her line of work, it wasn't uncommon to see people who'd gone through tragedy or violence start over. Choose a new life and identity. Could that be the case? If yes, then perhaps she should restart her search keeping that in mind.

Assuming Jack and Jill were not their birth names, all that left her was the basics: approximate age and cultural heritage. She tried the missing persons list first. It returned a number of possibilities, too many for her to sort. Dammit.

She rattled her fingers on her desk again, the rat-a-tat, annoying to others, but somehow helpful to her thinking process. What else did she know? No visible birthmarks or tattoos. No access to their dental work or doctor records. But wait. Didn't she hear mention of a brother. Sang, Sing, no, Sheng. She typed it in along with some variations and spelling. The database returned one hit.

Missing After A Fall in the Rockies

Sheng Chua and his sister, Jiao, are missing after an unfortunate rock climbing incident. The pair were last seen heading into the Saber region of Rocky Mountain park. It is believed they fell during the ascent, but their bodies were never recovered, nor was any of their equipment. If you have any information on this missing duo, please contact Park authorities or your local RCMP branch.

Stunned, Gina leaned back in her seat. What could this mean? Was Jiao, Jill? Had she and her brother faked their death? If Jill was indeed the missing rock climber, then who did that make Jack? Had Jiao perhaps lost her memories in the accident? Did Jack find her? Or worse, what if Jack abducted her and made her change her name and identity? What if he held Jill against her will?

Crazy assumptions – and possibly the basis for a movie she'd once watched – but farfetched or not, the cop in her had to know. Was Jack a criminal? Did Jill need rescuing?

Or the better question before she jumped to conclusions, was this Jiao Chua, Jill? Only one way to find out. The missing report, filed about six years ago listed an uncle as the only family contact. Gina dialed.

The phone rang several times before someone answered, with a low, "Can I help you?"

"Hi, I'm Gina Greco with the Ottawa police department. I am looking to speak with a Mr. Kaleb Chua."

A pregnant silence followed interspersed with heavy breathing before he answered. "This is he. May I ask what this is in regards to?"

No hesitation, or worry in his tone despite her claim of working for law enforcement. Odd. Most people had mini panic attacks when cops called, even if for benign reasons. "I'd like to ask you a few questions about your missing niece and nephew."

"Is there news? Have you found them?" He finally showed some animation.

"Not exactly, but your nephew's name, Sheng, came up in connection to another case I'm working."

"And who are you once again?"

"Constable Gina Greco with Ottawa Law Enforcement."

"I'd be delighted to help, constable. Anything to help bring my nephew home, where he belongs."

Encouraged at her possible lead, Gina asked Mr. Chua a few questions, and had him email a picture of the missing duo, something, oddly enough, the online report lacked. Staring at the Asian faces, the features nothing close to Jill, or Jack for that matter, Gina thanked Mr. Chua for his time and hung up, discouraged.

Another dead end. But she wasn't about to give up. The mystery of Jack and Jill begged an answer. Tapping her fingers again, she debated her next step. She needed to do something more than research. She called Chris's cell phone, surprised when he answered. Usually, she went to voicemail because he constantly forgot to charge the damned thing.

"Your timing sucks," he growled.

"Excellent. I do my best. So what are you up to?"

A rustle of the receiver followed by muffled voices, both which she recognized, made her brows lift. Now his disgruntlement became clear. Chris was busy entertaining another man's wife. Gina's emotions vacillated between outrage that Jack's wife would so blatantly cuckhold him, but at the same time, she no longer felt any guilt over the kiss she'd given the married man.

The hand left the mouthpiece and Chris came back on the line. "Sorry. I was just saying bye to Naomi and her kids."

"I thought I heard Jill too."

"You did. Naomi kidnapped her for a girl's night and wouldn't let me keep her." He sounded so irritated.

"I'm surprised you let her leave. Aren't you worried about the stories Naomi could tell about you?"

"Of course I'm worried. But, she'll find out eventually anyway. I'm sure mom already has the slideshow of my most embarrassing moments ready to go."

Gina giggled. "She does. And I helped her make it."

"I hate you."

"I know."

Chris laughed. "Brat. But I'm sure you didn't call just to drive me nuts. What's up? Do I need to bail a family member out of jail? Did Stu get drunk and streak naked again? Please tell me someone got pictures this time."

A snicker escaped her as she recalled the incident. Best part? She'd gotten Stu drunk in the first place and dared him to do it. Worst part? Her phone with its built in camera died before she could get a shot. "Nobody needs springing, yet, but the day is young. Hey, how's the water pressure at your house?" Code for, I want to say something and you might want to ensure no one hears me.

It seemed Chris remembered their trick from their prank days because a moment later the gurgle of water rushing from a tap and draining came through the line.

"We're good," he said in a hushed voice.

"I called because I wanted to let you know to be careful of your girlfriend."

"What do you mean?" he asked, his tone measured.

"Either Jack and Jill are in the witness protection program, are running from something, or they're illegal immigrants. I'm not sure which, nor am I willing to bet there isn't a possible fourth reason for the fact they don't exist."

"In other words, they're not really Jack and Jill?"

"Probably not."

"So are they even actually married?"

"Again, I can't be sure. But something is definitely wonky. So be careful."

"I will."

"That's it? Aren't you going to ask your girlfriend about it?"

"I'd rather not because I don't want her thinking I was checking up on her."

Seriously? Gina rolled her eyes. "You weren't. I was."

"She's a woman. Will she pay attention to that distinction? I'll wait and see what she tells me on her own. She's breaking the news that she's splitting to Jack tomorrow. I'm hoping once she can be with me openly that she'll trust me enough to tell me what she's hiding."

"And if she doesn't?" Gina left unsaid her great worry that an association with Jill could bring down something worse than an angry husband on their heads. If Jill belonged to a witness protection program, then did they need to worry about someone gunning for her? Would innocent bystanders and family members get caught in a line of fire?

"She'll tell me. Don't worry."

"If you say so, cousin. But don't ask me to visit you in jail when we find out you've married some mob lord's daughter and you get tossed in the slammer for guilt by association."

His laughter boomed through their connection. "You have got to stop watching those mafia movies and shows."

"But they have the best violence." Although, it wouldn't hurt to check out a few Jackie Chan flicks. Crisp fight scenes with a hot Asian lead? Hmmm, she'd have to hit a video store on the way home.

"You are one sick chick, Gina."

"No, sick would be me reminding you not to bend over when it's shower time in jail."

"That is wrong on so many levels," he groaned.

"I know. So you'd better hope whatever the hell is going on is on the up and up."

"I'll let you know what happens with Jack and Jill tomorrow."

"Yeah. Here's to hoping I don't have to fetch your body parts in a bucket."

"Thanks for the vote of confidence."

"You're welcome. Talk to you later."

Gina hung up and tapped her lower lip. So, as of tomorrow sometime, Jack would revert to single. How intriguing. Perhaps she should saunter over on Friday to his work and check on the status of her new car. Maybe tempt him to go out for lunch – on her, literally. Sure, he'd probably protest, but that's what would make it so much fun. What she didn't count on was him finding her first.

*

Kaleb hung up with the constable and leaned back in his chair, tenting his fingers over his stomach. *Well, well. The cat has resurfaced.* What an unexpected turn of events. Of course, Kaleb didn't know yet under what name Sheng hid, or if Jiao was still with him, nor did he have an address, but now he at least had a general area. Ottawa.

Stupid cop. In her search for answers to someone she obviously suspected, she'd given Kaleb enough information for him to reorganize his search for the missing pair. And to think he'd just about given up.

Leaning forward, Kaleb punched a button on his phone, activating the intercom.

"Did you require something, sir?" his secretary queried.

"Have my private jet fueled and brought via small jumps to Edmonton tonight." Because he liked to keep those watching him guessing.

"Destination for the flight plan?" she asked over the sound of her fingers tapping.

"Our nation's capital. Ottawa, but make the route erratic."

"Of course, sir. Unmarked sedans for transportation at all the stopovers to further muddy your travels as well, sir?"

"You read my mind." Damn but his new secretary was efficient. She knew how he liked his privacy. "And be sure to have the cages packed along with the tranquilizer kits. I'm going hunting."

And he wouldn't come back empty handed.

Chapter Nineteen

Despite the mini fight she had with Sheng about leaving the house, a fight she won, Jiao spent a fun evening with Naomi and Francine, who also ended up coming over for a girl's night. They talked a lot, well the she-wolves did, Jiao kind of listened, absorbing their stories, and envying their easy friendship. She didn't understand the name calling – bitch, wench, skank – but obviously, Naomi and Francine didn't take offense at the often derogatory terms uttered with affection and laughter.

Best of all, they acted like Jiao was already an accepted part of their group and family. A foregone affair. Now if only she didn't have to lie to her new friends.

Jiao did her best not to divulge too much; the fewer lies she told, the better. But evasions and misdirects didn't mean she completely escaped some uncomfortable moments such as when Naomi asked flat out how she and Jack got together.

Jiao stuck to a partial truth. "We knew each other as children."

"How do you think he's going to handle you asking for a divorce?"

"He's known this has been coming for a while." Jiao complained often enough. "And while he might be annoyed at first, he'll eventually understand it's for the best. We can't keep going on as we have."

Nope. Jiao couldn't fake it anymore, not when she wanted to spend every moment with Chris.

"If he tosses you out, and you need a place to stay, you're welcome to come here until Chris finds you guys a place."

"You'd take me in?" Jiao's eyes widened at the offer. "But you barely know me."

"My instincts about people are good."

Francine snorted. "Really? Because it took you a while to admit your two jocks were the loves of your life."

"I did that to keep them on their toes. A girl can't give in too easily, even if they're good looking. And persistent. And smarter than I initially gave them credit for."

Laughter followed and the uncomfortable moment passed. Next thing Jiao knew, she was back home, cheeks sore from smiling, her entire mood bubbly. It only took the loud click as she shut the front door to lose some of her elation pleasure. Shoulders braced, she prepared to face the inquisition.

Or expected to. Where was Sheng with a glower and a shaking finger asking her if she divulged any secrets?

She took a step further in, tossing her handbag on the side table and kicking off her shoes. She opened up her senses. The house smelt fine. The scents all belonged. Her cat didn't even stir. But something remained amiss. *Where is my brother?* He always greeted her at the door. She peeked into the living room and noted its pristine condition. She wandered into the kitchen. Again, spotless, and Sheng-free. A flicker of light in the hall caught her eye.

"Sheng?" She tried to sound confident but her query emerged low.

"I'm in the office."

Alone or a prisoner? "Are you hungry?" Prearranged code for 'Is it safe?'

"No. But I wouldn't say no to a bowl of ice cream."

All clear. Tension eased out of her, but puzzlement took its place. She stormed in to their home office and found her brother sitting at the desk, the laptop screen swirling the screen saver pattern. If he was fine then why did he act so strange?

"What the heck is wrong with you?"

Sheng whirled in chair and there was the scowl she loved. "Me? What makes you think anything is?"

"You didn't meet me at the door."

"You're a big girl. I'm pretty sure you know how to lock it after yourself."

"Aren't you going to ask me how my evening went?" She readied herself for the barrage of questions and the safety speech.

"I trust you said nothing I should worry about?"

She deflated. "Just our cover story."

"Good."

Good? Who was this alien and where was her brother? She stared at him.

"Did you need something?" His terse query raised her hackles.

"No. I'm going to bed."

"Sleep tight, ji☐ zǐ."

She turned to go, yet stopped. "Is everything all right?"

"Fine. Never better."

"Are you sure?" Because despite his assurance, she didn't quite believe him. But if they were in danger, she knew they wouldn't be talking. Sheng would have her packing. So if it wasn't danger bothering Sheng, what had him so perturbed? Had something happened at work? "You don't seem yourself. Are you hiding something from me?"

"Why the suspicion? Is someone feeling guilty?"

"Totally. I ignored my diet and totally pigged out on two bite brownies."

A ghostly reminder of the boy she once knew flitted across his face, a genuine smile there and gone in a blink. "Don't let yourself get fat now. The gym is almost here."

Ah yes the gym, and its handsome creator. "I can't wait." *Can't wait until I see Chris again.* Given Sheng's oddly mellow mood, should she tell him about Chris? About the fact she'd met her mate and wanted to tell him the truth so they could be together?

And ruin the first smile I've seen in ages?

Her needs could wait another day. She'd tackle her brother tomorrow after his meeting with Patricia. A hopefully positive meeting.

Fingers and toes crossed, Jiao wished with all her might that Patricia would have good news. In her fantasy, Sheng would come back and tell her they had nothing to fear. Jiao would admit Chris was her mate and that they needed to end the charade. Sheng would of course get mad, dig his heels in for a bit because of his lingering fear, but in the end he'd cave. They'd hug and everyone would live happily ever after.

Or, that was her fanciful plan. She should have known better than to expect easy where her life was concerned.

It started the following day with Sheng's decision to visit Patricia late in the day, real late which meant Jill couldn't spend any alone time with Chris, a fact he surely hated. Not that she saw him. Sheng kept a close eye on her and the basement. Drove her to her yoga class and waited for her. Watched her all afternoon making it impossible for her to sneak away under his scrutiny.

She'd actually given up hope of seeing Chris at all given she couldn't tell him of Sheng's change of plans. Chris left just before five, and with a satisfied smirk, that Jiao suspected had to do with the fact Sheng knew he'd foiled her plans, her brother left to meet with Patricia.

Grumbling about meddling brothers, Jiao locked the front door and stomped back to the kitchen. She made herself a dinner of leftovers, wondering if she dared dig up Chris's number and call him. Even if he couldn't come over, maybe they could talk. Or she could suck up her disappointment, wait until tomorrow and finally give him the answer he hoped for.

Tomorrow just seemed so darned far away, though.

Since her meal tasted like cardboard with her appetite hungry for something other than food, she dumped the remains and tossed the plate in the sink to join the other dirty kitchenware. Water running, the scent of dish soap heavy as suds floated, her mind churned angrily at her missed opportunity to spend time with Chris. *Stupid overprotective brother.* He treated her like a maiden in the middle ages. For that fact alone she needed to end the fake marriage. She couldn't stand him stifling her anymore. Not when they didn't have any evidence of a reason to hide other than his delusional theories.

Slamming dishes, and sneezing as a fluff of bubbles tickled her nose, she didn't hear or smell a thing amiss and thus screamed when a pair of arms wrapped around her middle. Her panic immediately calmed as Chris's tingling touch penetrated and his unique smell wrapped around her.

"You came back!"

"I never actually left," he admitted as he turned her in his arms. "I parked a few streets over and kind of hung out waiting. When I saw Jack get in his SUV, I followed and saw him get on the highway before coming back."

"Stalker."

"I prefer the term dedicated."

She gave a small giggle. "I'm glad, and sorry. He usually has this meeting in the city during the day. I don't know what happened to change his plans." However, she suspected. *He didn't trust me to stay alone with Chris.* How astute of her brother. But too late.

"As long as I get to spend time with you, who cares?"

A warmth spread through her at the sincerity in his words. Who cared indeed? She had her wolf for at least an hour or two. She might as well enjoy it.

"Can I make you something to eat?"

"How about I just take what I hunger for?"

His words sent a shiver down her spine and her breath caught at the intensity of his gaze. With a finger, he tilted her chin, then ran the digit along the

edge of her jaw to her ear. Her cat meowed anxiously in her head, begging for a scratch. As if sensing her feline's demand, he did rub the soft skin behind Jiao's ear.

Mmmm. Yeah, that merited a rumble of enjoyment. A short laugh left him.

"What's so funny?" she asked opening her eyes.

"You are so freakn' cute. I cannot wait to make you purr."

"Then you'll need to do more than scratch my ear," she replied with a saucy smile.

"I intend to." Hands spanning her waist, he lifted her with ease and sat her on the counter. Pushing his body against her knees, they spread and he settled between them. Slowly, ever so slowly while he kept his eyes locked to hers, he lowered his head until their lips almost touched. Their breath mingled. Her heart pounded so hard, she feared it would escape her chest.

He slanted his mouth over hers, dragging his lips across her own, sensually sliding over them, but not actually capturing them. She made a noise, more of a mewl really, and he chuckled low, the masculine sound teasing her already sensitized nerves.

With light kisses, he marked her skin – forehead, cheeks, the corner of her mouth, the tip of her chin, the soft spot under her ear. His fluttery embraces left her panting, her body aching and her fingers clutching as she tried to draw him nearer. She wanted to stop his erotic teasing and claim his mouth. Feel the heady passion his kisses ignited.

He tugged her lower lip with his teeth and growled, "What do you want, baby?"

"Kiss me."

"I don't know if I can stop at just a kiss."

She didn't think she could halt either. And no longer really cared. "Kiss me anyway."

"If you insist." He crushed his mouth to hers, and the humming arousal in her body burst into flames. Clinging to him, she wrapped her legs around his waist drawing his hardness against her. Even through their clothing, she felt him. Wanted him. She dug her fingers into his shoulders as she devoured his mouth, letting his tongue slide sinuously into her mouth to tangle with hers.

His hands, big, strong capable ones, caressed her, skimming initially over her t-shirt, but as the frantic pants and soft sounds of her pleasure escalated, he pushed up the fabric and touched her skin. Oh, sweet heaven. He dragged his calloused digits up her back, then down her sides, skimming her rib cage. With one deft flick, he undid her bra, and a moment later his hands cupped her small breasts. When his thumbs thrummed over her aching peaks, she tore her mouth from his as her back arched and a cry escaped her.

Before she could straighten and claim his mouth again, he ducked his head and claimed one of her buds, his hands making quick work of her t-shirt leaving her bare for his touch. Not that she cared she sat half-naked on her kitchen counter, not when he did such wonderful things to her body.

Hot, wet, and oh so decadent, he sucked on her nipples, pulling them with his lips. Pinching them with his teeth. Swirling his tongue around the tips as she cried out, her hips bumping and grinding against his lower body, caught in a mindless sexual fever.

The raging storm of arousal should have frightened her. But she couldn't stop it. She didn't want to. This was Chris who touched her. The man who haunted her every thought. The man who would claim her if she just said the word. *My mate.*

When his mouth trailed from her pulsing nipples down her stomach to the part of her that ached most, she didn't protest or ask him to slow down. Danger? Who cared. She would die if he didn't do something to cure the throb between her legs.

He cupped her through her pants and she moaned, her whole body trembling. But then he shocked her and managed to draw a short scream as his mouth pressed against the crotch of her pants. Oh, that felt good, but when he blew his warm breath?

No words could describe it. She lifted her hips when his hands tugged at the waistband of her pants. He tore the material away, baring her to his view, and utter silence reigned except for their ragged breaths. He didn't touch her, and she opened her eyes to see him staring at her, reverence clear in his gaze. He lifted his glance and she shivered at how his eyes smoldered with passion. A lust and admiration for her.

"So pretty and perfect," he murmured.

"Too small," she amended, lamenting aloud about her less than busty upper body. And possibly too hairy? She'd never had reason to shave her mound, but now that it was on display, she wondered if she should have. She'd read enough books and knew enough about today's culture to know trimming was expected.

"Perfect," he reiterated. "And mine." He growled the possessive word a moment before lowering his face and at the first swipe of his tongue across her sex, she couldn't care less what she looked like.

He lapped her, long wet strokes across her cleft, and she moaned. Trembled. Scrabbled at the smooth counter for purchase. Not that she was going anywhere with Chris holding her thighs apart so he could better taste her.

Need coiled inside her. Her body tightened. Something approached. She panted, feeling it just out of reach. Just a little bit …

Her orgasm hit, much stronger than expected. Her climax tightened her body into a bowed arc, her toes pointing, her mouth open in a silent wail. Her entire channel quivered. And still he licked her, stroked her, kept her quivering until she sobbed "Enough". Then he gathered her in his arms while she fought to regain her wits.

Basking in the glory would have to wait, though. The phone rang, insistent and distracting. But she lacked the strength to move, or care. Chris placed light kisses on her skin, working his way along her jaw to her mouth. Lightly he embraced her, not that her sensitized body cared as it shuddered and quaked with aftershocks of pleasure.

"Why does it feel like every time I touch you, it's the first time?" he murmured.

If he only knew. "I'm not very experienced," she admitted.

"But your marriage –"

"Is unconventional."

He leaned away from her and she lamented the loss of his sultry face, replaced by a suspicious expression replete with creased brow and tight lips. It made her feel guilty that she still kept a secret.

"What are you hiding?" He spoke aloud, but she didn't get the impression he truly asked her, more that he mused rhetorically.

"I'm going to tell you everything. Soon. Or as much as I'm allowed. In the meantime, I need you to trust me."

He scrubbed a hand through his hair and moved away from her. "Trust? You're making it hard. I've been open and honest with you since we met. I never hid my intentions except from your husband at your request. I've not done anything to make you doubt I am a man of my word."

"I know you're honorable."

"I hear a but?"

"But, parts of my life are complicated. Now that I've met you, I'm hoping that some of that will go away, but at the same time, I have to be careful. What I want isn't always what's best. And I don't want to see you hurt."

A sudden revelation hit her. *This is how Sheng feels!* She'd spent years with Sheng as her protector, but it was only now, face to face with Chris and the realization that her past could hurt him, that she truly understood how her brother felt. How helpless to know that the person she loved, cared for so deeply, might get hurt because of her actions, or in her case, the past.

I can't let anything happen to him. How she'd keep that vow, she didn't know, but she'd do her damnedest to keep him and his family safe.

"The only thing that hurts me is not having you permanently in my life."

"There are worse things. Believe me," she muttered.

*

Excuse me? Chris' mind tangled into a great big knot as he tried to follow her hints covered in subterfuge. How exactly had a moment of ecstasy – and yes it counted as such even if he'd not yet spilled – turned into a discussion of trust? And secrets.

"We're mates." He declared it as a proven fact. In his eyes, she was in every way except for the bite, the exchange of blood and fluid that would link them on a level higher than that of marriage or spoken words of affection.

"We are. But, because you're my mate, I must do everything I can to make sure I don't bring harm upon you."

"You think Jack might hurt me?" His lip curled at the suggestion.

"Jack is the least of your worries. He might shout and yell, but ultimately, he'll abide by my choice."

"Then what danger are you talking about? I don't understand and I'm tired of your allusions. I want you to trust me, dammit."

"I –"

Whatever she might have said next got lost in the ring of the phone. His eyes told her in no uncertain terms to leave it alone. Lips pursed, she answered it anyway. When she proceeded to engage in a rapid fire conversation that he couldn't follow, he resisted the urge to punch something.

Jack. Jack. Jack. Every time he turned around it seemed she chose her husband over him. *I am her mate.*

She should cater to him, not the dude who treated her like chattel.

But the real problem? Knowing he was her mate, and actually *being* her mate were two different things. A true mate, one who'd gone through the actual marking process and created that esoteric link had rights that superseded all others – including that of a husband who wasn't a true mate. But until he took that final step and claimed her, he was just the guy relegated to furtive kisses and meetings.

So perhaps it was time he took the next step. She already planned to break things off with Jack so what if Chris made sure it happened sooner rather than later?

She hung up the phone looking puzzled.

"What's wrong?"

"Jack won't be home for a while."

"Business?"

"I guess. He didn't really say."

"Do you want me to stay?" He would no matter her answer, but he wanted to hear her choice.

"Please. I'd like that very much. We've got at least another hour or two apparently. He told me not to bother waiting up."

Perfect. Just enough time to do what he should have done from day one. Time to meet the pussy behind the woman, and then mark her for the world to see. Make her his in every sense of the word.

And hope she didn't kill him afterwards.

Chapter Twenty

Meeting Patricia at the restaurant, Sheng stuffed his damp hands in his pockets. Nervous? Him. About what? Surely he didn't care that much about the outcome of their talk. Jiao was the one who wanted things to change. Sheng didn't have a problem with the status quo. Or so he tried to convince himself while he ignored how Gina's face kept popping into his head – wearing nothing but her cop hat and boots while swinging her cuffs.

If Patricia thinks it's safe to drop the ruse, I could technically take the she-wolf up on her erotic offer. Sate himself with her body so that she ended up evicted from his fantasies. However, Gina wasn't his only reason for wanting to end the fake marriage.

His sister needed a chance to find happiness, whether Sheng approved of her choice or not. He suspected Jiao snuck around behind his back and saw the wolf despite his orders. As if he couldn't smell the dog all over her. With fate intervening, Sheng knew he didn't have long before the inevitable happened and Jiao mated with Chris.

Ugh. A dog for a brother-in-law. How distasteful. Funny, though, how he didn't have a problem contemplating bedding the handyman's cousin, who also shared the same wolfish heritage.

The two are different. For one, Sheng had no intention of making it forever. As a mature male in charge of his own destiny, he wouldn't kowtow to some ridiculous notion that a hormonal reaction – or otherworldly force – would have him do something he didn't want or plan to do. And that's what it was. Hormones. Lust. A healthy dose of attraction easily cured with a few rounds of naked wrestling.

Meowrr! What the hell? His inner cat did not just snicker? Impossible. It seemed he'd kept his other half caged so long he now imagined things.

The bell above the restaurant door tinkled as he stepped in. The aroma of home cooked fries and sizzling burgers just about overwhelmed him and covered him in a light sheen of grease. How his RCMP friend managed to eat the calorie laden, artery hardening food, he still couldn't decipher, but, every meeting, she extolled him to join her at a new spot to taste the wares.

Spotting Patricia at a booth in the back, her short blonde bob distinctive, he made his way over and slid into the seat across from her. She'd already ordered him a Coke with no ice. How well she'd gotten to know him over the years.

She peeked up from the menu. "Hey Jack. How are things going?"

"I'm well thank you, and yourself?"

A wry twist of her lips accompanied a shoulder shrug. "Things are going. My boyfriend back west has decided he can't handle a long term relationship, so I might make the posting out here permanent."

"I'm sorry," he replied automatically. Not really though. Sheng met the guy once and thought him too weak willed for the strong willed RCMP officer.

"Don't be sorry. It's kind of a relief. I like it out here. More than I expected. The job is great. The place I rented is twice the size I could get out west. As for being single? Acquiring a new boyfriend is the least of my worries. But, who cares about me. How's it going with you and Jill?"

"It's going well. Too well. She also likes it here and is hoping we can drop the marriage ruse." Nothing like diving in and laying it all out.

A crease appeared on Patricia's brow. "Not so quick. If we hadn't already planned to meet, I was going to call you in. We might have a problem. I spotted some nibbles."

Sheng almost choked on a mouthful of soda as panic suddenly rushed up to consume him. "What do you mean by nibbles?"

"Someone pinged both yours and Jill's driver license."

"Who? And why?" And most of all, how? How had Kaleb found them? Were they in danger? Should he call Jiao and tell her to pack up?

"The who wasn't readily evident, but whoever it is works in the Ottawa area as a cop because the request for info came from a local precinct. As to why, you tell me. Have you spotted anything suspicious? Done anything that might have roused an officer's weird-o-meter?"

Oh, he'd roused a cop alright, a certain she-wolf in uniform who showed way too much interest in him – as a man. "I don't think you need to worry about it."

"How can you be sure? Do we need to contact my guy about getting some new id? Should I be planning for a relocate?"

Two weeks ago, Sheng would have said yes just for paranoia's sake. But, now? Now, he doubted Jiao would agree. He also wasn't sure he wanted to start over again. And, in all honesty, he didn't think Gina posed a danger. She showed a curiosity about a new couple in the shifter community, but she worked as a cop. Could he blame her?

Yes, but that was something he'd discuss with Gina. Later – while wearing clothes, despite what his dirty mind thought. Sheng turned the discussion to other things, as they ate the good, if bad for his health, food. When Patricia went to the washroom, he placed a quick call to his sister. Forget going home right after his meeting with Patricia. He had a stop to make and a discussion to have with a certain wolf. And no, he didn't plan to silence her by stuffing a certain part of his anatomy in her mouth – despite what his cock thought, and even if it was the only idea he came up with. But, he didn't completely veto it, because he never knew, he might need to go that route as a Plan B.

Chapter Twenty One

After Jiao hung up with her brother, and Chris agreed to stay, she wondered what to do with him. Her body still throbbed, but not with the hungry insistence of before. She also knew Chris didn't take his pleasure. Innocent perhaps in some ways, she still understood the basic mechanics of sex. Would he want to resume where they left off? Was she about to become a woman in all senses of the word?

The thought both excited her and roused her nervousness. Once they made love, there was no turning back. And no hiding her virgin state which would lead to more questions, valid questions she wasn't sure she could answer without betraying her brother's trust.

"Is your cat feeling frisky?"

His odd question took her by surprise. "My cat?"

"Yes, your inner kitty. Is it spinning right now? My wolf certainly is."

"Yes. My feline found our, um –" A blush heated her cheeks. "– activities quite invigorating. Why?"

"It's a beautiful evening. What do you say we take our inner friends for a run?"

Oh, the temptation. Damn the reality. "I can't."

"Why not? I'd love to see your cat."

And she'd love to let her cat out, but Sheng's warning rang in her head. "I can't," she repeated miserably.

His brow knit into a frown. "You'll have to do better than *I can't*, baby. What's the problem? Is it related to the fact you need a gym before the next full moon? Does your kitty have something weird going on like two tails, or no fur?"

"There's nothing wrong with my cat," she huffed indignantly. But her reply did nothing to chase the curiosity from his face. What could she tell him? How about a sanitized version of the truth? "My feline is not common to North America. If the wrong person sees me ..." She trailed off and let him draw his own conclusion.

"You're afraid?" he seemed slightly incredulous. "Baby, there isn't a soul who'll hurt you out in those woods. And not just because you'll be with me. First off, you don't have to worry about hunters. They're not allowed near the residential areas and it's not hunting season. As for someone seeing you, say like a human, they'll either assume you're a local species despite your coloring, or you'll become one of those urban legends like alligators in the sewers."

"But —"

"Trust me. I'll keep you safe," he winked. "Come on. It's already dark outside. No one will see a thing. We'll head into the woods before changing, and go for a little run. Stick to the shadowy areas and not a soul will be the wiser."

She shouldn't. It was dangerous. Stupid. Contrary to her brother's wishes. None of the excuses stopped her from following Chris into the shadowy forest.

The serenity of the woods quickly enveloped her. Dark, the scantily laden bows of the trees hung over their heads, a piece of wildness preserved among the suburbs. The scent of decay, the leaves and foliage of summer dying, tickled her nose. But it was interspersed with life as well. There was the subtle musk of a family of squirrels still frantically playing and storing before the true chill of winter.

Underfoot, the layer of dry leaves crinkled, their short lived beauty of green, red, and shades of yellow orange, all faded to a uniform brown, their last stage before crumbling back into the arms of the earth.

How quickly and easily she felt at home. Her cat purred in excitement, kneading her claws at the edge of her mind, raring to go. Jiao tilted her head back, closed her eyes and spread her arms. She inhaled deeply. "I love fall," she admitted.

"You do?" Chris sounded surprised.

"Oh yes, I do, because fall is the still moment before the deep hibernating chill. That moment where the earth finishes giving us her bounty, and if we've harvested her well, we'll survive the frigid grip of winter. Then, witness the renewal of the earth, as everything comes to life again."

"Gee, and I would have probably said I loved fall because of pumpkin pie."

"What?" Snapped from her dreamy thoughts, she blinked at him.

"See, I love fall too. But if I had to rank why it's so special, pumpkin pie would win first place. While jumping into leaf piles comes a pretty close second."

Jiao's mouth fell open and she stared at Chris. Shirt off, shoulders hunched, jeans hanging low on his hips, he gave her a sheepish grin.

"What can I say? While I think it's pretty, I'm a man. We're more tactile."

It wiggled its way out from deep inside, a giggle so liberating, she at first fought to muffle it with her fist. She didn't. Instead, she let her laughter burst free, growing in tenor, releasing the tension in her body. It eased something inside her, a heavy darkness, a suffocating fear, a crushing burden, and left her light. Buoyant and happy, and finally ready to shed it all.

To be free!

Stripping took her only a moment, a blink of an eye, then she changed and her cat rejoiced.

Landing on four feet, she didn't wait or look to see what Chris did. Off she went, leaping through the brush, streaking like the wind on furry paws. How she'd missed the freedom of her feline side. The crisp scents. The sharp vision. The great hearing. But best of all, she loved the chase.

Tail high as she whipped through the woods, she heard the rustle of someone following her, a certain wolf who yipped in excitement. If she'd still possessed her human mouth, she would have laughed with exhilaration. Instead, she contented herself with a chuffing sound of pleasure.

She slowed down, and let him catch up, then leapt away when he would have pounced. His rumbling growl conveyed his amusement at her maneuver. She tossed her head in triumph. He'd still missed.

Sprinting ahead, she ran full out before coiling herself and jumping up into a tree, her claws digging into the bark of a thick limb, her toes curling for grip. It might have been years since she last climbed a tree, but a body never forgot how. Perched in her hiding spot, she waited and watched the shadows below. Soon enough, a large shaggy shape came barreling through, then stopped short as he lost her scent trail. Nose to the ground, Chris sniffed while she watched.

She knew the moment he figured it out. His body stiffened, and he raised his muzzle. Brilliant eyes regarded her, and she flashed her teeth.

Surprise!

Leaping from branch to branch, she took off again, keeping to the heights while he followed on the ground. When she heard the sound of water, she slowed until she crouched on a thick bough overhanging a sluggish moving creek.

Chris didn't pause, emerging from the forest and splashing into the water. He changed shapes, one moment a wolf, the next a man, a very naked man with slick wet skin that shone in the feeble light filtering down from the stars and waning moon.

Jiao shifted as well. "Isn't that cold?" she asked with a shudder. She perched on the branch, legs dangling, the rough bark digging into her cheeks.

"Nah. It's more like invigorating."

"If you say so."

"Oh I do. You should give it a try?"

"No thanks." She wrinkled her nose. It looked pretty freakn' chilly.

"Don't tell me my kitty doesn't like water?"

"I like water, when it's more than ninety degrees. Anything less is barbaric." And reminded her too much of her nightmare swim down that raging river so many years ago. Having no desire to repeat that teeth chattering experience, she stuck to heated pools, hot baths, and scalding showers.

"So does that mean you won't come down and warm me up?" Chris slogged to the shallow end until he stood below her, hands on his hips, with his head tilted to peek at her. As for further below his waist, and in large evidence, jutted his cock, a proud prow.

She looked away, cheeks heating at his evident arousal. But, she couldn't glance away for long, not when the sight of him enthralled her. And enflamed her.

"Come down here." He crooked a finger.

"And if I don't?"

"You'd make a poor wolf climb a tree?" He pretended affront.

She laughed. In a move learned in her youth as part of the act, she swung down and landed with a slight bend of her knees.

"Nice move. Gymnastics?"

"Of a sort." Try high wire circus act whose sole purpose was to perform deadly stunts while flipping between forms.

"Just how flexible are you?" Chris murmured pulling her into his arms.

Gasping at his cold skin, she skirted his embrace. "You're freezing."

"So warm me up." He gave her a devastating smile.

Jiao almost gave in, but a chill breeze swept up and brushed her cooling skin, dimpling it. "Only if you can catch me." Off she dashed, keeping her human form for now, having ascertained during her run as her cat that nobody roamed the woods this night, well no one human, that was, according to her nose.

Streaking naked held a certain liberating quality. Different than when she wore her cat, she was more aware of her body instead of her surroundings, such as how the air kissed her skin. How a light sheen of sweat covered her. The sting of branches as they lightly whipped her in passing. The decadence of flesh against flesh when a certain long legged predator caught up and swept her into his arms.

Lacing her arms around his neck, Jiao laughed as he jogged back towards her house. She pondered her happiness, knowing it owed a lot to the man carrying her, but also a part to the freedom of their actions. For so long she kept herself from the small pleasures in life like shifting and going for a run. Chasing and playing for the sake of fun and laughter. How wonderful to know freedom tasted and felt so good.

And to think, passion tasted even better.

She didn't doubt for a single moment what would happen when they arrived at the house. Nothing would stop them from making love. And, despite their tangled mess, she didn't think she could stop herself from claiming this man. *I just hope he can forgive me when I can finally tell him the truth.*

*

Need burned deep inside Chris. If he didn't sink into his woman and mark her soon, he'd probably go insane – or burst. Or both. He'd thought himself blue balled after making her come on his tongue. Yeah, then she partially fulfilled one of his fantasies, shifting into a beautiful, sleek spotted cat, similar to a leopard, but like none he'd ever seen. Best part? She wanted him to catch her.

He chased her. Oh, the fun he had, trailing her through the woods. He would have enjoyed making love to her by the water, but he could see her trembling from the chill air. A protective need consumed him. If she required warmth, he'd give it to her because he definitely had heat to spare. His body fairly burned, but even ensconced in his arms, she shivered, although he would almost wager some of that had to do with desire, not just the cold. Not conceit, just plain fact.

It didn't take them long to return to the house, their wild dash through the forest close to a full circuit. Not being a complete idiot – even if his brain probably didn't have much blood left – he didn't just dash into the house, he stopped and despite the travesty of covering her body, he still made her dress, following suit which was rendered difficult by the erection straining to remain free.

That of course made her giggle again, a sound so addictive, he gladly suffered the indignity. At the edge of the woods, Chris hesitated. Despite his need, did he dare go back to her house and make love to her? He'd hate to end up a blurb on the morning news.

Christopher and Jill were found shot dead late last night when her husband Jack came home to find them making love and snapped.

"What's wrong?" she asked, stopping a few feet into the yard when she realized he didn't follow.

"If I go inside, I don't think I'll be able to stop myself from claiming you." Left unsaid, was the fact he left the choice up to her. He couldn't claim her without her consent. No matter how much he needed her, loved her, he wanted her to make the choice. *To choose me.*

"I know." She said it softly, her serious tone at odds with her recent laughter.

"So I guess I should go?"

"No. Stay. I can't watch you leave again."

The admittance of her need for him, the same agony he felt when he left her every day, shone clear on her face. It seemed fate was done waiting. They needed to be with each other. Now. Tonight.

Then, they would deal with the repercussions of their need, together.

But first, he would make love to a certain temptress.

Sweeping her into his arms, he crushed his mouth to hers, only belatedly calling himself a fool as he entered the kitchen before checking to see if Jack had come home earlier than expected. Lucky him, they had the house to themselves.

"Where to, baby?" he asked breaking off the kiss so he could locate a bedroom.

"Last room down the hall."

"Guest room I hope?"

"My room. Jack sleeps in the room by the kitchen."

Once again, she'd managed to surprise him, and then again, not. It seemed she didn't lie when she called her marriage unconventional. Entering her bedroom, one quick sniff told him that she was the one to use this room. Alone.

Good because he didn't think he could handle making love to her on the bed she shared with her husband. He did have some scruples left.

Tossing her onto the cover, he turned back around, shut and then latched the door. Before turning back to face her, he stripped. He heard her gasps. Smelt her desire. Staggered under the weight of his need.

Slowly, he pivoted to face her. She lay sprawled on her bed, watching him. Her eyes wide open, her cheeks flushed, and her need so thick it formed an almost tangible cord that flowed from her to him.

With measured steps, he approached her. "Get undressed. Show me your perfect body."

Give him a moment of admiration before he fell on her like a ravening, rutting animal. He'd flirted with temptation one too many times. He feared once he touched her this time, he would lose his mind. Lose his control. He wanted to make sure she was good and ready before that happened. And somehow without touching her.

Naked, she lay before him, her teeth tugging at her lower lip, her arms crossed over her breasts.

"Move your hands."

She obeyed instantly. Beautiful pert breasts appeared with puckered buds. His cock twitched.

"Do you know how many times I've imagined you like this?" he said after he swallowed hard. "How many nights I ached to be with you?"

"I know how many nights because I felt it too." A wry smile twisted her lips. "I thought I would go crazy washing my darned sheets."

"You too?" The admission made him laugh and drew the level of intensity down a notch. Not far though.

She nodded.

"You are so cute and perfect," he announced, before kneeling on the bed. He grabbed her leg and pulled, scooting her down a little, before leaning over and bracing himself on his forearms over her. "But you do need one more thing."

"And what would that be?"

"Me, as your mate." He lowered his mouth to hers, keeping his body aloft still. It didn't help much. He remained all too aware of the fact she lay naked beneath him. Naked and horny.

The kiss went on and on as he sought to recapture her breathless passion. When her breath came in pants, he knelt on the bed and allowed himself to explore; her taut buds, her slight indent at the waist, the lean curve of her hip, the thick curls. She writhed under his touch, squirmed and cried out.

He covered her mouth with his. "Shhh. Just in case." Risky reminding her of a possible interruption by her ball and chain, but it seemed the thought of discovery didn't frighten her. Or at least not as much as it excited her.

She wrapped her hands around his head and mashed his mouth to hers, using him to silence her cries as his hands continued to stroke her, arouse her.

The temptation of her smooth skin won and he plastered himself over her, pinning his cock between her spread thighs and butting it against her wet sex.

She squeaked, as if surprised, and he reared back.

"Is everything alright?"

"Um," she appeared worried. "It's been a while. Could you be – Um, that is…" She trailed off and bit her lip.

"I'll go slow, baby. Trust me."

Holding her gaze, he shifted himself between her legs. She trembled. He positioned himself, rubbing his engorged head against her damp sex and then rubbing it against her nub. She arched for him, and wiggled. But he played a while longer, dipping and rubbing until she veritably thrashed.

Then he covered her again and shifted the head of him inside the opening of her sex. She stiffened and he held in a groan at the tight feel of her. He pushed a little more forward and stopped as something impeded his path.

No. It couldn't be. He pressed a little forward, and she went rigid. A virgin? Jill was a freakn' virgin? How the hell did that happen? She was bloody married.

But then it penetrated. *She's untouched. Mine, and only mine.*

With a quick thrust, he broke the barrier, swallowing her small cry of pain. He held himself still inside her, letting her channel adjust to his girth, basking in the knowledge of the surprise gift she'd given him.

Staying still though, especially when encased in such a tight heaven, wasn't something he could do for long. Lips fervently stroking hers, he gyrated his hips, grinding himself against her until the tautness in her frame eased. Soon, her hips wiggled under him, a silent plea for more. Conscious of her tender state, he withdrew, then eased back in.

Holy freakn' hell. She fit him so perfectly. Welcomed him so eagerly. He caught her mounting cries with his mouth as he took them both to the edge. When she crested, her flesh convulsing around his length, her nails raking his back, he let himself go. Poured himself inside her, seed, heart and soul.

Ours. All ours. His wolf surged to the front while he basked in the post coital bliss. Canines descended and he ducked his head into the hollow by her throat, and marked her.

Teeth sunk into her flesh, her coppery blood on his tongue, she became his mate. And a moment later, once she'd eagerly taken her own bite, he became hers. Two beings, two hearts, in love and forever entwined.

Figured a phone call would interrupt the most important moment of his life. But then again, watching Jill jump out of bed naked, her skin flushed rosy, her hair a tangled mess down her back and her heart shaped cheeks peeking, when she grabbed the phone tempered his mood somewhat.

While she engaged in a rapid fire conversation with her husband – who was never her lover – Chris pondered the startling fact of his mate's virginity. Unexpected. Super surprising. More mysterious than ever.

He meant to ask her what it meant. Truly he did. But when she turned to him with a smile made to destroy his control – but arouse his lust – and his tongue got stuck. He might have recovered had his brain not left the room when she said, "We have at least an hour or more and my shower is big enough for two."

He'd question her later. Much later when the blood returned to his head. The one on top that was. Right now, his mate wanted his touch, and it would take a stronger wolf than he to say no.

Chapter Twenty Two

Dinner and social catching up done, Sheng left Patricia and exited the diner. It was then he finally allowed himself to dwell on Patricia's news that Gina pried into his private affairs. And he got angry.

How dare the she-wolf threaten his existence? It was one thing to taunt him with her body and for her to steal a kiss. But Gina went too far when she began digging in to his and Jiao's life. What if she'd accidentally notified Kaleb? She could have brought their tenuous existence down with just one misplaced phone call.

Luckily, Patricia noticed the searches and now, Sheng would deal with it. *I'll teach her to put her canine nose in other people's business.* What better time to confront her than now? He had access to her home address because of her recent car purchase. He swung by the car dealership under the guise of checking his schedule, but in reality, he scribbled her location down.

On his way over, it occurred to him to call his sister and let her know he'd arrive later than expected.

She answered after several rings out of breath. "Hello."

"Is everything alright?" he asked, slipping into their birth language. He drove onto the highway.

"Fine. Just fine. I was just downstairs checking on the gym and had to run to grab the phone. Are you on your way home?"

"No. That's why I'm calling. I have to make a stop and will probably be gone for at least another hour, or more." What he intended to do, he wouldn't admit to himself, but the bulge at his groin had a hard idea.

"I won't wait up for you then, if you don't mind. I'm kind of tired."

"I'll see you in the morning. Lock the doors."

"I will. Bye."

They hung up and Sheng frowned. His sister sounded happy at his delay, which made no sense, unless she planned something he wouldn't like. But then again, he couldn't really talk since he planned to do something about his own wolf problem. *Something involving handcuffs, no clothes, my tongue, and hours of erotic torture until Gina agrees to behave.* God, the fantasies she inspired. A part of him understood he wasn't in complete control at the moment. A part of him, a big part, honestly didn't care.

The she-wolf drew him. Taunted him. And he was tired of it. It ended tonight, even if he had to bury his cock in her a dozen times to sate his lust, one way or another, he wasn't leaving her apartment until he got the madness under control.

Arriving at Gina's place, a condo building in the east end of Ottawa, he regarded the locked front door with a frown. He didn't want to announce his presence, however, someone needed to buzz the portal to let him in. He tossed some change into the parking meter before strolling across the street, timing his arrival to that of a couple slowing in front. The older gent gave him a hard look when Sheng caught the door and held it open.

"I'm just visiting my girlfriend, Gina, on the fifth floor," he said, adopting his most benign expression.

"Gina, the cop, Gina?" the woman asked.

"That's my girl," he said with a wide smile. "You know her?"

"Who doesn't? She made sure the druggies in the park found another spot. It's so nice to go for walks now and not worry about the needles and other junk."

"Sounds like my Gina." Grin still plastered to his face, Sheng wondered if he looked as crazy as he felt. Apparently not, because the couple let him follow them in and got on the elevator with him. When he got off at the fifth floor, they even wished him a good evening.

Oh, I'm planning on a good night, so don't mind the screams and thumps.

Arriving in front of her door, he didn't hesitate or try to talk himself out the confrontation. He wasn't about to let one nosy wolf chase him out of town. Or keep him up any longer. He raised his fist and knocked.

*

In the midst of doing some yoga, Gina, currently bent over with her arms extended, frowned. Who the heck knocked? She rarely got visitors, and forget surprise ones. To access the building a person needed a key or have someone buzz them in. The impatient rap came again.

Curious, she unwound her body and padded over to the front door. Before opening it, she grabbed her gun off the sideboard and held it behind her before swinging open the portal. A cute, yet pissed off, Asian man pushed his way in past her.

"Won't you come in?" she said, with all the sarcasm possible.

"We need to talk," Jack growled.

"Fine, but do you mine taking off your shoes first. I just vacuumed."

Brows knitting together to form one annoyed slash, and lips tight, despite his annoyance, Jack bent over and removed his shoes. Grinning, she admired his ass as she slid her gun back into her junk basket.

"Good pussycat. I don't suppose you'd let the pants follow?" Darn but she'd never known a man to blush like this one did.

"I am not here for sex."

Odd, her cop radar said he lied. Awesome. "Plans change. People get naked. Sometimes sex happens. Or at least some hot and heavy oral." Gina tried not to laugh as he opened his mouth to speak but nothing came out. Yeah, she freely admitted to getting a perverse pleasure out of shocking him.

"You are the most uncouth creature," he finally managed to choke.

"And you are the most repressed. Holy smokes, pussycat. Relax a little. Can't a girl toss around a few dirty jokes? Maybe hope for a little no strings, sweaty action? Maybe a boob job?" She pushed her breasts together to further emphasize her words and wet her panties when he almost went cross-eyed. A girl did so enjoy knowing she turned a man on. And if she wasn't mistaken, her pussycat had reached the point of no return.

Unfortunately, he didn't ravish her, despite his obvious erection. "I can't relax," he snapped.

"Why not? Tough day at work?"

"It was my day off."

"Undershorts too tight?" she asked.

"I don't wear any."

Oh, no. He did not say that with a smirk. Her eyes shot to his groin, trying to x-ray the fabric and see if he told the truth. "Really? I don't believe you. Prove it."

He recoiled. "I will not prove it. Why would I lie?"

She shrugged and stepped past him into her living room, a chaotic space filled with a pair of overstuffed, brushed suede love seats covered in multi colored cushions rivaling the hues of a rainbow. Her Wii game system was paused as it waited for her to resume her yoga session. Grabbing up a remote, and ignoring her visitor, she selected the next pose and got in position.

"What are you doing?"

"Well, since someone won't show me his commando state, nor tell me why he's here, I'm going back to my yoga. Feel free to join me."

"We need to talk about what you did." He moved until he stood in front of her, his arms crossed over his chest.

Hands touching her toes, she peeked up at him. "Talk about what? The kiss? Don't be so anal. We shared one little smooch. Not a big deal. If you're worried about your wife finding out, then don't. I'm not the type to kiss and tell."

"This has nothing to do with the kiss. I meant the other thing you did."

Other? Seeing as how she'd not gotten drunk in the last few days and woken up in a strange bed with a fuzzy mouth and no recollection of events after a round of tequila shooters, she really had no clue what he meant. "You'll have to be more specific, pussycat. Although, I'm pretty sure if we'd done something else, I would remember it, unless you really weren't that memorable."

Oh no, he looked pissed now. "For the last time, this isn't about sex, but for the record, if I did do something to you, you'd remember it. Now stop playing stupid. I'm talking about your inquiries in to me and Jill."

How did he find out about that? Gina frowned and knew she should ask him, but dammit, he'd challenged her. And Gina Greco never turned down a challenge. "You think you're that good in the sack? I dare you to prove it. Personally, I think you're too repressed to be anything other than perfunctory, but I'm game to try."

"Perfunctory? I'm an excellent lover. I take a lot of care with my partners to ensure they enjoy themselves."

Gina buffed her nails on the edge of her shirt and pretended boredom. "Gee, I haven't heard that one before. Hate to break it to you, pussycat, but most men don't live up to their claims."

"And you would know, wouldn't you?" he spat bitterly.

Her brows arched. "If you're calling me a slut, watch out, because while I'll tolerate many names, that's not one of them."

"And what are you going to do about it?"

"I'm a cop. I know how to hurt you."

His lips curled into a smirk. "You're a girl. I'd like to see you try."

"You did not just say that," she sputtered at his chauvinistic remark.

"I did. It's a known fact women just aren't as physically capable as men. It's why we have to take on the role of protector."

"*Protecting*?" she asked, framing the word in finger quotes. "That's priceless. I can't believe your wife lets you get away spouting bullshit like that."

"My wife knows her place," he pompously asserted.

"I'm not your wife." And no, despite her wolf's whining, she didn't intend to apply for the position not even when Jill hooked up with Chris. The guy, while hot, was not her type at all. Cute yes. But also an obvious control freak. "Anyone ever tell you that you're a jerk." Not content to let words act as her only rebuttal, she also swept her leg at Jack's ankle and dumped him on his ass. Or meant to. He somehow got his hands out and managed to spring away and land on his feet.

Cool. And hot because it showed her another layer to Mr. Prim-and-Proper. "Martial arts?"

"Among other things," he replied.

Curious about the other things, she threw a pillow at him, and as he caught it, she dove at him. He caught her, twisted her so her back was to his chest while his arms pinned hers at her side. His breath fluttered against her ear lobe. "See. You can't beat a man."

"But I can hurt one," she snarled, annoyed at how easily he handled her. Jamming her foot down, she stomped him, then rammed her elbow at the part of his body that supposedly went commando. His arms loosened as his breath whooshed out. She leapt free and turned to face him, blood pumping and strangely aroused by their wrestling match.

"That was a low blow," he chided.

"Want me to kiss it better?"

His eyes flashed but not with annoyance. "I prefer my women more ladylike."

"I prefer my men without a stick up their ass."

"You are the most annoying she-wolf."

"Ditto, Mr. Irritable cat."

With each word, they took a step toward each other.

"Temptress." He growled it like an insult. It still made her cleft flood with moisture.

"Stupid stud." And with that, she kissed him.

Chapter Twenty Three

How they went from sparring with fists and words to locked in a frantic kiss, Sheng couldn't have said, but once his lips clashed with hers, he forgot his reason for coming over. Forgot why he disliked Gina.

But Sheng did remember every erotic fantasy he'd had about her. Like a tsunami, arousal washed over him and swept him in its grip. Awash in sensation, he could only struggle to breathe, frantic pants as he nibbled on her lips and sucked on her lithe tongue. Encased in his arms, she didn't struggle to escape. On the contrary, she held onto him just as tight, her rounded body, with its undertone of muscle, rubbing against him.

He wound his hand in her hair and pulled, tilting her face back. "This is such a bad idea," he growled.

Eyes heavy with languor, she licked her lips. "Yes it is. Now shut up and get naked or I'll get the cuffs out." She no sooner finished speaking than her hands tugged at his shirt.

As if he'd let her control the situation. He placed his hands over hers and helped her strip it off. For once in his life, Sheng gave in to something other than the right thing to do. He chose the path of pleasure instead of duty and made quick work of her clothes as she fumbled at his slacks. It took only a few frantic moments for them to denude themselves. Damn, his fantasies didn't do justice to her body.

Full hips, rounded belly, heavy breasts with a slight tan all over, every inch of her demanded worship, especially her large, brown nipples.

To his ego's manly delight, she sucked in a breath as she eyeballed him. "Holy shit. You are commando."

"And you talk too much." Grabbing her by the nape, he dragged her to him, something about the she-wolf bringing out his more dominant side. He devoured her mouth hungrily, nipping her bottom lip. God, he wanted to bite her so bad. The feel of her skin against his, rubbing and marking him with her scent had his cat yeowling.

His cat wanted her. Wanted him to bite her. Mark her.

Sheng retained enough sanity to know better. But not enough to stop himself from letting his mouth travel from her lips to her neck, then further down to her heavy breasts. Cupping large handfuls, so different than his usual experience, he mentally revised his previous dislike of big breasts. Smothering his face between them, squeezing the round globes was much more satisfying than he expected. And sucking on her prominent nipples? Almost as fun as the noises Gina made, guttural cries of pleasure as she yanked his hair, pushing him harder into her breasts. Rough, and vocal, and so responsive. A wet dream come true.

"Suck them, pussycat," she demanded. "Bite them too. Work that mouth."

So she thought to command the situation? To control him? Not likely. Sheng didn't have much say over many parts of his life, but when it came to sex, especially with this woman, he intended to call the shots. Capturing her lips again, he walked them until the back of her knees hit the couch. She toppled onto it, legs splayed. He stepped between them, his cock jutting forth at just the right height – in other words, even with her mouth. Even without its garish layer of color, the fullness of her lips beckoned him.

"Is this a hint, pussycat?" she asked, eyeing him coyly even as she grabbed his dick and stroked it.

"No hint. Suck it."

His frank order widened her gaze. "Or?"

"Or you won't get a turn." He flicked a finger against the dampness between her legs, fighting an urge to sink to his knees and bury his face. Not yet. First, he needed her mouth around his cock.

It didn't take her long to decide. Lips latched onto his swollen head and Sheng threw his head back with a loud groan. With an impressive suction, Gina drew him into her mouth, while her fingers kneaded his sac. She took every inch of him and then slid it back out. She bobbed her head along his length, fast and eager, but he still wrapped his hands in her hair, tugging at her. Controlling the pace, gagging her every so often to show her who was in charge. The minx enjoyed it too, groaning loudly, the rumble vibrating along the length of his cock.

Damn. If she didn't stop he'd come in her freakn' mouth. He wasn't ready for that, not when he had another destination in mind. He pulled free, not with ease as she tried to follow him, her lips not eager to relinquish their prize.

Before she could protest – and he gave in to the climax her sultry wet mouth promised – he dropped to his knees and buried his face between her thighs. Then he did what cats did best. He lapped at her cream.

*

Gina must have died and gone to heaven, or so she assumed as she moaned and thrashed on her couch as she got the most amazing oral ever, and from the most straight laced of sources. Who would have guessed the passionate nature hiding behind the scowl? The deft tongue flicking across her clit, its gentle rasp an unexpected delight.

She went straight from aroused, to the edge of orgasm in seconds. And then he purred.

Holy. Freakn'. Hell.

The vibration of his lips, and the sounds against her most sensitive of parts, sent her over the edge. Yelling and hips bucking, the climax tore through her body and left her just about comatose.

But her pussycat wasn't done yet.

He covered her body on the couch, inserting his hips between her thighs, the tip of his hard cock probing her still quivering sex. In he plunged. Hard, deep jabs, perfectly aimed shots that hit her g-spot and left her unable to catch her breath. A shame, because if she'd possessed an ounce of air in her lungs, the scream she would have loosed with her second orgasm might have shattered windows. As it was, she had to satisfy herself with arching against him, mouth open wide – and for once silent.

He, on the other hand, didn't hold back, and he bellowed her name as he came in hot spurts inside her that did nothing to calm the shock waves going through her entire body. Then his actions hit her, and she sat up, shoving at his chest.

"What the hell is wrong with you?" she yelled.

Wearing a bemused expression, he rolled off and landed on his knees on the floor. "Wrong?" His brow creased. "You came twice. What do you have to be mad about?"

She pointed to his semi erect, glistening dick. "Did you forget something?"

His eyes widened in horror. "Impossible. I never forget. Shit." He stumbled to his feet and ran a hand over his eyes, obviously upset.

Yeah, boo hoo. Gina wasn't feeling sorry one bit for her pussycat. "You know, if you're going to maul a girl, the least you could do is put a hat on."

"Maul you? You're the one constantly tempting me with your body and words. What else did you expect me to do? And besides, I didn't see you calling for a halt so I could throw on some protection."

Oh no he didn't! "Don't you dare try to lay the blame for this on me. I was perfectly content to give you head in exchange for some tongue action. But oh no, you just had to stick your dick in my hole and now you want to make this my fault you might have impregnated me?"

"It was only one time. I'm sure you'll be fine."

"And if I'm not? In case you hadn't noticed, you're married."

"Don't worry about that. If you end up pregnant, I'll do the right thing by you."

His stiff declaration pissed her off more and she jumped off the couch. "Right thing? Don't do me any favors, pussycat."

"You are obstinate."

"And you're an ass."

"I don't understand why my body and cat crave you," he snapped.

His cat wanted her? As much as her wolf wanted him. Uh oh. "I think you should leave." Before they both did something stupid.

"Yes, I should." But he didn't and he kept watching her. Then stepped closer. And closer. Before she knew it, they were in each other's arms again. And round two was just as barebacked, hot and furious as round one, and didn't cool down even during round three in the shower.

Chapter Twenty Four

Wet, from the shower, his body sated for the moment, an arm loosely draped around a drowsy she-wolf, Sheng pondered the madness.

What happened?

He'd come over with the intention of telling Gina to keep her nose out of his business. Instead, he'd had sex with her, three times without protection. Worse than that? A part of him didn't panic at the possibility she might have gotten pregnant. Nope, his cat rumbled in satisfaction at the idea of kittens, and he couldn't say he hated the idea either.

But with Gina? Crass mouthed. Scantily dressed. Always provoking him. Super sexy temptress. Oh damn it all to hell and back. He pressed his arm over his eyes as if that would hide the inevitable truth. Yeah, that didn't happen. Gina was his freakn' mate.

Unbelievable. How could fate want to tie him to a woman who drove him batshit crazy? But could he really state surprise? Despite his initial purpose in coming here, a part of him knew, and expected, he'd sleep with her. Where she was concerned, he lacked any sense of control. Any sense of propriety. And damn, did it feel good.

He wanted her again. And again. Possibly forever.

The tinny ring of his phone roused Sheng from his shocked revelation. Rolling out of bed, he padded naked into the living room and dug through his pockets until he found his cell. Patricia's number lit up the display. He answered. "Hey. Did I forget something at the restaurant?"

"Sheng, thank god you answered. You need to leave town. Now. Forget about packing. Just grab your sister and run."

An icy chill went through him. "What's happened?"

"Kaleb's here."

He sank on the couch as his legs suddenly wouldn't support him. "Are you sure?"

"A private plane just landed at an airstrip out of town. The guy in charge of refueling is a friend of my dad's. He called me because he saw cages in the cargo area. Silver cages."

A shiver went up his spine. "Could be anyone?"

"Could be, except the guy reported disembarking matches the description you gave me of Kaleb. I think it's safest if you disappeared for a bit until I can find out more about this plane and its passengers."

Sheng pinched the bridge of his nose, refusing to give in to panic. "I'm not at home, but I'll be there in a few. Can you call Jiao and let her know to get ready?"

"I've tried and it's going straight to voicemail."

The chill in his heart spread. *Oh, please let Jiao be safe. Don't let my one lapse of judgment cost my sister her freedom.* He hung up and started pulling on his clothes.

A very naked, tousle haired Gina strode from the bedroom. "What's happening? Where are you going?"

Too angry, and frightened, he didn't answer her. Didn't trust anything he might say while his emotions ran so high. He sat down and pulled on his socks instead of resorting to balancing on one leg.

Rather than retreat from his silence, she frowned and forged ahead. "Are you ignoring me? Seriously? After what we just did the last couple of hours, don't I deserve some recognition?"

"I need to go."

"Where?"

"Away."

"What do you mean, away? Like home away? Or away-away on a trip? Was that your wife on the phone?"

Her numerous questions loosened his tongue. "That was the agent in charge of my case. I need to leave."

"Okay, pussycat, you're giving me more questions than answers. What agent and case? Why do you need to leave?"

Striding to the door, he would have ignored her, but she threw herself in front of him, blocking the portal. "You are not leaving until you answer me, dammit." She stamped her foot.

He snapped. "You want to know what's happening? I'll tell you then. You and your meddling helped him find us."

"Helped who? I don't understand."

"Of course you don't, because it was meant to be a secret. But oh no, you just had to dig and dig until you set off one of Kaleb's traps. And now, he's here. He's come to get us, and it's all your damned fault!"

Chest heaving, he spat the last part, so angry, and not just because Gina brought Kaleb to their doorstep, but because dammit, he didn't want to leave. Despite the fact she'd blown his and Jiao's cover, Sheng still wanted the damned wolf. Wanted her so freakn' bad it hurt. Wanted her because she was his mate.

What an idiot he was for not recognizing it from the get go. Deep down, he'd known this for days, probably since the moment they'd met. But he denied the link between them, not wanting to deal with it, and what it meant. He actually hoped, just like his sister, that perhaps they could drop the charade and once again live their lives as themselves. What a foolish fantasy.

As Sheng predicted, Kaleb would never let them go. Would never let him live free. *I can never claim Gina as a mate because then she would be in danger too.* What Kaleb would do if he ever got his hands on Sheng's mate, he preferred not to think of. Worse, just how far would Sheng go to protect Gina if Kaleb ever threatened her? He'd after all seen what his father did to keep his own mate safe from harm.

He should have never come here. Never let her get so close. "Move away from the door," he ordered in the coldest voice he could manage.

Didn't work. She-wolves were a tenacious and fearless breed.

"I am not accepting responsibility for anything," she yelled. "It's not my fault you look more suspicious than a drug smuggler clenching his cheeks tight because he's got a load in his pants. I'm a cop. What did you expect me to do? Turn a blind eye to the fact you and your wife didn't exist until a few months ago?"

"And just why did you even bother to investigate? We broke no laws. We did nothing to call attention to ourselves. Why? Why stick your nose where you weren't wanted?"

Her lips thinned into a line. "I had my reasons."

"What reason was good enough to blow my cover? Huh? Can you explain that to me?"

"I was trying to help Chris."

"My contractor? Why?" Sheng figured he already knew the answer, but wanted it confirmed.

"Chris thinks your wife is his mate."

"Dammit. I was afraid of that."

"You don't seem too surprised or hurt," she snapped. "Do you care so little for the woman you promised to honor, cherish and obey?"

"I care, just not in the way you think, because Jill is not my wife. She's Jiao, my sister."

"Your sister …" If he'd not seen her wide open mouth in action earlier, under much more pleasurable circumstances, he would have been impressed. As it was, he stifled the memory of those luscious lips wreaking havoc, and pushed her away from the door.

Finally quiet, Gina didn't resist, and despite the inner howling of his cat, begging him to stay, Sheng slammed out of her apartment. Once in the hall, he didn't allow himself to look back. He ignored his feline's meows of displeasure. He stifled his urge to run back, grab Gina, and drag her along with him into hiding.

She didn't belong with him – even if every part of him screamed she did. He'd not marked her. Maybe she still had a chance of escaping the mating curse.

With Sheng out of sight and out of mind, Gina could forget all about him and move on. Date a shifter without a curse over his head. Tease and please another male. Sheng growled as he stabbed the elevator button.

Actually, he growled all the way home and didn't relax until he walked into his house, his untouched, scent free home.

A pity. He'd have welcomed a fight.

But no, his neighborhood bore no unfamiliar parked vehicles. His driveway sat empty. A porch light lit his way and the pristine interior showed no signs of intruders or violence. For now.

Undiscovered and in no danger it seemed for the moment, Sheng still didn't relax – and his fear didn't abate – until his disheveled sister appeared in the hall in answer to his yells for her to get her lazy butt moving.

Thank freakn' God. Jiao was safe which meant they stood a chance of escaping. Whether she wanted to or not, though, was a totally different question. And he feared, judging by the aroma of wolf wafting from his sister's direction, she wouldn't have the answer he wanted.

*

A knock at the door had Gina flying to open it, wondering if her pussycat returned, hopefully to apologize for being an ass.

What was wrong with the man? Making her body sing one minute, then yelling at her like she was evil incarnate the next. She didn't do it on purpose to bring his subterfuge to light. Could she help the fact her cop brain saw something suspicious and insisted she look in on it? He should thank her for the concern she showed her family. How was she supposed to know he was in some kind of witness protection program and not just a criminal in hiding?

Shifters didn't really have a governing body, even if rumors abounded of a secret council who kept an eye on their general affairs. So who hid him? The RCMP, the Americans, or someone else? And again, still not her fault if she found his cover suspect. Whoever was in charge of his case should have their head examined for using Jack and Jill as their cover ID.

Swinging open the door, she prepared to give Sheng a piece of her mind, but the words died on her lips as a beefy pair of guys dressed in suits, shoved their way in, pushing her backwards.

"Hey! What the hell are you freakn' doing? Get out of here."

It didn't surprise her when they ignored her request, which was why she dove at the table she kept in her front hall, and scrabbled in her basket. Before she could pull out her gun, one of the gorilla's – real ones if her nose wasn't mistaken – grabbed her arm and stopped her short. The other wrapped a beefy bicep around her middle and carried her further into her condo.

"You're making a big mistake, boys. I'm with the Ottawa police department."

"We know."

Not good, but not over yet. Whipping her head back, Gina cracked it off the guy's face, hearing the satisfying crunch of a nose breaking. At the same time, she slammed her foot down, her bare foot doing little damage as it slid off his polished leather shoe. The elbow rammed behind her didn't even cause an 'oof'. Nothing she did loosened the manacle around her waist and when she opened her mouth to yell, gorilla number two shoved a wad of fabric in – *eew, not my dirty undies!* – stifling her.

Okay, now she could panic. Who were these guys and what did they want? And why did she suddenly remember Sheng's taunting assertion that a woman needed a man to protect her? Stupid jerk. As if anyone could guard themselves against thugs the size of cars. In a battle like that, forget strength. These were gun odds.

While they attached her hands together, using the duct tape they'd thoughtfully brought along, she tried furiously to think of how she could escape. It definitely wouldn't happen while the two giant goons watched her. She'd have to wait for a moment of inattention. If they didn't kill her first.

Hands trussed in front of her. Legs taped together. Mouth sealed shut as well, as they replaced her underpants with a length of tape, it occurred her to that even if they left the room she was royally freakn' screwed. Her only hope was shifting into her wolf in the hopes the violence of the change would snap her bonds.

"There is no escape, dog. I've been working with your kind for years, and trust me when I say, I've wrangled with better and come out ahead." The speaker, a barrel chested man with a sneer on his face, came to stand in front of her. Gray hair thinning on top, his eyes a flinty grey, she saw no mercy in the human. "I'm sure you're wondering who I am and why

I'm here. I am Kaleb. Perhaps you remember me? We spoke yesterday about Sheng."

The dude who claimed she had the wrong person? What the hell did he want?

"I'm afraid I misled you. The picture I sent you wasn't exactly accurate. But this one is, if a few years old. Recognize him?"

Gina's eyes widened in shock at the younger version of her cat before she thought to school herself. Too late. Kaleb caught it.

"I see you do know who this is. Excellent. And this one?" He held up a picture of a young girl, but this time Gina expected to see Jiao's face and didn't react.

"I see we're pretending ignorance now. No matter. You will tell me what you know of Sheng and his sister, starting with where they live. Nod once for yes and I'll free your mouth."

Gina didn't move.

"A stubborn girl, eh? A pity. I guess I should mention now that I only tolerate obedience. Has anyone ever taught you to listen? Probably not, given your poor manners. Lucky for you, I can fix that. See, some people don't believe in hitting women," Kaleb remarked as he peeled off his leather gloves. "I'm not one of them." His backhand caught her cheek and slammed her head sideways. As shots went, pretty damned good.

"Still feeling silent?" Kaleb queried after he'd yanked her by the hair to face him.

As if one tap would loosen her tongue. She'd grown up with a shitload of rowdy cousins, followed by chauvinistic dicks while she trained as a cop. She could handle a hell of a lot. *Bring it, jerkoff.*

Apparently, he read the message in her eyes because he smiled. "So be it." He followed his words with a slap. She needed more color in her cheeks. Smack. Some women paid to plump up their lips for that full look.

"Hey boss."

Kaleb stopped his methodical damage to her face as one the gorillas beckoned him from her bedroom doorway. Uh-oh. How good was their sense of smell, and would they recognize Sheng's scent, formerly known as Jack, on her sheets?

Judging by the wide smile on Kaleb's face, they did.

"It seems you've held back. My men say you entertained the cat here and not long ago." The big man wandered around her living room, his cold eyes taking in everything. He headed to her spare bedroom with the computer and her books. She wanted to curse up a blue streak when he emerged with her folder on Jack and Jill. *Nice job, Gina. I just handed him and his sister over to the psycho. He's right. I should have minded my own business.*

Waving the file, Kaleb smiled. "So kind of you to provide an address. But, it seems I no longer need it. I have a much better plan to capture my missing pets. You see, Sheng always did have a soft spot for helping damsels in distress. You should have seen the lengths he went to just to protect his sister. What do you say we see how he reacts when he finds out I've stolen his lover?"

Should I tell him he'll probably say good riddance? Her one night stand, passionate as it was, wouldn't inspire Sheng to do anything dramatic for her. Not when he already planned to skip town with his sister. His protection of women only extended to one person, and her name didn't start with G.

A shame really, because despite her tough exterior, Gina always wondered what a damsel getting rescued felt. And if she ever needed a knight to come to her rescue, right about now would work. Although, she'd recommend an Uzi semi-automatic instead of a sword, because the gorillas looked like they could take a licking and keep on beating the crap out of a person.

They also had rock solid fists her jaw discovered. Not that she pondered it for long since they knocked her unconscious.

Chapter Twenty Five

Jiao woke to the slamming of the front door and loud shouts. She recognized Sheng's voice as he stomped around, in the grips of a hissy fit, bellowing for her like a madman. While she'd usually not reply and would wait for him to find her, she kind of had a big problem. A really, really big problem, and it was naked in her bed with an arm slung around her waist.

Oh no – oh yay – Chris fell asleep with her. But how to make sure Sheng didn't find her mate? And kill him? Somehow, she doubted her talk of 'I think we need a fake divorce' would go over well with the reason so blatantly sprawled in her bed.

Although, Sheng didn't need to know who slept under her covers if she headed him off. Sliding out from under Chris's arm, she held her finger to her lips when he opened his eyes. They opened even wider as Sheng's ranting got closer.

"Stay here," she whispered before sliding on a robe. Concerned her scent would give her away, she held her nose and also doused herself in body spray. Smoothing her hair down, heart pounding in fear of discovery – and her tummy doing back flips because Chris leaned back in her bed, letting the sheet fall low enough to display an indecent amount of flesh – she went to find her brother.

She found him in their office area, stuffing papers into a garbage pail. She recognized his plan by the smell of gas and barbecue lighter on the desk top.

"What are you doing?"

"What's it look like I'm doing? Covering our tracks. Pack a bag. We need to go," her brother growled.

"What? No. I can't leave."

"You don't have a choice," Sheng snapped. "We've been found."

"Found?" Her heart stuttered to a stop. "Are you sure?"

"Gina, you know that girl you met at the dinner? She's a cop and she checked up on our identities. I don't know how she did it, but somehow she managed to catch Kaleb's attention and accidentally gave us away."

"Kaleb's coming?" Her heart stopped.

"Kaleb's here," he answered grimly.

"No! He can't be. I won't go back to the compound!" Raw panic threatened to overcome Jiao and she dropped to her knees, tucking her head down as she hyperventilated.

Arms came around her and Sheng adopted a soothing tone. "No one's taking you away, jiě zǐ. I won't let him."

Pressing the heels of her hands in her eyes, Jiao tried to calm herself. Tried to think past the thick fear fogging her mind. "Are you sure it's him?"

"The description matches and the airplane he arrived in holds silver cages."

Jiao shoved away from her brother and sprang to her feet. Like a panicked animal, her gaze roved around the space; seeking escape, expecting an enemy, looking for help. She licked her lips. "We'll hide. Hide until Kaleb thinks he's mistaken and leaves."

"No."

"Yes. We have to. I can't go. I won't let Kaleb chase me away."

"Are you insane? We need to do more than hide." His gaze narrowed. "Is this because of that wolf?"

Jiao saw the curl of his lip and heard the disdain in his voice. "Yes," she replied meekly.

"Forget him. We've leaving before it's too late." Sheng dropped a match in the pail and the contents lit up, small flames dancing while an acrid streamer of smoke curled upward.

Jiao dug in her heels when Sheng would have pulled her after him. She yanked her arm from his grasp and straightened her back. A defiant stare met her brother's angry one. "No. I'm not leaving. I'm tired of running. Tired of hiding and putting my life on hold. This stops now."

Sheng's lips tightened and she mentally braced herself for his upcoming harangue. Except it never happened. A body inserted itself between them. The broad back of her lover – bare, muscled perfection – hid Jiao from her brother's view as Chris rumbled, "Dude, calm down." Despite the grave situation, she peeked down and almost sighed in relief as she noted he'd at least put on pants. Not that it would help. It seemed the cat, ahem the wolf, was out of the bag, or in this case, bed.

"What are you doing here?" Sheng asked, his query much too quiet.

Jiao winced as she could just imagine her brother's red faced apoplexy at seeing the wolf, in their home, at this hour, wearing her scent. It was official. The marriage was over. Unfortunately, given the situation, she couldn't muster the joy she'd thought she'd feel.

She jumped to Chris's rescue before her brother could completely go off the deep end. "Chris is here because I asked him to stay."

"I see." Two words spoken in such a way as to make her feel about two inches tall. Yeah, she'd hurt and disappointed her brother. But did he leave her any choice? "We will talk about this later. Get dressed. We're leaving."

Jiao gaped at him. Did Sheng not grasp things had changed? That she'd changed? He'd also not counted on her mate. As if her lover would let Sheng make an announcement like that and then step aside.

"Leaving? No one's leaving. Baby, what's going on? Why does he want you to go?" Chris turned to ask her.

"I—" The truth caught in her throat.

"This doesn't concern you, wolf."

Chris whirled back to face her brother. "Oh, but it does. Jill is my mate."

"Find another. Because she leaves with me."

"Listen dude. I understand she's your wife and all, but, truth is, she's my mate. I can show you the mark. Now, I know you might find this hard to handle, and I'm real sorry to spring this on you like this but—"

"Jiao! Is this true? Did you mate with the wolf?"

Peeking around her lover's body, Jiao muttered a low *"Yes"* and watched her brother's incredulity grow.

"It changes nothing. We still need to leave."

"What part of she's my mate didn't you get?" Chris bristled, and fearing violence, Jiao stepped between her brother and mate.

"I heard. I just don't have time to listen about how you've been running around behind my back. Betraying me." He aimed the words at Jiao and she bit her lip as she hung her head. Faced with her brother's disappointment, she couldn't help but feel the chagrin at having hurt the one person who'd always loved and stuck by her.

"I'm sorry, Sheng," she whispered.

"Sheng? I thought that was your brother?" Chris's gaze bounced between Jiao and Sheng.

The moment of truth arrived, and of course didn't unfold at all like she'd hoped. Was there an easy way to say *'Hey, my husband is my brother and we're running from a demented ring master?'* Hallmark really needed to expand its selection of cards. "Chris, I wanted to explain. I truly did, but I couldn't. I promised to keep the secret."

"Explain what?" Chris looked between Jiao and Sheng. She noted the moment understanding dawned. "You're not freakn' married, are you? You're brother and sister. But why? Why pretend you were a couple? And why not tell me? Do you have any idea how I struggled with my feelings for you thinking you were married? How hard it was for me to come to terms with it?"

"I'm so sorry. I wanted to tell you. Believe me. I did. But I couldn't. Sheng and I needed to keep up our fake marriage so that anyone spying for Kaleb wouldn't tell him where we were."

"Who's Kaleb? And what does he have to do with all this?"

Showing no patience for their lover's quarrel, Sheng interrupted. "We don't have time for this, Jiao. Patricia called and said Kaleb landed hours ago. He's come to find us and it's only a matter of time before he shows up here." Sheng clenched her arm and began to pull.

Chris caught her other limb and halted him. "She's not going anywhere."

"Oh yes, she is. This doesn't concern you," Sheng replied, his eyes flashing darkly as he tugged.

"It does too bloody concern me. She's my freakn' mate! And she is not going anywhere without me." Chris yanked Jiao free and tucked her against his side.

Sheng stumbled back, the hurt in his eyes creating an ache in her heart. "Is this what you want?"

"I didn't mean for it to happen, Sheng. But from the moment I met him, I knew Chris was my mate. I couldn't fight it, nor did I want to."

"But the danger of discovery ..."

"Seemed worth it if I could have a chance at happiness. I never meant to hurt you."

Sheng sighed loudly and spun on his heel. The fire in the garbage can now licked a foot or more in the air, as it consumed the dry paper. Cursing, Sheng grabbed the pail and marched it past them into the kitchen, dousing it with the retractable sprayer. Jiao followed, her fingers laced with Chris', who while surely full of questions, remained silent as she dealt with her brother.

"What are you going to do?" she asked. Left unsaid, was would Sheng leave her? She hoped not, but not because she needed him for protection. It was time she stood up to her past and stopped letting fear dictate her future. While she couldn't be sure of how, she trusted in Chris enough, even with the secret that finally came out into the open, that he would stand by her side. And she wanted Sheng there too.

"What can I do? I won't leave you alone with only a guard dog to watch your back."

"You'll stay?"

"Of course I will. You're my little sister. I promised to always protect you. I can't do that if I'm not around."

"Don't do me any favors, dude. I can keep her safe," Chris interjected.

Sheng snorted. "I'm sure you will do your best, even if it's not good enough. And if we somehow make it out of this mess in one piece, be warned, I'll be watching you. Hurt my sister and –"

"Oh would you both stop with your threats and posturing. Kaleb is still out there looking for us. For all we know he could be outside our door."

Two sets of eyes veered to the kitchen window and Jiao sighed. "I didn't mean it literally. I'm just saying we need to make plans. Warn the community. Just because Kaleb's come looking for us, doesn't mean he'll be content to leave with only us."

"We'll need to –" Whatever Sheng prepared to say got interrupted as a phone rang and Sheng dug his hand in his pocket and yanked his cell out.

While her brother answered his call, Jiao stepped closer to Chris. Relief suffused her when his arms wrapped around her. She'd feared his anger when the truth came out. Feared he'd reject her when he found out just how she'd lied, even if her reason was good. But it seemed he could look past the things she'd withheld, although she was sure later, when they were alone, he'd expect an accounting.

A whispered, "No," came from her brother, and she turned her attention from her mate to her brother. Face ashen, Sheng took the phone from his ear.

Icy fear squeezed her heart. "What's wrong, Sheng?" What had him looking like tragedy struck?

"They've taken Gina."

"Gina, as in my cousin, Gina?" Chris asked.

"Yes. That Gina. Kaleb says unless Jiao and I give ourselves up before dawn, he'll kill her."

"Like freakn' hell he will," Chris snarled.

"Agreed. I will give myself in exchange," Sheng said, straightening from his slouch. Grim purpose shone in his eyes. "But, you must take Jiao and hide her until Kaleb departs with me. Even better, disappear. Start anew if you can. Patricia will help."

"Sheng, no," Jiao cried. "You can't do this."

"I must. You have found your mate, and while I never claimed her, I found mine. It is only right that since I inadvertently led Kaleb to Gina, that I give my life for hers."

Chris clapped. "Bravo. Nice speech. Now, if you're done getting all melodramatic and sappy, why don't we come up with a real plan? One that involves getting my cousin back. Keeping you here. And letting Jiao live with me openly."

"And how would you suggest we manage that, wolf?"

"You and Jiao are family now. And to the Grayson's, that means everything. We don't let anyone in the pack fight alone."

"While the offer is honorable, it will be dangerous. Kaleb and his men are likely armed. We can't allow your family to get involved any further."

"Armed or not, they won't get away with this. And you don't know us too well if you think we'll just sit back while some prick kidnaps our cousin and holds her for ransom."

"What are you going to do?" Jiao asked. "Call the police?" Contact the shifter secret council that Patricia reported to?

Chris though, had another plan. "I'm going to call my mother."

*

As declarations went, Chris could understand Sheng's snicker. After all, his mate's brother didn't understand what his mother was capable of. If anyone could organize a rescue operation and take down a villain, dear old Ma could. And provide food for after.

The first call he made was to his mother. He gave her the basics, listened to her coldly spoken, "He's a dead man," before hanging up.

"So?" Sheng asked, still looking uptight, but Chris could forgive him that. One, because Sheng wasn't married to Chris's woman – *no threesome for me, yay!* – and two, because Chris could see the fear in Sheng's eyes that only appeared when he heard of Gina's capture. Anyone willing to trade themselves for that hoyden deserved some respect. Or at least a free pass from a fist in the face for being a jerk the rest of the time.

"Now we wait for my brothers to arrive with my dad. They'll make sure the neighborhood is clear before we head over to my house."

"Why there?"

"Because chances are this Kaleb person doesn't know about Jiao and I being mated yet, so my house is safer than yours. Pack a bag of clothes, but stay away from windows. I'd hate for a hunter to take a potshot. Come with me." He directed his last order to Jiao, tugging her by the hand to her room.

She immediately understood what he wanted and pulled a suitcase out from under the bed. She presented it with a flourish.

"While I do prefer you naked, don't you want to pack some clothes?"

A wan smile crossed her lips. "It is already packed in case of an emergency. I was really hoping to never have to use it."

"I'm sorry, baby."

"Why? It's not your fault Kaleb found us. I just wish I hadn't dragged you into this mess. I don't want you, or anyone for that matter, to get hurt."

"Everything will work out." It had to. He'd not just found the woman of his dreams only to lose her. But he did have questions. "So, Sheng, who's not Jack, is your brother, and you are …?"

"Jiao. It means, dainty or lovely."

Chris rolled her name around on his tongue. "I like it. It suits you. Next question is, how long have you and Sheng been pretending to be married?"

"Just over four years. The first two, we played the part of orphans but we stood out too much."

"You've been hiding for six years? But why? Who is this Kaleb fellow and why does he want you so bad?" Not that he'd want her for long after Chris got through with him. Anyone who could inspire the level of terror he sensed in his mate needed a serious ass kicking. Or more.

"Kaleb is a rich human who somehow discovered shifters exist. He kidnaps them, especially the rare ones like me and Sheng. But others as well, anyone he has a use for."

"So he's a collector?"

"Of sorts. However he's not content to just put us on display."

"How does he use shifters? It's not like we have special skills other than changing into an animal."

"Smart animals," she gently corrected. "Wily animals who know how to evade hunters eager for something a little wilder than just a safari."

"He freakn' hunts our kind?" Chris didn't even bother to hide his shock.

"Hunts. Awards some of us as prizes to his friends, or sells us like cattle. Yet others, rare breeds like Sheng and I, became attractions in his perverse version of a circus. Sheng and I worked the high wire when Kaleb retired my parents. We had to perform all kinds of acrobatics, dozens of feet in the air while flipping from human to cat."

"Holy shit. So who rescued you?"

"No one. When Kaleb announced his plans to sell me for breeding, Sheng came up with a plan for escape. Six years later, we're still alive. And I thought safe."

Forget ass kicking. This Kaleb person needed to die. "Not thought – are." He pulled Jiao into his arms and rested his chin on her head. So small and delicate, it appalled him to learn the truth she could finally reveal, a past more complicated and horrifying than he could have imagined.

While she recounted the period of her life in captivity in a quick monotone, he could sense the hurt and fear beneath it. He freely admitted to not fully understanding the awfulness of it, he just didn't have anything to compare it to. But he did know that from now on, no one would ever hurt her again. And, he'd make sure he gave her reasons to laugh and smile. Starting with now.

"Hey, I just thought of something." He held her out at arm's-length. "I'm mated to a circus lady. A flexible circus lady. My buddies are going to be so jealous."

"This isn't funny."

"No, but it's damned hot. Did you have to wear one of those skimpy outfits?" He waggled his brows and her lips twitched.

"Yes. A skimpy two piece bikini that left little to the imagination."

Chris frowned. "And people saw you in it?"

"Yes. That was the whole point of the show."

He was afraid of that. "Will you visit me when I go to jail?"

She cocked her head. "Why are you going to jail?"

"Because I need to kill the audience."

"So you're going to go on a murderous, jealous rampage?"

"Maybe."

"Do you think we can get conjugal visits? Maybe even share a cell? Because the way I hear it, a lot of the female population saw what belongs to me." She said it with a dead pan tone, but her eyes twinkled.

He winced. "Who said something? Gina?"

"And Naomi. And Francine. Oh, and a few of the ladies themselves boasted about it at the Thanksgiving dinner. You're lucky I didn't unleash my claws then and there."

"Is this your way of saying we're even and we should leave it alone?"

"I'd much rather spend every night in bed with you than staring at bars. I stared at those enough when I was a kid."

Ouch. That slapped his attempt at mirth in the face. His chagrin must have shown because she threw her arms around his waist. "Oh, don't look like that. I got over it. I just don't want to return to it."

"You won't have to," his mother announced appearing in the bedroom door. "Sorry, but I overheard the last part. And believe me dear, when I say no one will ever put you in a cage again. You're family now and family doesn't stand for that kind of shit."

"I take it the coast is clear?" Chris asked.

"Clear as a blue sky. So let's get out of here before that changes."

"So have you got a plan?" he asked, as she led him through the house out to the cavalcade of waiting cars.

"Of course I do. But, it's going to require a little patience, my son."

"Uh oh, we're screwed," Jiao muttered.

Their laughter, while wildly inappropriate for the occasion, provided an ease to the tension in his body, and that of his mate's. Sheng on the other hand looked like he'd packed an extra stick – up his butt.

Chapter Twenty Six

Sheng's mind boggled at the number of people who showed up when they found out Gina was in trouble. Even harder to wrap his mind around, they just accepted him as the newest member of the family. It didn't matter it was his sister mated to the wolf. Or that he remained standoffish. His back got slapped. Shoulders hugged. And he was reassured by a ridiculous number of dogs to not worry, they'd take care of him, because despite the fact he used a litter box, he was family.

A more emotional man might have wept. But Sheng was a rock. Rocks didn't get sappy, so Sheng took himself outside and stood in the shadow of the house taking deep breaths, fighting tears.

Men didn't cry. He'd not cried when his father died. He'd not cried when his mother took her life. He'd not once cried when punished for not performing well. Nor shed a tear, even in frustration when they escaped and found the path to freedom arduous.

But now, surrounded by people, so willing to accept him, to come to his aid and help end a nightmare he'd lived with for years … Bloody freakn' hell, he couldn't help the hot moisture pooling in his eyes, although, he tried his best.

"What's wrong?"

Having scented his sister before her question, Sheng didn't jump, but he did attempt to hide his unmanly tears. "Nothing. I got something in my eye."

"Liar. There's no shame in showing your emotions."

"Whatever," he grumbled, scrubbing at his face.

"You're worried about Gina."

"Very. She's my mate. I have to do something. But I'm scared." He admitted it softly, as if ashamed to let the words slip past his lips. "How do we know this plan will work? What if –" He swallowed hard. "What if I can't set her free?" What if he failed to save Gina like he failed to save his mother?

"I believe in you."

"But –"

Jiao clasped his hands in hers. "No buts. Six years ago, you saved a scared sixteen-year-old girl. Then put your life on hold to keep me safe. You did that."

"Patricia –"

"Gave us the tools, but you were the one who used them. If anyone can free Gina, it's you. As it should be. You are her mate, after all."

"I doubt she'll care after the things I said to her. I acted like a jerk."

"So grovel for forgiveness. Although, if you ask me, coming to her rescue like some hot Samurai hero of legend will probably work in your favor. I hear she used to have a thing for Bruce Lee."

Sheng snorted. "Seriously? That's just wrong."

"Or a sign of fate. Don't doubt yourself, Sheng. I never did."

Sheng hugged his little sister. "How did you get so wise?"

"Watching Dr. Phil."

And that was how her wolf mate found them, giggling like idiots while hugging.

"Family hug!" Chris yelled.

The next thing Sheng knew, not only did Chris's arms surround him and Jiao, but another pair, and another, until he almost couldn't breathe so many bodies crowded in for the hug.

Damned touchy feely family. He wouldn't cry again – even if the acceptance felt great. Nope. No more tears. Not until he saved Gina and could shed tears of relief. Or pain as she hurt him for letting her get captured in the first place.

Chapter Twenty Seven

Nothing like stripping naked in the predawn hours of a crisp October morning to get in the mood for a rescue operation. After the shocks of the past few hours, Chris found a certain comfort in communing with nature. Although, if given a choice, he'd have preferred to stay home, in his bed, with his new mate, sticky and sweaty as he showed her the many ways he loved her. As it was, despite her pleas – initially tearful, then angry and hot – he'd left her behind with the other women as the men embarked on their mission.

He consoled himself with the knowledge when he rescued his cousin, he could come home and collect a celebratory kiss – and more. Lots more because he doubted a single kiss, a single climax, actually anything that entailed touching his mate, would ever be enough.

Now, however, wasn't the time to get a woody, not when he stood buck naked with another dude. Chris dumped his clothes alongside Sheng's neat pile. He could tell his new brother-in-law wasn't sure about the plan concocted over coffee, Coca Cola, and his mom's freshly baked chocolate chip cookies. The guy took life way too seriously, and yes, while Gina's plight deserved some degree of decorum, the Grayson family could no sooner stop themselves from their boisterous ways than they could beating the hell out of the idiot who took Gina. Sheng didn't get that yet, but he would. Their ways would grow on the little dude, like a fungus. Sheng would also learn Chris meant what he said. Family took care of family. And that included a sour puss Asian.

"You remember what to do?"

Sheng rolled his eyes. "Yeah, because it's so complicated. Walk up to the plane, tell them I'm there for the exchange. Hand myself over and try to get them to release Gina."

"And if that doesn't work, don't do anything stupid, like fight. We'll come for you. No matter what. Remember that. Your biggest job is to protect Gina until we arrive to the rescue."

"That goes without saying. I also assume, if I don't make it out of here, you promise to keep Jiao safe?"

"First off, you'll make it back. Your sister would kill me otherwise. She might be tiny, but she's got claws." His back bore testament to that. "And second, dude, I know we might not have gotten off on the best foot, but it's only because I'm crazy for Jiao. She's my mate. My life. I'd do anything for her. Keeping her safe is only a part of what I intend to do."

"Ick. No more. I want to keep my lunch thank you," Sheng grimaced. "Thanks though. And good luck. You'll need it. My sister has a temper."

"I'm sure I can handle anything she dishes out." Chris grinned. "Ready, my newest brother?"

"No. But let's do this anyway."

Chris clapped him on the shoulder. "May the force be with you."

"Geek," Sheng snickered, but with a smile.

Stepping back, Chris just hoped he could keep his word and rescue both Sheng and Gina without harm. Despite his blasé attitude, he knew they'd have a fight ahead of them. And an evil bastard to take down.

*

Despite the danger of the situation, a part of Sheng couldn't help a giddy excitement that he could roam the outdoors, free and in his feline skin. Tail bobbing, whiskers twitching and paws gripping the earth, he bounded across the strip of grass bordering the tarmac of the runway.

A lone plane sat in the open with its cargo bay door wide open. Approaching it, Sheng sniffed, and couldn't help a growl at the familiar smell of Kaleb and his goons, gorilla mercs imported from South America and loyal to whoever paid their salary. Traitors to their kind.

As if thinking of Kaleb conjured him, the broad chested man appeared in the opening of the plane and held his arms wide. The wide grin on his lips though never reached his eyes.

"If it's not my long lost kitty, returned at last. But where is your sister? I thought I made myself quite clear that you were both to come?"

In a blink of an eye, Sheng shifted to his human shape, proud and tall despite his nakedness. He stood before the man who'd haunted his nightmares for so long and realized something. *Kaleb is just a man.* Not a super being with powers. Not a deadly shifter. Just an aging human with a god complex – oh, and a gun. But Sheng wasn't here to fight him – yet. "Jiao is gone. You just missed her. She eloped with her wolf lover when I wouldn't give my blessing."

"Liar. She wouldn't leave you."

Sheng shrugged. "She found her mate. You should know by now the mating bond isn't one we can fight for long."

"Ah yes, the infamous mating fever. Funny you should mention that. Imagine my surprise when I met up with the officer who tipped me to your whereabouts. It seems we missed you by only moments. A she-wolf, though? I'm surprised at you, Sheng. Tainting your blood line like that."

Ice water ran through his veins and Sheng fought not to shiver and give away how Kaleb's words affected him. His cat didn't like the implied threat to their mate at all. "I don't know what you're talking about."

"Really? So, she's not your mate then?"

"She's not even my type," Sheng lied and hoped he did it well. No denying, he'd gone through a radical change in the last week. According to his mind and body, only short, curvy and mouthy would do. But he couldn't let Kaleb know that. Couldn't admit to anything that might jeopardize Gina further.

"Well, in that case then, you won't mind if I give her to my boys. She put up quite the fight and they're eager for retribution. And they're horny. I just hope they don't damage her too much. I have clients who like a girl with spirit."

"Don't you dare." Sheng growled before he could stop himself.

An arched brow accompanied Kaleb's, "I thought you didn't care?"

"The deal was me for her. It has nothing to do with caring or not. I wouldn't leave anyone in your sick clutches."

Kaleb shook his head. "Liar. You care for the she-wolf, else you'd have no problem sacrificing her to save yourself and your sister. Enough talk. Get in the cage." He pointed towards an open silver cage, the bottom lined in plastic.

"Let her go, first."

"I think not. Since you didn't bring me your sister, I'm going to need some extra female bodies to use as incubators. Congratulations, my precious cat, you are going to get to play stud. Even if all the babes you father don't come out clouded leopards, I can still sell the extras. It's amazing what people will pay for genuine shifters."

"No."

"As if you have a choice. Grab him."

Sheng struggled against the hands reaching out to snag him, but not too hard. He needed on the plane, close to Gina so he could save her. Forget implementing the defensive and offensive moves he'd learned over the years. He kicked and thrashed as ineptly as possible without giving away the fact he wanted to get caught.

Moments later, he ended up tossed into a cage. He winced as he hit the bars, the silver burning his exposed skin before he rolled away to the center, away from the poisonous metal. Kryptonite for superman, silver for shifters. Every hero owned a weakness. His mate sat in the cage alongside his shaking her head.

"Jack?" Gina, a little bit bruised, but none the worse for wear, stood. She wore a t-shirt and shorts that didn't cover enough. The exposed skin displayed splotches of color, a visual map of her resistance, and fuel for his simmering rage. No one could say she lacked courage. But it pissed him off she'd needed to defend herself in the first place.

Gina approached the bars of her cage but refrained from touching them as she stared at him. "What are you doing here?"

A wan smile curved his lips. "I was making an attempt at chivalry and thought I'd trade myself for you."

Despite her situation, she met him with an answering grin. Did she not own an ounce of common sense?

"I don't think it worked."

"I hadn't noticed. Are you okay?" He drank her in, noting the burns that spoke of her attempts to free herself from the silver prison.

"I've been better. So what's the plan?"

Conscious of the watching eyes and listening ears, Sheng sighed loudly. "The plan failed. Kaleb was supposed to trade you for me, but he lied. But don't worry, I'll figure something out."

"Bullshit. You are too methodical to not have a backup plan B."

Sheng noted the empty cargo space, but still didn't trust it. He gave her a hint. "Eyes and ears."

"And mouth and toes. Why are we singing a kid's body part song?"

Thankfully, he didn't have to answer what seemed obvious to him.

A howl rose up outside the plane, the ululation of dozens of wolves. The cavalry implementing part two of their plot.

Kaleb bolted back in to the plane, his two goons following more slowly and taking up position at the foot of the ramp.

"Shit. The fucking cat didn't come alone. Close the bay door and get this piece of metal into the air," Kaleb yelled.

"Aren't you going to do something?" Gina hissed as motors whirred to life.

Sheng didn't reply, watching instead as Kaleb grabbed a rifle and primed it, but didn't use it. The door to the plane shut, minus one of the gorilla mercs, cutting off the sounds of snarls, but not quite muffling the distinct cracks of guns going off. Gina's face turned ashen, her usual spirit cowed at the violence erupting outside the plane.

Ignoring the sizzle of pain as he slid his arm through the bars, Sheng reached for her, and to his relief, she gripped his hand, squeezing his fingers tight.

"Please tell me everything will be alright,' she whispered.

"I can't because I made a promise. No more lies."

"Since when?"

"Since I left you after acting like a jerk because you caught on to me. From now on, I'm going to give you nothing but the truth."

"Seriously? You couldn't have decided that days ago, before I began looking into you? Or last night, when you ran off without explanation?"

"About that, I'm really sorry. Patricia called and said my sister was in danger and –"

"Whoa. Back up. Sister? Aha. I knew it. You are Sheng and Jiao, not Jack and Jill, husband and wife."

Still clasping her hand tight, despite the burns on his forearm from the bars, he told her the story;

from his capture with his parents, to their deaths, to the escape and their years of hiding.

"I'm so sorry," Gina whispered when he was done. "If I'd have known, I would have never done a search."

"Not your fault. My sister made a very valid point about my paranoia and instinct to act standoffish brought us more attention. If anyone is to blame, it's me. I put the target on us by refusing to blend in and make friends."

"You're right. It is your fault. So fix it."

"I intend to." He lowered his voice, not worried as much anymore about anyone listening because of the noisy vibrations all around them. Gina needed something to keep her mind occupied, and guess who had the perfect distraction for her. "Just so you know, once we get out of this mess, I'm claiming you."

Tearing her fingers from his, she took a step back. "Excuse me?"

"We're mates. Hence, I am going to claim you."

"Gee, how romantic. Especially the part where you asked me. No." Eyes flashing, she crossed her arms over her chest in a defiant – but very cute – pose.

"No?"

"You heard me, no. I want a man who thinks of me as an equal. That man isn't you. I've heard your theories on women."

"Backed by science and brute strength tests."

"Oh, you're incredible."

"And smart," he added smugly.

"Definitely not modest."

"Why, when I have nothing to be modest about?"

Such a subtle, yet blatant reminder of his cock and her enjoyment of it, and oh, she reacted beautifully. Her cheeks flushed, her eyes smoldered and her lips rounded into a beautiful 'O' perfect for …

"You've got to be kidding me. You have a boner!"

An unfortunate aspect to the life of a shifter; nakedness, because clothes were such fragile, easily lost items. Rule number five in the guy shifter handbook, though? Unless you can do something about it, pretend you don't see the erect evidence. Ignoring his wildly inappropriate hard on – her fault, she turned him on after all in the first place – he forged ahead.

"There is nothing wrong with a virile male showing appreciation of a pleasing female form in the most visible compliment available."

"Pussycat, you ever get a hard on for another woman in front of me, and you'll sing soprano in a girls voice."

"Jealousy. It is the sign of a true mating." He said the words in his best wise sage voice – the one atop the mountain, smoking a pipe, cross-legged with a beard down to his knees.

"Would you stop that?"

"Stop what?"

An inarticulate snarl came from her before she gave him her back. Sheng stifled a grin. How utterly amazing. Here he was, stuck in a cage, his mate also a prisoner, on a plane to who knew where, and yet, he smiled. Not a cold smile, or a wry one, but a genuine, happy in the moment smile.

Now, a person could argue that his misplaced humor, during such grave circumstances, emerged because of his need to protect his mate. A need to prevent her fear. But given their situation, caged in a metal bird, a few thousand feet in the air thing, yeah, he needed something better than, 'Don't worry, I got this.' Come on, a daring escape attempt with her under the current conditions was on par to racing on foot in front of a tornado. Doable, but with a highly unlikely survival rate. Escape was out until they hit solid ground.

But he couldn't let her panic, or cry. He hated it when his sister cried and suspected he'd hate it even more with Gina. Not that she appeared anywhere close to crying. Nope, she ignored him and studied the wall of her cage.

A part of him felt kind of bad he couldn't say anything. Yet he was also loathed to reveal too much in case Kaleb or his men possibly eavesdropped.

Still, though, making a joke, and about mating – which he took very seriously – had he completely lost his mind?

Yes, he had, and it felt great. He'd spent so long in his serious shell, mistrusting the world, not letting people get close. It hadn't done him an ounce of good. Miserable wasn't how he wanted to spend the rest of his life. Funny how a change in scenery and a chance encounter could change a man so drastically so fast. However, meeting Gina didn't cause the entire reversal of his previously held notions. He'd realized a lot of things recently as his sister questioned his true motives behind his paranoia. Honesty within himself oozed forth to shock him.

I'm scared.

Before his capture by Kaleb, the first time when he was still just a boy, Sheng remembered the happy times. The smiles and laughter. The love of his family. Then, in one fell swoop, his bright and shining world was ripped away. He survived. He protected his family best he could. He failed with his parents and escaped with his sister. However, his one victory didn't appease the fear or bring back those happy days, a past where he didn't constantly look over his shoulder. *I fear.* Jiao hit it square in the head when she questioned his reasons for hiding. Forced him to see.

To compound his already fragile mindset readjustment, he met a certain she-wolf determined to get under his skin. Happiness beckoned, but required him to find the courage to grasp it.

But what if I lose it again? What if I can't keep Gina safe? If I fail …

So many doubts. Time to stop letting fear make his choices. Time to live life, instead of envying it. Time to claim his mate and a chance for happiness.

Gina might fight him now, but she didn't stand a chance. *I want her in my life.* Even if she drove him nuts, he'd have to make sure not to claw the furniture. Gina did, after all, own a gun. He could see plenty of fireworks and head butting, but at least life would never lack action. And if lucky, he'd get to live in love.

Chapter Twenty Eight

Stupid freakn' silver cage. Too small for her to pace properly, too silvery for her to touch, Gina couldn't properly vent her frustration by wearing a groove or hitting something. A sane person would have blamed her dilemma on the situation – kidnapped and flown to God knew where – but no. Gina didn't doubt her family would come to the rescue. They wouldn't rest until she was found, so if she just sat back and kept herself from getting killed, they'd spring her at some point.

No, her problem napped in the cage beside her. Lying on his back with his knees drawn up and his hands crossed over his naked stomach – taut and defined with washboard abs she'd licked less than a day ago – Sheng slept. How could he sleep? Especially after telling her he intended to claim her ass as his mate – and sporting a very complimentary boner. The things she could do – and had done – with that perfect dick …

Stop. She couldn't think that way. He'd smell her desire for sure then. Back to the reason for her annoyance. *I'm his mate, or so he says.*

Not likely. Sure, he pushed every single one of her buttons and made her orgasm like nobody's business – more than once, all three times they'd screwed – it didn't mean she'd tie herself to a guy who thought women were inferior to men. He'd made his beliefs clear.

I could show him differently.

If she cared. Let someone else teach the jerk that women were just as, if not more than, capable of taking care of themselves. So long as the person who taught him wasn't a woman. *Ours*, her wolf snarled. Ours indeed. If the idea of him with another woman made her want to neuter something, then something big was afoot.

Damn. Stupid cat got it right. He was her mate. She could deny it and fight it all she wanted. In the end, the fever would consume her and she'd crawl to him begging for his mark.

Screw that. Gina Greco didn't get on her knees for anybody. Okay, unless she was giving head. But that was different! So how to solve this dilemma? She knew enough of the mating fever to know once it struck, the clock began ticking, faster and faster until they gave each other the mark in a mindless frenzy. There was only one acceptable solution.

Bite her pussycat first and claim him on her terms. And if he pulled any of his macho bullshit, she'd chase his feline ass up a tree.

Sitting hunched, she must have dozed off because she woke to a rude, "Still awake, bitch?" Her captor sidled up to her cage.

Oh, if she could have one shot, just one, perfectly timed punch to the face, she'd erase the smirk Kaleb regarded her with. "You'll regret doing this, human."

"Ooh, I'm shaking in my boots."

"You should because if I ever get out of this cage, I'm going to find you. Handcuff you to a chair –"

"Sounds kinky, no wonder my little Chinaman likes you," he interrupted with a leer.

"– strip you."

"This is getting better and better."

"Then I'm going to wrap dental floss around your balls, and pull it so freakn' tight, those babies will turn black and fall off."

"And then?" Kaleb smirked, not at all bothered by her threat.

"I'll make you eat them."

"Lay one finger on me and I'll show you how many ways there are to torture a person and keep them alive.

It seemed Sheng didn't nap after all because he said, "I don't think so. You want to use me as a stud, then you'll leave my woman alone."

Kaleb whirled from Gina to her pussycat. "Oh ho. So the cat finally admits she's his. Should I punish you for your earlier lie?"

"Not if you want me to cooperate."

"If I agree to leave her untouched, you'll breed her?"

"Yes." Sheng didn't look too happy, but he agreed to Kaleb's terms.

"Prove it. Take her, right here, right now. I'll have my men toss her into your cage."

Okay this took voyeurism to a level Gina didn't like. "Excuse me, but I don't do live sex shows. And I don't care what video some people say they saw on YouTube. It wasn't me."

"What's she's trying to say, in her usual delicate fashion, is no," Sheng added. "I won't be watched like an animal. Any breeding we do, we'll do in private."

"Only? That kind of sucks. Public sex can be so much fun." Gina pouted.

"Would you shut up?" Sheng hissed.

"A lover's quarrel, what fun. While I'd love to watch, you're distracting me from my work. How about you decide on the whole public sex thing after a nap."

Gina would have said she wasn't tired, but something pricked her in the side. She peeked down to see a feathered tuft sticking from her skin.

"Drugs don't wor–" she couldn't finish the thought, darkness grabbed her so quickly.

*

Mouth tasting like a toilet – a fact Gina unfortunately knew due to party years (still ongoing) – Gina raised her head and peered blearily around her. Blink. Stare. Blink. Stare.

Nope, still definitely the weirdest place she'd ever woken up in. It looked like a cross between a dungeon, and a cage. A big cage, but still a freakn' cage.

What the hell?

Up she sprang, swaying a little as her sluggish body fought to catch up. Gina whipped her head from side to side, checking out the joint. Then flicked her gaze back left. Yup, a much too relaxed Sheng – if you ignored his semi erect cock that twitched higher the more she stared – lay on the floor, naked, rumpled haired, bristly jawed, and looking like the most luscious piece of ass ever. She couldn't help the heat between her legs. Her naked legs. Shit, who undressed her?

Clarity returned quickly as the possible answers narrowed themselves into equally distasteful options. Nothing sore. Sniff. No strange smells on her skin. It looked like someone stripped her but left the goods alone. "Where are we?"

"Kaleb's compound in the mountains. Welcome to the lowermost level of Castle Hell, or at least that's what we called it when I lived here with my family. These are not his best accommodations though. Say hello to the training model. If we behave ourselves while here and follow the rules, we get to move on up to something a little less rustic with an actual bed."

"This is seriously insane." She fought down panic. Gina Greco didn't do girly wimp. "This place is awesome. I am so going to suggest it for next year's Big Brother Have-Not Room." Ignoring his shocked expression, she peeked around.

The floor, if you could call it that, since it consisted of concrete covered in itchy, scratchy hay, was about ten by ten, enough for some movement, but small enough to drive her crazy real quick. Stone blocks comprised the back and side walls. The only source of light provided by a window high up and covered in thinly spaced – bet you they were silver – bars. The three cement block walls appeared unwashed and scarred with scratches and splotches she preferred not to dwell on. The fourth edge, at her back, comprised floor to ceiling bars. She could feel the tingle of silver in them from two feet away. Shudder.

Furnishings were a one star hotel, hole in the ground replete with a stack of paper, a blanket, and an annoyed looking Asian man.

"Have you gone into shock?" Sheng asked.

"No. I'm just assessing the situation. Looking for a way out, and something to use as a weapon."

"Shhh." He slapped his hand over her mouth and dragged her close. "Be careful what you say. They are listening."

Shit, she'd not even thought of that. Bad cop. Hmmm, now there was an idea for role-play later. But for now, while warming quickly at the slight brush of his skin against hers, she instead opted to slant her head until she whispered back in his ear. "Well duh, but if I don't act in character, a.k.a. new prisoner looking for escape, then they'll think I'm up to something."

"Are you?"

"Am I what?"

"Up to something," he snapped, only to clamp his lips when he realized he practically shouted.

"Of course I am." She rolled her eyes. "I'm not going to let my family have all the fun when they come to the rescue."

"They are not coming to the rescue."

A raspberry on his chest told him what she thought of his reply. "Don't be silly. Of course they're coming. It's my family. Like they'd pass up a chance for some fun."

"Fun?" he choked out.

"Yeah, I guess this is a little more serious than a party. How about, they couldn't pass up a chance to hit something? There are a lot of boys in my family. The testosterone can get a little heavy. People to hit, outside of family members, are encouraged."

"So in other words, at Christmas dinner I should wear a jock?"

"And a helmet. My mom's coming. It should be better than UFC 271."

"That good, huh?"

"Better. But back to my family getting ready to rescue me, since I don't want to have to listen for the rest of my life how they had to rescue my fat ass –"

"Absolutely tempting ass," he corrected.

"– and my cuddly little pussycat from the bad guys. We can't let that happen. I'll never hear the end of it."

"Excuse me? You did not just call my leopard cuddly."

"Leopard? How interesting. And here I thought you might be a Siamese."

"A domestic hairball?" he sputtered.

"Well you are rather snobbish, and I'll bet you're high maintenance. But between the baton and my cuffs, I think we can cure those habits."

"Cuffs?" His gaze took on a smoldering intensity that sucked her breath away. Never had a man ever looked at her with such hunger. And need.

She wanted to feed both. She wanted him.

Gina could see now the whole picture – the rigid man, no more than a boy when he started his hard life, protecting the only thing left to him, a sister. She could see the lover who struggled with his needs, looking for someone he could trust and finally relax with. And finally Sheng, lost and hurt, who needed to learn how to regain his identity, his life, and smile again – *right after I hurt him for being such a dumbass*.

"Oh pussycat, we are going to have so much fun when we get out of here. However, if you're going to be my mate, you'll have to understand a few things."

"Mate? What happened to *hell no*?"

"I'm not stupid. I know you belong to me. But just so we're clear. I don't share."

"Me either."

Yeah, Sheng looked the possessive – borderline stalker – type, which worked, because she had trust issues too. "Oh, I wasn't talking about you. Although, that goes without saying. I meant I don't share my steak, or my ice cream, or my chips. Actually, if you want to earn sexual brownie points, bring me home some chips, with dip if you want me to lick it off you."

"Fair enough. I don't share the remote."

"Typical," she muttered. "Now for the ground rules. One, I am a cop, not a very important one I'll admit, I mostly patrol parks, the downtown strip and hand out tickets, but still, one day, I might make it to one of the cool squads, and if I do, I expect you to respect that even if it's dangerous."

"Or I could keep you barefoot and pregnant." Surely he feigned that level of nonchalance?

She gaped at him. "You did not just say that."

He grinned, mischief dancing – a huge cucaracha with flamboyant can-can dancers – in his eyes. "We'll get a big house that you need to clean too. Maybe a tiny yappy dog we can name Skittles."

She opened her mouth to retort, but then got it. "You're joking with me?"

He snickered. "Of course I am. I might be a little rigid, but even I have kept up with woman's rights. And besides, can you see me owning a dog? I'm much more a cat person."

"If you're Mr. Joe Cool, then what was all that crap about women not able to protect themselves?"

"Best pickup line ever when I was in the circus. Don't forget I was a teenage boy while cooped up. There weren't many girls close to my age, but there were some. Challenge a girl to prove she's tough and you get to cop a feel. From there …"

"You used a pickup move on me?" Gina breathed the question, not daring to believe his nerve.

*

Sheng wondered if he should duck, because there were two answers to that question. One got him killed, the other yeah, it probably got him killed too. "Yes, I did."

"Why? You acted like you didn't even like me."

"I hated what you made me feel, but that was because I liked you too much. I don't get close to people."

"Understatement of the year," she muttered.

"I wanted to be with you."

"Aw, nice line. Is this the part where I say that is so beautiful and swoon in your arms?"

"Not a line. The truth."

"So what if I say I want to claim you right now? And to hell with who might be watching?"

Sheng winced. Straw left the itchiest marks on the skin. "Can't we wait for somewhere a little more comfortable?"

Gina approached him, hips swaying, gaze taunting. "Why don't I just claim you without the sex? After all, it's the mark that counts."

Not acceptable, because, dammit, he wanted his cock sunk deep inside her when he finally gave in to his need. Preferably while climaxing.

Stupid camera. He wanted Gina, but not enough to give anyone a show.

Whirling, he took a few short running steps, jumped and twirled in the air, his foot arcing and hitting the lens of the camera nestled in the corner of the wall. A sharp crack made him smile as he landed on his feet in a partial crouch, facing his woman.

"What was that?"

"I call that move the we-have-about-five-to-ten-minutes so get over here."

Her breathing hitched and the scent of her desire made his mouth water. "We should be looking for a way out."

"Come here," he growled. He needed to keep her distracted until he heard a sign. With only his body at hand and no other verbal bombshells ... he sacrificed himself.

"Or?"

"There is no or." He yanked her to him, slanting his mouth over hers.

"Still. No. Bed." She managed to gasp between caresses.

"The back wall is cold, but smooth."

She grasped his intent, when he lifted and carried her across the room.

"This is insane," she hissed as he pressed her against the stone.

"Totally. Feels great!" He hoisted her until her legs clasped his waist while her arms looped around his shoulders. One arm anchored around her torso, he ran his free fingers down her soft skin until he reached the spot between her thighs. Thank freakn' God she already wanted him. Slick digits slid easily into her heat. He stroked her. Shuddered against her as she moaned and her body tightened.

The distant pop, pop, pop, didn't stop him. Not now. Just a few more minutes. Screw the signal the assault commenced. He wouldn't take long to come but he'd have to hurry her along.

Sheng thrust into her, the warm sheath of her body pulling him in. Heavenly. But only with her. Only because of the connection he felt to her. A trust and ease that he wanted more than anything. A passion he would die for.

Gina didn't protest his minimal foreplay. On the contrary, she urged him on, bouncing on his length, growling "More" in his ear. He gave her what she wanted. Hard. Fast. Slapping strokes. In and out. A fast piston that she rewarded with nails, raking across his back.

The twinge of pain made him yell. So close now. But he didn't forget his primary purpose. He nestled his lips against her throat, and felt her mimicking on the other side of his. A sharp pinch on his side, a flex of his dropped canines on her, the metallic taste of blood hit tongue as he continued to thrust into her. The ripple of her orgasm triggered his, a wicked climax that never stopped as he sucked her skin, making her his … forever.

Quivering and shaking, hot and sweaty, happy, so freakn' loopy from the ecstasy, they clung together for a moment, basking in the wonder of their union. Coming to grips – holy shit – with their mating.

And then his new wife just had to ruin it.

"Are you freakn' purring?"

*

For a second, Gina wondered what her new mate would do. He seemed so taken aback, even puzzled by the sound. He said nothing for a moment, but the purrs continued.

"Um, Sheng? Are you alright."

"I'm purring." He sounded surprised.

"Yes you are. And I like it so long as that's not your, I'm about to eat you, sound."

"Eat you? Seriously?"

"Well, who can tell what with you being a big tough jungle cat and all?"

"Are you mocking me? Or is this a not so subtle hint you want something?"

"I would never mock my mate. Much. But I do want something." She wiggled against him, holding back a self-satisfied grin at his stirring cock. Now wasn't the time for round two, though, not with the sound of gunfire in the distance. "You say you're not a Siamese, but I've yet to see your cat. Hint. Hint."

"Soon, my she-wolf. I think the cavalry arrives."

"Duh. I told you they'd come, but don't tell me you're going to just sit here and wait for them? Do you really want Chris and the rest of them to constantly remind you they had to save your naked ass?"

Sheng peered down. "Good point. But give me one good reason why I should risk your ass out there when it's perfectly safe in here?"

"Wait a second. Back up a second. Are you implying you know a way out?"

Her mate shot her a supercilious look. "Of course. There isn't a cell alive that can hold me."

"Then get us out."

"Out there," he said while pointing, "is dangerous to you. In here isn't. I'm doing the right thing. You can thank me later."

"You mean, I'll thank my family. Some of whom are second and third cousins who'll expect some *gratitude*, which isn't illegal in most states you know."

"Nice try. But I'm not falling for it."

"So much for your words of no sharing. I would have thought you'd want to participate in the take down seeing as the gorilla boys copped a feel while stripping me. Most mates wouldn't stand for that. But then again, you're just a cat."

One moment he stood still, the next he spun, flashed his fists a few times, and like some magic show featuring a sexy dude in tight black pants – her naked version being much hotter – the door swung open.

"Wow, remind me to get better cuffs." She didn't even bother to hide her awe. Martial arts – and old Kung Fu movies – were such a turn on.

"We're out. Happy now? Keep up and stay out of trouble." He gave her a hard kiss to go with his order before stepping away and morphing into a gorgeous cat. A dark gray fur, deep and lustrous, covered him and was spotted with ebony patches across his whole body. His whiskers twitched and he flicked his tail as he stood proudly for her perusal.

"So do you go crazy for catnip?" she sassed. Then squealed as he licked her thigh with his raspy tongue.

He then snorted and bumped her with his head. She snapped into her wolf shape, landing on four feet and shaking her fur. Hmmm, cat. She nosed him. He swatted at her head. She nipped his tail. He yeowled and took off running.

Yay. Tag and he was it!

Chapter Twenty Nine

Jiao paced the living room. *Leave me behind indeed.* While Chris's concern for her wellbeing warmed her, his decision not to allow her to go on the trip, pissed her right off. *Sheng's my brother. Who does he think he is making decisions for me?*

Her mate. *My mate* … The concept still hadn't sunk in yet. They'd claimed each other. Now until they died, they would belong to each other. She guessed that kind of gave him a little say in her protection, but she wouldn't let him stifle her like Sheng had.

Poor Sheng. She only hoped he didn't suffer while in Kaleb's grasp.

She could admit the plan had merit. Send Sheng as bait, wearing a GPS transmitter. Track him back to Kaleb's lair, then not only take care of the ringmaster, but dismantle his compound and free the other prisoners as well.

When Jiao questioned Chris under her breath about numbers, laughter erupted from all around. "Don't worry about us. We have enough Grayson's and extended family to take over a small country."

But cocky confidence wouldn't stop a bullet. *Let Chris stay out of the path of speeding missiles. And pretty girls.* It didn't hurt to hedge her prayer.

"So, let me get this straight," Naomi said, hoisting a baby to her shoulder for a vigorous back pounding meant to make the child burp. "You used to live in Thailand, but your parents migrated to Canada when you were about eight years old. You got accepted into a group of shifters in the British Columbia Rocky foothills, and that's where this Kaleb fellow found out about you."

Staring out the bay window at the darkness cloaking the front yard, Jiao nodded. "Yes. Kaleb had plants in many shifter communities, people who would tell him about loners no one would miss, or in our case, rare breeds that could fetch good money."

"But he didn't sell you," Francine piped in. "He trained you instead to act like circus acrobats."

"My family and I, because of our agility, were the high rope act. We used to have to flip between our human body and our cat while fifty feet up in the air. No net."

"Damn. Did you ever fall?" Naomi swapped babies with Francine.

"Once, when I was young. My dad caught me. After that I was super careful."

"That's just awful. I can't believe he's been living in Canada this entire time and we've never heard of him." Francine shook her head, not in disbelief. No one doubted Jiao's story. No, none of them could believe they'd never even heard a rumor of Kaleb's activities.

"Only those with money to burn in large quantities knew what he did. And they weren't about to tell."

"Okay, I don't like it, but I get it. What I don't understand is why did you pretend to be married to your brother?" Naomi wrinkled her nose. "I could never pretend something like that with any of mine. Heck, I can't figure out how you and Francine could even consider being mated to one."

"It wasn't easy. Sheng is somewhat straitlaced. But I got even in my own way. I spat in his coffee, put starch in his laundry and short sheeted his bed as a way of venting my frustration."

"Oh boy, are you ever perfect for Chris," Francine giggled.

Naomi grinned. "You should try putting plastic cling wrap over the toilet seat. It makes a bit of a mess, but the bellow of disgust is so worth it."

Despite the gravity of the situation, and her worry, Jiao grinned. "I'll remember that."

"What about some hot sauce in their toothpaste?" Meredith added, entering the room with a tray laden with cups, a spouted Thermos and a plate of cookies.

As they poured coffee and continued to discuss dirty tricks to get even with their big shifter mates, Jiao continued to stare outside.

With the plane landed as of their last phoned check in, the men would arrive at the compound any minute now if their plan worked. Or at least so they assumed given Kaleb needed his hideaway within driving distance of the airplane. Soon, Sheng and Gina, along with whoever else resided in Kaleb's dungeon, would get their freedom. However, at what cost? Kaleb's guards would not give up easily. Heck, she still had a hard time believing he'd left without looking harder for her.

A flicker of movement outside caught her attention. The ball of dread in her stomach, that acidy fear which had grown all day, doubled in size. And grew some more as a figure stepped out of the shadows and let the pale gleam from the window hit him.

"Kaleb."

She didn't even realize she'd whispered his name aloud until Naomi replied. "What about him?"

"He's here," Jiao exclaimed as she whirled from the window. "He didn't leave on the plane. Oh no. The babies. Everyone. You have to hide."

Nobody moved.

"I am not hiding in my own home," Meredith said in a much too calm tone. Of course, her serene statement might have had a lot to with the shotgun she pulled from under the couch.

Naomi's lips tightened. "Francine, take the babies to mom's room. No one can get in the window there." And then, the she-wolf hauled out her own gun.

Francine pouted. "But I wanted to watch."

"You are such a horny bitch," Naomi muttered, which made no sense to Jiao. "But this time, you'll have to content yourself with your imagination. Take the babies. Don't make me yank your fat pregnant ass up those stairs."

"I'm going," Francine grumbled, a baby on each hip. "But just so we're clear, my ass is not fat, it's freakn' fluffy."

"What are you doing?" Jiao whispered as Naomi flipped off the safety on her gun.

"We are not letting some twisted ringmaster steal you back."

Jiao's brows arched so high they almost merged with her hair. "You suspected he might do this?"

Naomi snorted. "Duh. It's why we had a backup plan."

"And you didn't tell me because?"

Coming alongside her, Chris's mother patted her. "We didn't want you to worry."

"I'm not worried." No, she was stark raving mad. How dare one human with too much money to spend treat her worse than an animal? Even his pet hounds got more care than shifters did. And now, he had the nerve to come here and threaten her new family and friends.

Like freakn' hell.

Marching to the front door, Jiao tore outside.

"Jiao, get back here," Naomi yelled.

"Leave her be," she heard Meredith caution. "She needs to face this demon on her own."

Face him. More like kill him. She wouldn't let Kaleb terrorize her anymore. She stalked right up to him, inches from his remembered bulk and annoying smirk.

"If it isn't my little kitty cat."

"What are you doing here?"

"Picking up my property of course. It took me a little snooping to figure out who your wolf mate was, but as you can see, I found you. And from what I spied, you've got a houseful of friends as a bonus."

Up whipped her hand. Jiao cracked it across his face. Then she screamed. "Why? Why damn you? Couldn't you have just left us alone?"

Rubbing his cheek, Kaleb's gaze turned malevolent. "Why, because I can. Filthy half-breed. You'll regret your actions."

"Really? Then I might as well regret this too." Out jabbed her hand, a hard direct shot to his chest. Kaleb choked and hunched over. Her satisfaction at hurting him didn't mean she missed the sound of a gun cocking. "Once a coward, always a coward," she remarked as a shadow detached itself from a tree and approached, rifle pointed at her chest. She shot the gunman an imperious look, daring him. She didn't fear getting shot. Tranquilizer darts were the usual fare when looking to capture a shifter.

Kaleb straightened with a smirk. "Surprise. As if I'd tangle with a she-cat alone."

"I won't let you take me." Jiao stood her ground despite the fear that wanted her to run.

"Brave words, except I know your boyfriend and the others are gone. Following my plane back to the mountains. As if a handful of wolves could take down my compound. You'd need an army."

"Not an army. We prefer the term family," rumbled a voice from the darkness.

Was that…?

"Shit." Kaleb cursed and shoved Jiao. He attempted to run, but a shadow dropped from a tree and Geoffrey, an older grizzled version of Chris and the voice she'd heard, cold cocked him. Before she could blink, a yelp of pain to the side distracted her. The thug with the tranquilizer gun fought against Mitchell and Alejandro. Well, more like Francine's mates toyed with him, sharp jabs, lightning quick, staggering the large fellow. Shirtless and dressed in low hipped pants, Jiao finally understood what Francine meant when she talked about watching. Her mates really knew how to move.

Veering her gaze she saw Javier pounded another paid goon while Ethan held him, looking bored. A prickling sensation at her back could only mean …

"Chris?"

"Hey baby. Miss me?" he asked with a grin as he sauntered from the side of the house.

"What are you doing here?"

"My job."

She stared at him blankly.

"Protecting you. Mate rule number one."

"But you were supposed to get on a plane and follow Kaleb."

"I did, and I followed him when he hopped flights back to Ottawa. Aren't you glad to see me?"

Yes, but she had a more pressing concern. "Where's my brother?"

"Oh, he went on to the compound as planned."

"He what!"

"But I'm sure he's fine. Stu, Kendrick and the gang were meeting up with the cousins out there last we spoke. Shouldn't be long before we get the all clear."

"You knew this would happen? That Kaleb would come back for me?"

"Not one hundred percent sure, but I had a feeling."

"So you were here the entire time. When were you planning to let me know? Before or after Kaleb dragged me off?"

"Oh, it wouldn't have come to that. I had my eye on you the whole time. I just thought you needed to speak your piece before I stepped in. Nice shot to the ribs by the way. Good thing I still have my hockey equipment. You could cause some serious damage if you wanted."

Nope. She wouldn't let his flattery melt her yet. Not until Sheng was safe and Kaleb taken care of.

A cell phone rang. Chris answered with a hello. He looked grim. Jiao's heart stopped. Soundlessly, he handed the phone over.

"Ji□ zǐ, are you okay?"

"I'm fine." Her eyes flooded. "How are you? And Gina? And the others?"

"Fine. We're all fine. Only a few scratches that will heal. And a mating that'll leave a mark."

"You and Gina?"

"Yes. Sorry, but I won't be around as much to drive you crazy."

"I'm sure I'll survive," Jiao remarked dryly.

"I hear you guys caught on to Kaleb's sneaky plan. Do me a favor and give him a punch from me?"

"You bet." They hung up and the last of her tension eased. Sheng was safe. Mated. The compound discovered. It left just one more item to deal with.

"Where did Kaleb go?" He no longer lay on the ground, but neither did anyone hold him prisoner. Jiao whirled and saw the man staggering off. As if she'd let him escape that easy. "Going somewhere?" she called. Her claws flexed as she scented his fear.

"I'm done with you and your family," Kaleb blubbered.

"I think that goes without saying, asshat," Chris said, his body braced behind her, offering his support, but Jiao now knew she could face the trembling human on her own. Chris gave her the chance to confront her demon, a man she once thought was big and tough. Older, wiser and not willing to take his crap anymore, she realized he was just a coward without his paid guards. Now who held the upper hand? If only her father and mother could have lived to see this moment. Hopefully they watched from heaven since she planned to give them and all the other victims poetic justice.

"Hey Kaleb. Since you love sports, I'm going to give you a five minute head start," she sang.

"What are you doing?" Chris muttered as she stripped off her shirt.

"Hunting. Care to join me?"

"Would I ever!"

In the end, with the exception of Francine – who was forbidden by her mates – and Meredith, who offered to watch the babies, they all went on the chase.

Wee baby hunting, kitty's going hunting, and when she finds a human treat, she'll bring her mate a bloody treat.

Actually, it ended up a clean hunt. They ran after and tortured the human all night until he crawled and sobbed for mercy. And then they gave him over to Patricia who uncovered a human smuggling connection and buried Kaleb in the legal system – also known as a cell full of biker shifters.

The Hell's Angels had nothing on the Grizzly Northern Bikers down on a binge from the remote territories. Poor Kaleb. The courts declared him insane with all his crazy talk of werewolves.

But that was much later.

Within the hour of the hunt ending, Jiao found herself slumbering in Chris's arms as he carried her back to her house.

"Now what?" she asked through a yawn.

"Well, seeing as how we're already freakn' mated, I thought we'd start with a nap."

"A nap?" For some reason his suggestion woke her up. "Isn't this still technically our honeymoon? I mean it's only been just over a day since you claimed me."

"I know, and I'm aching for you, baby. But it's been a roller coaster of a day and night. You need your rest."

Rest on the first hour of her new freedom and life? Um, no thank you. "What I need is you."

"Thank freakn' God. I was so hoping you'd say that." His mouth caught hers in a torrential kiss, one she could fully enjoy now that the danger, the lies and all the rest were done with. Starting that moment, and forever, she could finally live, and love, and best of all, laugh. Laugh until she cried at Chris's expression of frustration.

"This is not funny," he growled, staring at the destruction inside her house. It seemed Kaleb didn't visit the Grayson home first.

"We don't need a bed do we?" she asked, trailing her fingers down his chest. No, they didn't or so he proved when he buried his face between her thighs while she sat on the small, squat table that survived the chaos and then again when he bent her over the arm of the torn up couch.

Later, collapsed on the floor, cuddled in his arms, in a pile of clean bedding they salvaged, she giggled and he asked, "What's so funny?"

"I thought getting the dust off that stupid glass table was annoying. But ass print?" Their laughter rang loud and beautiful.

This was freedom. This was worth fighting for.

*

Over in the Rocky Mountains …

The compound secured, the guards taken care of and the prisoners released, Sheng finally shifted back to his human shape and took the pants someone handed him, but not before he covered Gina in a long shirt that did more to display her assets than he liked.

Thank God it worked. He'd initially balked at the plan to return to Kaleb's stronghold. His first instinct was not fear for himself, but for Gina. Sure, as a cop, her first instinct would probably involve saving the victims, but Sheng had a duty to keep his woman safe. But as Chris and his brothers' so eloquently put it, "If you tell her no, she's going to do it just to prove you wrong. And kick you in the balls for good measure."

All was well that ended well though. Kaleb had finally met justice. Sheng no longer needed to fear, capture at any rate. His new family on the other hand though …

"Just how many people stayed behind in case Kaleb tried something sneaky?" Sheng asked.

"A couple handfuls. Mom thought Kaleb might not leave so easily. The gang following on the second charter knew for certain when the plane they followed landed for no apparent reason and took off again," Stu replied.

Peering around at the groups of tall men, the stench of wolf overpowering, Sheng made sure to mutter in a voice only Gina could hear, "Exactly how big is your family?"

The laughter wasn't what he'd call reassuring, but he forgave it because of the kiss that followed. Despite the sure craziness of the future, for better and better – because he'd already lived with worst – he would have his freedom, his woman, and a shitload of wolves to torment.

"Are you purring again?" she asked.

"Yeah. You got a problem with that?" If she called him a cute kitten again …

"Um, I think I saw an empty office over there. Care to put that rumble to good use?" She arched a brow.

And that quickly, they lost the crowd, he pounded between her thighs, and thanked the gods he owned nine lives because it felt like he died each time he came in her arms.

Epilogue

The Christmas celebration rocked the house while music about Santa ho-ho-ing, jingled, and lights twinkled. Garish decoration abounded with every cliché known to mankind displayed from snowmen, to mangers, to a little village of penguins dressed in pointy red hats. God she loved it. Loved the chaos, and noise, the goodwill and food.

Jiao maneuvered through the bodies, all shifters and mostly wolves given Chris's family dominated the place. But she did catch the occasional whiff of cat as Javier and Alejandro, accompanying their mates, mingled as well, their swarthier tones offsetting that of the predominantly Caucasian crowd.

A handsome fellow, someone she'd not met before, bumped into her. His eyes lit with interest. "Well hello there, cutie. You must be new. I'm Joel."

An arm curled around her waist possessively, and Chris growled. "She's already freakn' mated, Joel, so go pour the charm on someone else."

"No. Not you too?" Joel's eyes widened in mock horror. "Another good man bites the dust."

"Ha. Ha. Funny man. Just wait. One day, it will happen to you."

"Perish the thought." Joel shuddered.

"Perish what?" Kendrick asked coming up alongside them.

"I was just hoping Joel would meet the mate of his nightmares," Chris joked.

Kendrick snorted. "Might be kind of hard where we're going. All male, jungle expedition. We leave Boxing Day for the Amazon."

"Why all male?" Jiao asked.

"The clan we're going to find is very patriarchal to the point any unbound woman is free game, human or shifter. Even mated females aren't safe if one of their warriors take a fancy."

Chris laughed. "Maybe you'll meet the warrior of your dreams then, Joel."

Jiao felt the impact of the blow through her mate's body. She hissed at the cause and Chris tightened his arm. "Now you've done it. You made my wife angry."

"She gonna beat me up?" Joel taunted.

"Not her. Me."

Joel whirled as someone tapped his shoulder. Seconds later, he groaned on the floor while Sheng looked down on him. "No one upsets my sister," he announced. With a nod in Chris and Jiao's direction, Sheng placed his arm around Gina's waist possessively and moved away.

"I am liking your brother more and more," Chris said with a grin.

"And I think he likes you too." Or so she guessed amidst Shengs glower's and taunts asking if Chris wanted a Milkbone for dessert. While Sheng might have given Jiao her freedom, and put her safekeeping in Chris's hands, he still played an active role in their lives. A very active one, but as Gina confided to Jiao, "He trusts Chris to protect you. But old habits die hard. Just wait until you have kids."

Jiao couldn't wait, but judging by the way Sheng hovered over his mate, and how Gina powered down the little sausages wrapped in pastry, Jiao already lost that race, and she couldn't be happier. Not just because of a possible niece or nephew to spoil. It warmed her through and through to see her brother in love, smiling, and happy. So freakn' happy, tears made her blink.

"Hey, none of that," Chris whispered.

"Tears of joy," she sniffed.

"Oh, and here I thought they were because mom burned the sugar pie." Chris looked so woebegone, she giggled.

"I love you."

"I love you more."

"Someone kill me now," Stu choked.

"Right on it," Kendrick hollered.

"Don't you dare," Meredith warned.

"Put down the cranberry sauce," yelled some aunt.

"I'll save the pie!" Chris yelled.

"Too late. I ate it," Geoffrey, her new father in law, taunted.

Chaos erupted, her mate in the middle of it. Jiao sighed with happiness.

Wasn't family grand?

(The End...only of this story)

The fun continues in the Freakn' Shifter series with:

Delicate Freakn' Flower, Already Freakn' Mated, Human and Freakn', Jungle Freakn' Bride, Freakn' Cougar, Freakn' Out

See EveLanglais.com for more details.

CPSIA information can be obtained
at www.ICGtesting.com
Printed in the USA
BVOW06s1306291116

469203BV00014B/129/P